"Damnation woman. Stop your struggling before you bring the bloody guards down on us."

"Morgan?" she mumbled through the warm hand clapped over her lips.

"Who the bloody hell do you think it is?"

"I bloody well thought you were a murderer. Now, let me go!"

She stomped down hard on his booted foot, and spun around. Stretching up on tiptoe, she got within inches of his face. "You touch me like that ever again, and so help me, Morgan Farrell, I'll get that damned cutlass of yours and run it through your scurvy hide. Do you hear me?"

His lips slanted into a grin. "I hear you, Katie," he whispered, caressing a strand of hair away from her mouth. " 'Tis an angel you are, to fill my ears with such sweet affirmations of your devotion."

PATTI BERG

Looking For A Hero

AVON BOOKS  NEW YORK

AVON BOOKS, INC.
1350 Avenue of the Americas
New York, New York 10019

Copyright © 1998 by Patti Berg
Published by arrangement with the author
Visit our website at http://www.AvonBooks.com
Library of Congress Catalog Card Number: 98-93175
ISBN: 0-380-79555-8

For Bob,
my own special hero

Prologue

Time, the avenger! Unto thee I lift
My hands, and eyes, and heart,
and crave of thee a gift.

LORD BYRON
CHILDE HAROLD'S PILGRIMAGE: CANTO IV

A long, long time ago . . .

Satan's Revenge creaked and groaned as mountainous waves pummeled the heavily armed vessel. Salt water and hurricane-force winds buffeted the sails and shredded the canvas, while the warship listed, bucking and twisting in the brutally churning sea.

Black Heart listened to the clash of thunder, the crackle of lightning, the howl of the hurricane, and the rapid beat of his own empty heart. *Death will surely come this night*, he mused, laughing darkly at his fate. Drowning was a hell of a lot better than swinging from the yardarm, and a far sight more desirable than having his body bound in chains and put on display until it rotted.

'Twas obvious his band of cutthroats felt the same. Gripping the wheel, he watched as one by one the crew abandoned ship, jumping to a certain death in the tumultuous waters below. To hell with the lot of them. Not one man out of fifty-two was brave enough to stay on board and let the Devil determine his destiny.

In spite of his anger, he turned to the heavens and prayed, "God have mercy on their souls." And then he silently asked forgiveness for himself, afraid that this prayer, like all his others, would blow away with the wind.

Thunder rang out as another wall of water smashed against the ship. The mizzenmast groaned, wind battered the ragged sails, and broken rigging whipped about the quarterdeck like a school of writhing eels.

Black Heart fought for balance, wrapping an arm around a spoke of the wheel as he ground his boots into the slippery deck. He was exhausted from fighting the storm. *Satan's Revenge* was tired, too. She'd never suffered such a brutal attack, not from man, God, or the Devil. She'd never felt a cannonball in her hull, or a fire in her hold. She'd never lost a man—until today.

She'd been his life for the past six years. She'd outraced privateers and the Royal Navy's warships. She was his family, his comforter. If they

couldn't make it back to his island, he'd spend
eternity with her at the bottom of the sea. "I'll not
abandon you," he whispered.

A contemptuous laugh broke through the din
of the storm, and out of the corner of his eye, he
saw the flash of a curved steel blade. Black Heart
pivoted as the cutlass slashed through the air and
struck the wheel just inches from his hand.

God forbid! Thomas Low had escaped his
shackles.

The bloody bastard sneered as rivulets of salt
water coursed down his face. " 'Tis time you die,"
Low hissed.

Black Heart drew his cutlass and skillfully
blocked the next blow of Thomas Low's sword.
Steel clashed hard against steel as Low struck
back, then parried the next thrust of Black Heart's
weapon. "We'll go to hell together," Black Heart
laughingly tossed back. "I can't think of a better
way to spend eternity than watching you burn."

Low's brows furrowed in anger. "There will be
no hell for me, not this day nor any other," he
snarled, swinging his cutlass fiercely at Black
Heart's elusive body.

Black Heart swung, catching the steel of Thomas Low's blade, sending it high in the air, then
down to the slippery deck. He lunged, the tip of
his cutlass grazing Low's throat, drawing a drop
of blood that washed away instantly in the down-
pour. He coaxed the frightened man backward,
pinning his quivering body to the mizzenmast.

"I'd planned a slow death for you," Black Heart

threatened. "Something equally as vile as what you inflicted on my family, but I've tired of this game of chase we've been playing."

"It's been no game. I want what you stole from me."

Black Heart lightly fingered the golden links around his neck, smiling as he touched his most precious treasures—his sister's cross, and his mother's wedding ring. Low had taken the cherished band once before, but never again.

A resounding roar bellowed directly overhead and a bolt of lightning flashed down from the darkened sky, striking the broad side of his blade. Shock ripped through his hand, up his arm, through his entire body. He jerked backward, his fingers still gripping the handle of the vibrating cutlass. He tried to breathe, but he couldn't suck air into his lungs. His heart ceased its beating, and pain exploded through his chest.

Once more he heard Thomas Low's mocking laughter. He looked at the man he hated and watched helplessly as Low pressed a boot against his stomach and sent him crashing into the railing.

Low swept his sword from the deck and advanced. There was nothing Black Heart could do. He had no strength to defend himself.

"This ship is mine now," Low declared. "I'll take those items you wear around your neck, too."

Never! The word screamed in Black Heart's mind, but it never had a chance to cross his tongue.

Lightning skittered across the sky, and one

strong bolt struck the topmast. Low stumbled away as the yardarm and sail toppled down to the deck and smashed just inches from Black Heart's legs. The rigging snapped and squirmed between the two men, and Low stood back, proud, victorious, his arms folded across his chest as he sneered.

Black Heart knew he was trapped. There was no escaping now. All he could do was muster what little strength he had to thwart the blows of unrestrained blocks and tackle while he glared hatefully at the man who mocked his plight, the man he should have killed years before.

"I'll not rest until I see you dead," Black Heart shouted through the squeal and groan of the cracking mizzenmast.

An evil grin crossed Low's face, and he ducked out of sight as the towering mast careened toward the stern.

Black Heart had little time to react. He raised his arms and cushioned the blow of the powerful pole as it smashed violently against the side of his head.

Fighting for consciousness, trying to ignore the pain, he grabbed the mast and held on tightly as it slid across the deck. It whipped back and forth and at last broke free of its rigging and sails. In one wild sweep, the mast hurtled over the side of the ship, carrying Black Heart with it into the turbulent depths of the unforgiving Atlantic.

Chapter 1

I had a dream which was not all a dream.

LORD BYRON, DARKNESS

Into the present . . .

A monstrous wave rose from the belly of the ocean, churning and foaming as it sped toward the strand. The teeming water crashed into the shore, tossing a bedraggled body mercilessly onto the beach. Salt water swirled over and around the man's legs, chest, and head, and slowly his limp, nearly lifeless fingers reached out and clawed at the sand to keep him from being dragged back into the cruel sea.

Black Heart gasped for air, crawling inch by inch up the familiar beach as he fought the pull of the ocean and the push of the hurricane winds which wanted to claim his last ounce of breath. But he refused to give up.

Stabbing the cutlass he hadn't relinquished to the sea into the sand for leverage, he struggled further from the water, then used the sword as a crutch to pull his weary body up from the ground. His legs wobbled beneath his weight. He'd exhausted most all his strength fighting for life in the raging Atlantic. He had little energy left to make it to shelter, but he'd find the power somewhere.

The wind blasted him from all sides as he pressed against the storm. Shielding his eyes with his hand, he could make out the grove of palms where he'd sought refuge many years before. Further inland was the fortress of rock, shell, and mud secluded in an oasis of moss-draped cypress, wind-twisted pines, and palmetto palms. If he could just make it to his hideaway, he could rest. There was rum stashed inside which would quench his thirst. If he drank enough, it might also numb the throbbing ache in his head and force him to sleep.

When he reached the palms that bent as easily as blades of grass in the wind, he wrapped his arms around a prickly trunk. Resting his cheek against the surface, he waited for the howling storm to calm. He prayed for just one moment of peace, one minute of rest.

Instead, nausea overwhelmed him and a dizzying array of colors swirled before his eyes as the earth spun around and around. Pain pulsed at his temple. He didn't need to reach up and touch the spot. He could easily envision the swollen, blood-clotted gash beneath his hair. The wound should have killed him. Hell, he should have drowned in the angry sea, but he was too stubborn to die. And he'd be damned if he'd meet his Maker, or the Devil himself, before wreaking revenge on Thomas Low.

'Twas that vengeance that drove him onward. Taking a deep breath, he pushed away from the tree and stumbled as he fought the wind, the bite of drifting, pelting sand, and the palm fronds and cypress branches that flew helter-skelter through the air.

Suddenly he halted. The pain in his body swept to the center of his heart as he surveyed the ravages before him. *Dear God Almighty.* Like the rest of his life, his home had been destroyed. Portions of the roof were gone and the walls looked as if they'd been blasted by cannonballs. The place where he'd hidden from his enemies was now just a skeleton, only a meager frame of the stronghold he'd built with his own two hands.

He raised his fist and his eyes to the darkened sky. "I won't let this defeat me. I swore revenge and I mean to get it, no matter what obstacles You or the Devil shove in my way."

Thunder bellowed, and a heavy sheet of rain crashed down from the clouds.

I won't be beaten. I won't.

He staggered through the main entrance, into an empty room. A cynical laugh rumbled in his chest. Furniture he'd taken from Spanish galleons and the carpets he'd traded diamonds and rubies for while traveling in ancient lands were gone. Hammered gold platters and fine Chinese porcelain no longer graced the shelves of mahogany cabinets. The rock floors he'd intricately laid had grass peeking up through gaping holes, and fine white sand had drifted into dunes along the base of the walls and covered most of the floor. And the relentless rain poured through ragged openings in the roof to form pools on the ground.

There was no need to search further for his belongings. He knew he'd find only the same bleak emptiness.

How could all this have happened in just one short year away? He shook his head in wonder. He thought he'd accomplished much on this latest voyage. Now he'd lost everything. The proof was in the island's empty harbor and in the crumbling ruins he was facing now.

None of that mattered, though. Once before he'd lost everything—everything but his life. He was still alive, he could rebuild, and he could again hunt Thomas Low. He prayed that his enemy had survived the storm. Without revenge, there'd be little left in his heart to keep him going.

He wound his way through the maze of rooms, while the wind howled through the battered rooftop and cracked walls, chasing him like banshees desperately trying to drag him to hell.

I'll not go easily, he warned, as he sought the place where his massive four-poster bed once had been. The heavy velvet drapes were gone, as was his leather sea trunk, and the Spanish dressing table and chair where he'd always sat to remove his boots. All the comforts he'd known before had disappeared.

Having nowhere else to lay his head, he collapsed against the rough shell and mortar wall and glared straight ahead.

This was the place he'd escaped to when the cruelty of life, when the horrors of all that he'd done in the past years had become too much to bear. This island where he'd buried his sister had become his home.

Now it was as empty as his soul.

He rested his head atop his drawn-up knees. He had to sleep. To heal. Tomorrow he'd rebuild his life—again.

He closed his eyes. Like a lullaby sung by demons, the pelting rain and the whine of the storm dulled his senses. His eyes grew heavy, as did his breathing, and when he thought he'd finally sleep, he heard the faint traces of childish laughter.

A ghost? His eyelids jerked opened. *Had Melody come back to keep him company?* Lord knows he'd prayed often enough for her to return.

He tried to calm his breathing and shut out the storm so he could once more hear the voice. And then it came to him.

"No, Mommy. You're telling it all wrong."

It *was* a child, and the first taste of comfort he'd known in days, maybe even years, consoled him.

He turned to the gaping hole in the wall that

connected this room to the quarters where his in-
frequent guests had stayed, and placed his ear to
the mortar, keeping completely out of sight so no
one would know he was about. There was a price
on his head, and many a man wanted the ample
reward.

Laughter drifted through the opening, a sweet,
warm voice wrapping around him like the finest
of furs. A woman this time, not a child.

"Okay, let me try it again. Long John Silver
swaggered into the inn with a great treasure chest
under his arm. All eyes turned toward the door,
and frightened men shivered in their boots when
the man with a parrot on his shoulder bellowed,
'Yo-ho-ho, and a bottle of rum!' "

"No," the child stressed, and a grin touched
Black Heart's lips at the sound of her frustration.
"Long John Silver was the one with the peg leg.
It was the old sea-dog living at the Admiral Ben-
bow who sang those words. Don't you remem-
ber?"

"You know I always get them confused."

"Then you should read the book again. Daddy
read it to me all the time!"

The voices were real—not imagined or ghostly.
Sweet, heaven-sent voices. Still, he bristled at the
thought of uninvited guests on his island. Where
there was a woman and child, there was bound
to be a man. He gripped his cutlass tightly in one
hand and pulled his dagger from under his belt
with the other.

Standing quietly on guard next to the jagged

wall, he listened for other voices, but all he heard was the incessant storm and a giggling child singing like a drunken buccaneer.

"Fifteen men on a dead man's chest. Yo-ho-ho, and a bottle of rum!"

Black Heart's lips angled into a smile. He hadn't heard a child's laughter in years. Surely this was all a dream, a delusion caused by the blasted blow to his head. And if so, he wanted the fantasy to continue.

"Why don't you let me tell *you* a story, Mommy? I know you like to try, but you don't have any imagination—not like Daddy and me."

Ah, a feisty little thing. He liked that in a child. He liked it in his women, too. But, bloody hell, ladies cowered from him now, and barmaids wanted only his booty.

What a sad state of affairs he'd brought upon himself, where he had to hide from the world, and seek comfort by spying on women and children.

"Why don't you tell me one just like your father would have told?" the woman said, her words laced with a hint of sadness he could detect even without seeing her face.

"Okay, but it's going to be scary."

The little girl giggled, sounding so much like his beloved Melody.

God, how he missed his sister's laughter, her smiles, the soft touch of little fingers in the palm of his hand as they'd walked the streets of London, he a respected young gentleman, she a child with bouncing black curls.

It seemed a thousand years since they'd shared secrets, since they'd sailed with their parents from England toward the West Indies—since he'd held Melody's limp, lifeless body in his arms and buried her in the midst of a grove of palms.

He shook his head, shoving that memory from his mind. Her death had driven him to vengeance; remembrances of her life kept him sane. And it was sanity he needed most of all now.

Pressing his cheek to the cool battered wall, he listened as the child in the next room cleared her throat, the same thing he'd often done when he'd sat down before the fire to begin one of his tales, with Melody snuggled in his lap.

"Listen up, matey," the child announced, in a deep, exaggerated voice. " 'Tis a vile story I tell you now, of the most infamous pirate to ever sail the seven seas."

Warmth touched his heart as he sank to the floor, resting his weary head against the wall while he listened to her tale.

"Some folks say Blackbeard was the scurviest of pirates, but my story is about a buccaneer who was even worse. He had a big, ugly scar on his face and when he wasn't wearing his patch, his right eye hung from its socket. Some people say that he ate babies for breakfast and picked his teeth with their bones."

"Don't you think you're exaggerating a bit too much?" the woman interrupted.

"No, Mommy," the girl said innocently. "It's true. Cross my heart."

A rumble of laughter caught in Black Heart's chest. He'd embellished many a tale to the delight of his sister, even to a drunken crew. He'd been the best of storytellers, and now it appeared he was meeting his match.

"Did he have *any* good qualities?" the woman asked.

"Of course not," the girl said indignantly. "He was a pirate! His hands were grimy, his finger-nails were broken. His pigtail smelled like rotten fish and his clothes were so dirty that even the ship's rats hated to get close to him." Her voice lowered, and Black Heart scrambled up from the floor and put his ear close to the opening so he could hear her story over the ceaseless winds. "If you've heard anything good about this man, don't believe it." Her voice raised again, and her words hit him loud and clear. "Black Heart was the wick-edest cutthroat to ever set foot on earth."

"Lies!" Black Heart shouted, but his protest was drowned out by a rumble of thunder. 'Twas one thing to embellish a story. 'Twas another to slan-der a man who'd once had an admirable name. He had half a mind to storm into that room and point out all of his sterling character traits, but nausea gripped him again. Swirls of darkness and light whipped around his head, and once more he rested his brow on the cool, damp wall.

The pain at his temple intensified, but he man-aged to peek cautiously through the jagged hole to see if the child who repeated such contemptible hearsay had horns protruding from her head.

He wasn't quite prepared for the sight he saw in the gloomy room. The storyteller chatted on and on as she cuddled in her mother's arms, dressed in scarcely a stitch. She was just a wee bit of a thing, with wide eyes the color of a tranquil sea, a turned-up nose, and a mass of blond ringlets. From the looks of her she should have a halo suspended over her head. A tilted halo. One that burned with Satan's fire.

"Aren't you leaving a few things out of your story?" the woman asked. "Like the fact that Black Heart robbed from the rich and gave to the poor?"

The child rolled her pretty blue eyes. "That stuff's no fun."

But it's the truth! Black Heart spouted inwardly, wanting to vindicate himself. He had to stay quiet, though. Hidden. A woman and child would not be on the island alone, and he couldn't risk being seen. Should their man return, a man interested in the bounty on his head, he would not have the endurance to fight.

Nay, he must remain silent. On guard. Watching his surroundings. The scantily clothed child. The inadequately attired woman.

Ah, the woman.

She had a damn fine face. One of the prettiest faces he'd seen in many a year. She had a mighty fine body, too, and he could see nearly every scandalously revealed inch. The child's head rested against her mother's bosom, a pillow of comfort if ever he'd seen one. Her plump round breasts came close to spilling out of the bright blue corset she wore. At least he assumed it was a corset, the way it hugged her waist and belly. He'd never seen one quite like it. Naturally, he'd seen many a corset in his day, but this one had no bones to keep the woman's back stiff, no hooks or laces to cinch her body into an unnatural shape and make it difficult for her to breathe, much less talk or eat. Instead, the fabric glistened like the finest of silk, and it smoothed over an already slender body. A damn fine body!

And the face. A grown-up version of the child's, with fair skin, the pinkest of lips, wide eyes that, even in the gathering gloom, sparkled like emeralds. Her wavy hair was the color of honey, and it hung far below her shoulders, looking windblown, tousled, as if she'd just been making love.

What a beautiful woman like that was doing on his island was hard to fathom.

Unless she was a gift from the gods.

Or an outcast. He looked around the room where she and the child huddled and saw nothing to sustain them. There were no baskets filled with cheese and bread, no flasks of water, beer, or rum. They had nothing with them save the few scraps of fabric they were clothed in.

Perhaps someone evil had left them alone on the island to die. Perhaps they'd had the misfortune of meeting someone as vile as Thomas Low.

A sudden attack of nausea and dizziness overwhelmed him, and he doubled over to thwart the worst of the sickness. Blood rushed to his head, to the gash across his skull. He forgot all about the woman's perfect body, about the child's angelic looks and her devilish lies. The incessant howl of wind and rain battered his eardrums, sending most thoughts from his mind.

Weakness overcame his muscles as a thousand pinpricks of pain jabbed at his skin. His fingers turned cold and numb. His shoulders drooped, and he felt as if they could no longer bear the weight of his neck and head.

He needed to sleep, to let his body heal. Perhaps when he woke he'd realize that the woman, the child, and the destruction of his home were nothing but a dream. Life would return to normal. *Satan's Revenge* would be anchored in the harbor. His fortress would be whole again and his riches would be in their rightful places.

Thomas Low would be in shackles.

And the godforsaken pain would be gone.

He prayed for oblivion, and smiled when a bolt of lightning flashed in the sky and thunder shook the ground. Slowly he crumpled to his knees. For one moment he thought he was going to die, and he clutched at the chains he wore about his neck, touching, one more time, his mother's ring and his sister's cross, before the blessed darkness enveloped him and the hard, sandy floor rushed up to meet his face.

Chapter 2

🗡️

The waves lie still and gleaming,
And the lulled winds seem dreaming.

LORD BYRON, *STANZAS FOR MUSIC*

"Are you okay, mister?"

The child's words were but a whisper against Black Heart's ear. Too many years had passed since he'd wakened to something so sweet, and the voice of the little girl he'd seen earlier pleased him more than fair winds ruffling the sails on *Satan's Revenge* or the lap of gentle waves against her hull.

"Can you hear me?"

Aye, he tried to say, but his mouth was much too dry for speech to come. It seemed as if he'd swallowed half the sand his face was resting in. Opening his eyes proved an impossibility, too, and the mere thought of nodding his head brought back the pain, as strong and relentless as the hurricane that had attempted to take his life.

"Wake up, mister."

He managed to groan, a horrendous, guttural noise that to his ears sounded like the wail of a cow.

"Did you say something?" the child asked. He could feel her warm breath against his cheek, her tiny fingers lightly prodding his shoulder. She was a brave bit of a thing to come so close, especially when she imagined him to be a man who ate babies for breakfast.

"Are you dead?"

"I'm . . . not . . . quite . . . sure," he mumbled. With great effort he rolled over on the rocky floor, and somehow he worked open the eyelid that wasn't covered with a patch. Blond ringlets bounced before his nose, and two frowning blue eyes studied his scar.

"Are you a pirate?"

He didn't respond. Instead, he asked, "Are you a castaway?"

"No. I'm Casey Cameron. But you didn't answer my question. Are you a pirate?"

"Aye." The word slipped from his lips with no thought of their consequence. He should have answered, "Nay," and told her some far-fetched story, but it was too late now.

Her eyes widened, followed by her smile. "I knew you'd come," she whispered, and then her voice rose with excitement. "I knew it! Mommy's never going to believe this. Not in a million years."

She started to run.

Bloody hell! He had to stop her before she brought back her mother and any others who might be on the island with thoughts of collecting the bounty on his head. He jerked up, and the dizziness once more overwhelmed him.

"Wait," he called out to her, his voice just as unsteady as his body, his throat as scratchy as the sand embedded in his skin.

The child stopped in the doorway and twisted around. "I'll be right back." But she didn't leave. Instead, she frowned, her gaze traveling to the cutlass lying on the floor, then upward, pausing just long enough to study the pistol and dagger tucked under his belt.

She bit the corner of her lip, then met him eye to eye. "You *are* real, aren't you?"

"Aye."

The angelic smile returned to her face. "Then don't go anywhere. Please."

She disappeared into the sunlight outside, and for one brief moment, he contemplated honoring her plea. But he couldn't stick around—not for her, not for anyone. Hiding was a way of life, one he practiced well.

Drawing in a deep breath, he struggled to stand. The room spun around him as if he'd been on a week-long drunk and was just now regaining his senses.

With a faltering sweep of his hand, he retrieved his cutlass from the ground, shoved it into its scabbard, and willed himself to move.

One foot dragged across the sand, and then the next. He was gasping for breath by the time he reached the doorway, and for just an instant, he rested his cheek against the craggy stone wall. Then he pushed on, forcing himself to go faster, skirting the palms that rustled in the waning wind.

The storm had calmed, but it had left its mark upon the land, making it even more difficult for him to maneuver. He trudged through puddles of water and over uprooted trees and finally collapsed behind a pile of storm-tossed vegetation that had mounded against a tall drift of sand.

A cool breeze brought some relief from the heat and humidity of the day, and carried with it the child's voice. She was close. Much too close. How could he possibly have run toward her—when he'd meant to run away?

"I knew he'd come, Mommy. I knew it!"

"Calm down, Case. What are you talking about?"

"The pirate. When I said my prayers last night, I asked God to send me a pirate—and He did."

Ah, the woman's laughter again. If only he could capture that sound as it drifted through the air, and keep it with him always.

"It's not funny, Mommy. He's not funny, either."

"Is he mean?"

"I don't think so, but he's not the kind of pirate I wanted."

"You had something specific in mind?" the woman asked.

"Well, I wanted a nice-looking pirate. One you might like, but this one's ugly. Really big and really ugly, and he has a big red scar down the whole side of his face. I guess that means he must be mean."

"You can't always judge someone by his appearance. It's what's inside that counts."

"Oh, I know all that. But if you saw this guy, you'd probably be really scared."

"Were you afraid of him?"

"Heck, no. I think he was asleep, and when I touched him, he just sort of grunted, then he kept saying, 'Aye' . . . 'Aye,' you know, like real pirates say."

The woman was silent for too long a time. He imagined her eyes scanning the island, looking for an evil buccaneer, wringing her hands in dismay, anxiously hoping that her own man would soon return.

And then her sweet, melodious voice touched his ears again.

"You're sure you didn't imagine the pirate, Case?"

"No, Mommy, you've got to believe me."

He remembered the child's words. *Mommy's never going to believe this. Not in a million years.* He wondered why his presence should seem such an impossibility, when a multitude of brigands roamed up and down this coast.

Then a thought crossed his mind. Perhaps

they'd been in search of a pirate, desperately needing to collect the bounty on his head. It seemed a foolhardy venture for a woman and child, but the price for capturing Black Heart was enough to tempt anyone.

Claiming the reward, however, would prove most difficult. As soon as nightfall came, he'd find a way to escape the island. Until then, he'd rest quietly on the dune, and listen to the woman, the child, and keep an ear out for others.

"Tell me more about the pirate, Case. Did he have a peg leg?"

"No, just a patch. I bet he doesn't even have an eye behind it. Somebody probably cut it out when they were fighting."

A laugh rumbled deep in Black Heart's chest as he reached under the patch and rubbed his right eye. Perfectly intact, just as it had always been. He readjusted the piece of black satin he'd worn—or not worn—to confuse his pursuers, then traced his index finger lightly down the length of the scar that ran from the outer corner of his right eye, over his cheek, and curled just under his lower lip. It wasn't all that big and it wasn't all that ugly, simply a razor-fine slice left by the tip of a very sharp blade.

Thomas Low's blade. Damn him to hell! The blackguard hadn't been satisfied with carving a deep scar on his soul; he'd maimed his body, too.

He shoved memories of Low away. He was confused enough by what he'd found on his island without clouding his thoughts with the deeds of that murderer. There were other things to think of now—like the unprotected woman and child, and the possibility that there might be others stalking the island, looking for him.

Climbing to the top of the sand dune, he caught sight of the curly-haired child.

And the woman.

She was on her knees in the sand, her hands on the child's shoulders. Behind her was the sleekest sailing vessel he'd ever seen, lying like a beached whale on the shore.

The ship was finely built, but it was the woman who caught his fancy. She was far and away the most winsome female who'd ever come into his line of vision. Definitely a woman to be gazed upon with two good eyes, he decided, flipping up his patch.

He imagined her age to be close to a score and four, perhaps as much as a score and six. She had the creamy skin of a girl not long out of the nursery, but the lusciously rounded body of a goddess—Tethys, maybe, the beautiful queen of the seas, the titaness he'd often asked to protect him as he and *Satan's Revenge* sailed the oceans.

Bloody hell! She was not a goddess, she was merely a woman, a petite bit of perfection who'd have to stand on her toes just so the top of her head could reach his chin.

A woman who could easily tempt a man to wish for a wife, and babes, and a permanent home, if he was foolish enough to contemplate leaving the sea.

A thought that would never cross his own mind.

"We have to go to him, Mommy," the child cried, tearing Black Heart's attention away from sentimental thoughts, and turning it back again to the child, and the beautiful woman shaking her head quite adamantly.

The child shoved her fists into her hips. "But he could be dying."

"He could be dangerous, too," the woman stated flatly. "No, Case, we're better off staying here in the open. That way we can keep an eye out for him."

"You don't believe there's a pirate, do you?" the child asked. "Daddy would have believed me."

The woman turned her head, looking out to sea. "Daddy was a dreamer, Case. He believed in a lot of things. . . ." Her words drifted away, just as the child drifted from her touch.

"I wish Daddy was here. I would have prayed for him to come instead of a pirate, but I've tried before and it doesn't work."

The woman reached out to touch the child, but she jerked away. He could sense the woman's hurt, the rejection she felt, as she looked at the back of her daughter's head. God knows he'd seen his own mother look that way many a time.

In spite of her daughter's withdrawal, the woman approached her again, wrapped her arms around the girl, and rested her cheek against her curls.

"Daddy's not coming back," she said gently.

"As much as we want him to, he can't. It's just you and me, Case."

He watched a tender smile transform her face from sad to wistful. "If Daddy were here. . . ." Even from the distance he could hear her sigh. "If Daddy were here, the blasted boat wouldn't be lying on the beach and we'd be home by now."

Slowly the woman ran her fingers down her daughter's sides, and with a sudden change of mood, she tickled her waist. She laughed as the little girl erupted into giggles.

For long minutes they chased each other around the beach, and as Black Heart watched their gaiety, he sensed they were alone, that there were no men on the island. He could easily make himself known to them, but then he'd no longer be able to watch their play, and it did his heart good to know that there was still great happiness in the world he'd abandoned.

He watched while they scampered through the water, kicking at waves, diving into their depths, then coming out at last to lie on the beach.

"Do you think we're going to be stranded here forever?" the child asked. "Like Robinson Crusoe?"

"Of course not. The storm just shoved the boat a little too far up on the sand, but as soon as the tide comes back in, we should be able to get it back out to sea."

The child looked inland, toward Black Heart's stronghold. "My pirate might help, if we ask him nicely."

Frowning, Casey's mother sighed as she looked toward the center of the island. He imagined she was wondering how much truth there was to her daughter's words about a pirate being in the fortress. She scanned the groves of palm and the deserted beach, and her gaze swept right over the dune where he hid. Finally she turned back to the child.

"Pirates aren't very trustworthy, Case. I know how much you'd like to have one for a friend, but this time I think we'd better take care of ourselves, and right now that means we try pushing the boat."

The woman shoved up from the ground, brushed sand from her hands, and moved gracefully toward the vessel. She was a beauty, parading about in only that bright blue corset and some sort of pantaloon. Her slender thighs, her rounded hips, and her blessed bottom swayed when she walked, and when she applied that part of her anatomy to the side of the boat and pushed, her glorious breasts nearly spilled from the small bit of fabric she was wearing.

Ah, but she made his body ache.

"Come on, Case," the woman pleaded to the child who stubbornly sat on the beach. "I really do need your help."

Black Heart could hear the child's frustrated sigh all the way across the beach, sounding so much like his own beloved sister who'd often sighed when she couldn't have what she wanted.

The old familiar pain stabbed at his heart. God,

how he missed Melody's little-girl giggles, her
bouncing black curls, the way dimples formed at
the corners of her lips when she smiled.

He'd never see those smiles again. Never hear
her laughter, or wrap a curl around his finger as
he bounced her on his knee.

He'd never again hear her say, "I love you."

Thomas Low would pay for what he'd done,
but, bloody hell, he could do nothing until he got
off this island.

He looked at the boat the woman was struggling to move. 'Twas just what he needed in order
to find *Satan's Revenge*, and it appeared it was not
going to leave the island until the tide came in.
'Twould be nearly impossible, even then, for the
woman to get the boat off the sand. 'Twould be
difficult enough for him, but he'd deal with that
problem when darkness fell and the ocean rolled
high on the beach. The woman and child would
be asleep by then, and he would take the boat
unbeknownst to either of them.

An ounce of guilt tugged at his heart. Perhaps
he should take them with him, but he had more
important matters to concern himself with now,
and he didn't need either of them in his way—or
under his skin. He had no doubt that they'd be
safe on the island and, being a gentleman by nature, he would send someone back to rescue them.

Sliding down on the dune, he banished the
woman and child from his thoughts. With the
blazing sun beating down on him, he rested his
dizzy head on palm fronds and cypress branches,

and allowed just one thought to consume his mind—revenge.

Soon even thoughts of Thomas Low left him, and once again he slept.

Kate pressed her back to the hull and attempted to shove the boat at least one miserable inch through the sand, but it wouldn't budge. "Damn!"

"You swear too much," Casey admonished, peeking over the side of the boat. "Aunt Evalena says—"

"Aunt Evalena says a lot of things," Kate interrupted, "and she's going to say a whole lot more if we don't get home soon."

"Why?"

"Because I didn't leave a sailing plan."

"Why?"

"Because the weather report was good. Because I didn't expect a hurricane to come up out of nowhere, and because I didn't want Evie *or* Aunt Nikki to know we were going to the island."

"Why?"

Kate smiled at Casey's one-word refrain. "They don't believe there's treasure here, and they'll think I've lost my mind if they find out I went hunting for something that might not exist."

"But it does exist. And when we find it, we'll be rich; then you won't have to take care of all those other kids anymore."

Casey jumped down to the sand and skipped to the water's edge before Kate could remind her that treasure or no treasure, she wasn't about to give up her day care center. She loved taking care of a house full of kids. They made her happy. She'd wanted half a dozen of her own, children she could love the way she'd wished her own parents had loved her, but she and Joe had been blessed with only Casey.

Maybe if he'd lived longer . . .

She let that thought drift away. She doubted that anything would have changed if Joe had lived longer. They might have had more children eventually, but he'd still be fun-loving Joe, the boy who didn't want to grow up. She'd still love him, of course. It was impossible not to. But she had no doubts that he'd still be searching for treasure, he'd still be obsessed with pirates, and he'd still be spending money as if they'd had it to burn.

She collapsed against the eighteen-foot sailboat that Joe never should have bought, and gazed at the storm-ravaged island—one more of Joe's impractical and expensive whims.

Joe was a doting father, a decorated cop, but he'd spent a portion of every paycheck buying things they didn't need, like the crossed swords he'd hung over the mantel in the living room, the eighteenth-century pistols he polished monthly and kept in a locked cabinet in his office, and the leather chest that rested at the end of their bed. It had once held a bounty of pirate treasure, or so Joe had told her. "We can't afford it," was all she had said, but he'd only laughed. "There's always money if you want something badly enough."

She remembered so well the call from the antique store the day after Joe's funeral. "We're sorry to bother you, Mrs. Cameron, but Joe was here the other night. He bought a trunk and said he'd pick it up later. We'd like you to have it. We'd like you to have the money back, too. It's the least we could do, considering. . . ."

Joe had wanted that trunk so badly it had cost him his life. Now, instead of giving him pleasure, it held some of the things Kate treasured most— the uniforms Joe would never wear again, his medal for bravery, and the badge he'd honored.

If Joe had listened to her when she'd said they couldn't afford it, he wouldn't have been in the antique store. He wouldn't have walked outside just in time to see the kid robbing the convenience store. He wouldn't have been blown away by a sawed-off shotgun.

And Nikki wouldn't have suffered so much remorse for emptying an entire barrel into the chest of the seventeen-year-old boy who'd murdered her brother.

Kate had forgotten all about the treasure after that night. She had a daughter to support, a home to take care of, and fanciful thoughts about pirates and buried treasure were the last thing on her mind.

But last night Joe had come to her in a dream. He'd told her to go to the island. "The treasure's there. I know it, Kate. Please, baby. Go and find it."

She'd listened to him because even in sleep,

she'd seen the sparkle in his eyes, and it brought back so many memories, like the way his face had beamed the first time they'd sailed to the island. "Black Heart used to live here," he'd said, speaking the pirate's name almost reverently. "Remember me telling you about him? He disappeared in a freak summer storm."

Kate laughed, wondering if that freak summer storm had been anything like the one she and Casey had just survived.

"What are you thinking about, Mommy?"

Casey's voice brought Kate back to the present, and she turned to the little girl who was a dreamer—just like her dad. "I was thinking how much your father would have enjoyed this adventure."

"He wouldn't have wasted so much time trying to get the boat back into the water when he could have been spending time with a pirate."

"No, I suppose he wouldn't. In fact, I don't want to spend any more time worrying about the boat, either."

"Then can we look for the pirate?"

Casey's eyes brightened when Kate nodded.

This would be the third imaginary pirate in her life. The first one she'd named Mr. Bones, the second she had called Captain Jack. They'd kept her company after Joe had died. They'd had make-believe sword fights with her in the living room and helped her dig for buried treasure in the backyard. Kate had never discouraged Casey's imaginative streak, and it was time to give in to it once again.

There was nothing else to do on the island—so they might as well have fun.

"So, Case, where do you think we'll find your pirate?"

"In the fortress."

"Great. Wanna race?"

A wide smile crossed Casey's face. "Yeah!"

"Last one to the fortress is a rotten egg." Kate sprinted away from the boat, listening to Casey's giggles as she ran close behind. They dashed across the beach, past an immense pile of palm fronds and cypress boughs that had blown against a sand dune, and jumped over puddles of water left from the storm. They laughed, as if the hurricane had never occurred, as if they had nothing at all to worry about.

Blocking Casey's way when they reached the entrance to the ancient island stronghold, Kate bent over, hands on knees, and took a long, deep breath. "Okay, Case. Let's not rush. He might still be inside."

She took Casey's hand and together they crept into the cavernous fortress.

"This way," Casey whispered, tugging Kate through the maze of empty rooms.

The light breeze whistled through holes and cracks, making the place seem eerier than it was. She tried to imagine the stronghold as it had looked hundreds of years before, with a pirate captain leaning against the wall and half a dozen of his crew standing about swilling rum and stout, while buxom wenches swirled their skirts and touted their wares.

Casey's pull on her hand tore her from her imaginings.

"He's just around the corner," she said, and Kate suddenly began to believe Casey's pirate might really exist.

Kate stilled her daughter and put a silencing finger to her lips.

Gripping Casey's arms, they cautiously peered around the opening and into . . . an empty room.

Under her fingers, Kate could feel the sag of her daughter's shoulders, her disappointment. In her own heart, she too felt a nagging sense of defeat.

"He's gone, Mommy. I *told* you we should have come earlier."

Maybe they should have, but it was too late now.

"I doubt he's gone far, Case. There's no way off the island, except in our boat, and it's not going anywhere."

"Do you think we'll see him tomorrow?"

"I don't know about you, but after the stories you told me, I'm bound to have nightmares about him tonight."

Casey finally laughed. "Did I tell you he had rings in both ears? Did I tell you about his cutlass?"

A picture of Casey's pirate was beginning to form in Kate's mind, and she definitely wasn't seeing Errol Flynn.

"I think you told me everything about him except his name. Do you think it might be Black Heart, the pirate who used to live here?"

Casey's lips twitched back and forth as she thought. "He didn't look at all like the pictures in Daddy's books."

"Those sketches aren't very good, Case. They're old, and they were usually drawn from someone's imagination, or from what they'd heard about a person."

"Well, if it is Black Heart, do you think he might be watching us, waiting for us to fall asleep, so he can snatch us up and take us prisoner?"

"Oh, I don't think that's likely to happen."

"But that's what pirates do, Mommy." Casey poked her head through the gap of a window that looked out on the approaching darkness.

"Do you think his pirate ship might be off shore somewhere?"

Kate walked across the room, curling her arms around her daughter, giving her comfort, seeking the same for herself.

"What do you think your father's answer to that question would have been?"

Looking up with a smile on her face, Casey cleared her throat, and said in a voice much lower than Joe's had ever been, "Well, Casey, if there's a pirate ship off shore, I guess it's our lucky day. Maybe we can thumb a ride back to St. Augustine."

Casey giggled, and warmth radiated through

Kate for her daughter, for the man they both had
loved.

God, how she missed him.

Throwing her arms around her mother's neck,
Casey pressed a hard, loving kiss on her cheek.
"I'm going to sleep," she said in a rush of words.
"I'm gonna dream about pirates," she added,
skipping out of the room, happily singing *"Yo-ho-
ho, and a bottle of rum!"*

With all her heart, Kate wished that a pirate—
a good pirate, she amended—would walk into the
fortress and make Casey's dreams come true. As
for her own dreams, she had let them die right
along with Joe. Now she was beginning to want
them back.

The caw of a bird turned her attention outside,
to the sounds of the night. Wings fluttered overhead as island birds stole from tree to tree. In the
distance she could hear the gentle lap of waves on
the beach, and the crackle and snap of fallen
brush, as if some night creature were stirring from
its daytime abode.

Could it possibly be a man? she wondered. *Casey's
pirate?* No, that was impossible. She'd just allowed
her imagination to run wild. Even now she was
seeing fairies dancing across the cobbled floor,
when it was only the rays of the rising moon glinting through the window. And the ring poking
through the sand was only. . . .

She moved toward the emerald glow and knelt
so the moonlight could still illuminate her find.
Calmly, deliberately, she scooped her fingers un-

derneath a band of gold and shimmering jewels, and let the sand sift away.

"Oh, my God."

A long, slender chain of golden links slid over her hand and dropped to the floor, but the ring settled in the center of her palm, staring up at her in all its glory. The emerald, if that's what the radiant green stone really was, had to be nearly the size of a dime. It was set in a wide band of filigreed gold, with a trio of diamonds glittering like luminous stars at either side.

It was the most beautiful piece of jewelry she'd ever seen, and certainly the most wonderful—and valuable—she'd ever touched. Could it possibly be real, and not just a piece of costume jewelry someone had once left behind on the island?

She slid the ring on her finger, covering the tan line where, until a few days ago, she'd worn a simple gold wedding band. It seemed sinful to put another ring on that finger, when Joe's ring had meant the world to her. But this new ring fit perfectly, as if it had been made just for her.

She looked about her, for some odd reason afraid that someone might be watching. Afraid that she'd just fallen in love with a ring that rightfully belonged to someone else. No one was around, though. No one watched her. As far as she knew, the ring had been buried under the sand in this fortress for hundreds of years, a treasure waiting to be found.

Perhaps it was the treasure Joe had sent her to find.

A lone tear slid down her face. With all her heart she wished Joe had been the one to find it.

Wiping the tear away, she swept the chain from the sand, studying the intricacy of the links, and the break where the unending circle of gold had torn apart. It looked like so many of the antique pieces of jewelry Joe had purchased, only this wasn't dull from over a hundred years of wear. Instead, it sparkled like new.

Were there more pieces buried beneath the stones?

Slipping the ring from her finger, she tucked it and the chain into the pocket of her shorts and went in search of other treasure. She carefully brushed sand away from the cobbles, digging her fingers between the cracks, hoping the moonlight would stay with her a little while longer.

Wouldn't Casey be thrilled to know the treasure her father had always talked about was right under their noses?

She pulled one of the stones up from the floor, but there was only sand beneath it. She dug deeper. Still nothing.

She tore up another stone, and another, until the moonlight ceased to shine on the spot where she'd found the first of the treasure, but there were no more rings, no more chains.

Crawling to the last bit of floor that was still lit by moonbeams, she started to dig, but her fingers came to a sudden stop.

A footprint seemed to rise up from the sand.

The heavy impression of a man's boot. There

was no mistaking the heel, the rounded toe. Or the size.

Oh, God!

Another print rested beside it, and another at a different angle. She turned and saw the remains of another print—one that she'd crawled through. Even in the darkness, she could see more prints crossing to the door, some appearing as if the man had stumbled and dragged his feet across the floor.

She felt her heart begin to beat hard inside her chest. Faster. Faster.

She stood, jerking quickly to look out the window, then back once more to the floor. Her body trembled, goosebumps rose on her arms, and slowly she put her bare foot inside one of the prints.

So large. So very, very large.

Her lips quivered as she again looked out into the dark. Night had crept in far too fast.

And someone—a stranger—was on the island.

Chapter 3

There was a laughing Devil in his sneer,
That raised emotions both of rage and fear . . .

LORD BYRON, *THE CORSAIR: CANTO* I

The dizziness had gone, but Black Heart woke from a deep, dreamless sleep with a gnawing in his belly so strong that he no longer thought about dying from the wound to his head or the hangman's noose. Hunger alone would surely do him in.

Darkness had rolled across the island, and with the night came his chance to move around undetected, a skill he'd learned many a year ago while hiding from Her Majesty's men. Someday he hoped he could again set foot in the homes of the gentlemen who'd once called him friend, sup at their tables, drink their wine, and romance their daughters. But he imagined that day would not come anytime soon.

He'd made too many enemies. Lost all his friends.

He laughed at the irony. *Such is the life of a pirate*, where the only friend he needed was a steady ship beneath his feet.

An armed galley like *Satan's Revenge*. He had to get back to her, and suddenly he remembered what he had planned before falling to sleep.

Cautiously he peered over the top of the sand dune, hoping no one else had come to the island while he'd slept. Hoping, too, that the woman and child had retreated to the fortress to spend the night.

Across the beach he could see the vessel resting on her keel. She hadn't been moved, there were no signs of anyone around, and the incoming tide rapidly approached her hull.

He smiled, knowing he'd soon be on the open sea, back on course once more.

Slipping away from his resting place, he crossed the deserted beach, keeping his ears and eyes attuned for any sign of trouble.

He neared the vessel. Her white surface glimmered in the moonlight seeping through the clouds. Hesitantly he touched her hull, marveling at the wondrous wood, sleek and smooth, like the jewels encrusting the hilt of his blade. Her mast was constructed of the same curious material, and her sails . . . by God! Her sails were extraordinary, made entirely of a fabric he could only liken to silk. The finest and richest of silks, like the bolts he'd taken off a merchantman bound for Spain.

He longed to test this small craft on the water. How easily he could envision the feel of her beneath his feet, the flap of her sails as they filled with wind, speeding her across the waves.

Water lapped against her side, at his ankles. Soon she'd right herself, or at least be deep enough in water that he could push her off the sand. And then he'd take her out to sea. He'd commandeered greater vessels in his time, like *Satan's Revenge*, once the pride of the French East India Company. But no vessel except *Satan's Revenge* ever gave him the satisfaction this small sailing boat did. She was a beauty, a ship you'd take out on a balmy spring day, with a bottle of wine and a willing lady.

For one moment he forgot about the boat and looked toward his stronghold. A woman and child rested there, a woman and child who'd be stranded if he took their vessel. He planned to send someone back for them, but his conscience stabbed at him, making him think of the fear they'd feel when they found their boat had disappeared.

He might be a pirate who consorted with some of the meanest scum God had inflicted upon the earth, but he still considered himself a gentleman, and gentlemen didn't leave helpless, defenseless women and children all alone.

He swept his fingers through his hair, turning back to look at the sea, at the water rapidly inching up his boots.

Bloody hell! He was a pirate, not a gentleman.

He had to get off the island, he had to find his ship, and he had to capture Thomas Low.

The blasted wound to his head, the woman's sensual body, not to mention her heaven-sent voice and a curly-haired child, had come too damn close to turning him soft. He couldn't do a thing about his injury—it would have to heal on its own. But he could get away from the two people digging at his hardened heart, the two people who could cause him more trouble than an entire fleet of Her Majesty's ships.

The woman and child were not his concern, and they were bloody well fortunate that he was going to send someone back for them.

Night droned on, the longest, fear-filled night Kate had ever lived through. No, that wasn't true; there'd been that night she'd been awakened by a knock downstairs. The old grandfather clock had chimed one when she'd opened the etched glass door. Nikki had stood there, her face stricken, her police uniform streaked with blood. "Joe's been shot," she'd said. "Get Casey. We need to hurry."

There'd been no time for sentiment, for Nikki to ease out the words. There'd been time only for Kate to imagine the worst as the siren roared and Nikki drove like hell to the hospital. She remembered the lieutenant and sergeant standing somber-faced outside the swinging doors that led to the operating room, and their words of encouragement: "He'll be all right, Kate."

She'd smiled faintly and pulled Casey close into

her arms as she paced the stark white hospital hall that smelled of alcohol and pine cleaner.

Even now she could see the gurney being wheeled out of the room, could see the gray color of her husband's face and the vast assortment of tubes in his nose and leading down his throat. She remembered the tear falling from her eye to his cheek, and someone pulling her away. She remembered the way Nikki's lips quivered as she lightly touched Joe's fingers with hands still covered with his blood.

And she remembered clutching Casey as they stood next to Joe in intensive care. "Don't go away, Daddy," she'd cried. "Please. Don't leave me, Daddy."

She'd been only four, much too young to lose the father she loved so dearly. But in spite of her pleas, Joe had left them. He'd said goodbye after dinner the night before. He'd kissed his daughter, swung her up in the air, and hugged her for the longest time before sending her off to her room to play. He'd grabbed the thermos of coffee Kate had made, brushed a quick kiss across her cheek, and rushed out the door. They'd argued that night. He'd wanted to go to the island the next day. For the first time—and the last—she'd told him she was tired of going to the island. She was tired of looking for a treasure that didn't exist. She wanted to stay home and work on the house. She wanted him to patch the roof, to paint the faded trim. She'd wanted him to be less of a dreamer and more of a realist—because they were growing up;

they weren't kids anymore. But he'd only laughed. "There's plenty of time to work on the house. Humor me, won't you, Kate? We'll pack a picnic. It's going to be a beautiful day for a sail."

And he was right. The sun and the bright blue sky had peeked through the blinds in his hospital room when morning came, and moments later Joe unconsciously took his last breath, and quit fighting to hang onto life.

Casey cried. Nikki put her head down on the pillow next to her brother and tears openly flowed down her cheeks. Lieutenant Ryan and hard-boiled Sergeant Crichton crept into the room and wept.

Kate had stood against the wall, cradling Casey in her arms, and stared at it all, eyes dry, too stunned, too heartbroken to cry.

She reached up and wiped away the tears that now fell from her eyes, tears that had taken weeks to come after Joe had died. He'd been the love of her life, he'd been her dearest friend, and she hated the fact that memories of him were starting to slip away from her, when she was trying so hard to hold him close.

Oh, Joe, if you were here now, I wouldn't be so afraid. I wouldn't be sitting here wondering if a stranger was standing just outside the battered walls, looking through the window.

Watching me.

Watching Casey.

A shiver of fear raced through her, and she

prayed for daylight to wash away the fear of another endless night.

Kate stretched, and the abrasive sand beneath her scratched at her skin. Overworked muscles cried out for rest, but they'd already gotten more than they deserved. She'd fallen asleep when she should have kept a vigilant watch all through the night. Still, morning had come and she was alive.

Rolling over, she reached to draw Casey into her arms, but her fingers touched only sand.

"Casey?" she called out, sure the child was somewhere near, but her daughter's sweet voice never answered. The only sounds that came to her were the screams of gulls and the familiar grunts of pelicans diving offshore for food.

"Casey!"

Anger and fear rolled through her as she pushed up from the floor and rushed through the maze of ruins. This wasn't the first time Casey had struck out on her own. She was headstrong and fearless—and that scared the hell out of Kate.

"Casey!"

She rushed toward the ocean.

"Casey!"

She ran between the clusters of palms, through puddles, and over the devastation left by the hurricane, at last reaching the wide, sandy beach, where tiny footprints trailed toward the water, toward the sailboat—her sailboat—that was anchored not far from shore.

How had it gotten off the beach? Who had dropped the anchor?

Terror knotted in her throat. The answer was obvious: the stranger lurking on the island.

The one-eyed pirate with a scar on his face.

"Casey!"

It seemed as if it took forever for her to reach the water, and she prayed that Casey would peek out of the cabin, that blond curls would magically appear over the side of the boat and she'd hear her daughter's voice calling back, "Hi, Mommy!" But she heard and saw nothing, only the birds overhead, the lap of salt water at her feet, the sailboat bobbing gently on the waves, and not too far up the strand, a set of boot prints headed inland. And the impression of a pair of tiny bare feet padding along behind.

"Avast, matey!"

Black Heart woke from a peace-filled sleep with the pressure of cold steel at his neck and the voice of an angel ringing through his ears. Holding his breath lest the steel pierce his skin, he cracked open his unpatched eyelid and saw Casey's tiny hands struggling to hold the cutlass she'd stealthily stolen from his scabbard.

Bloody hell! If he'd known this was the thanks he'd get for thinking more about the woman and child than his own plans for revenge, he'd have sailed during the night instead of waiting for morning, when he could take the castaways with him. There was no doubt he'd lost his senses at the same time he'd lost his ship.

Now a wee bit of a thing with the cunning of a panther had taken him—reputedly the most illusive pirate to sail the seas—captive. He'd laugh, but he didn't find his current situation humorous. If the blade slipped from the child's fingers. . . .

Damn! That was a possibility he didn't want to consider.

Nervously he smiled and eased into a nonchalant conversation with his captor. "And a good day to you, Mistress Casey."

"Don't move. I don't want you to disappear again."

" 'Tis not my intention to move, child. As you can see, I'm perfectly content to lie here on the sand." At least until he could retrieve his cutlass. "Pray tell, is it your intention to skewer me with my own blade?"

The girl's eyes narrowed, and the heavy sword trembled in her hands, making a zigzag pattern merely an inch above his neck.

"I don't want you to go away. I want my mommy to see you."

"And what of your father?" he asked. The woman had said he wouldn't be coming, that they were all alone, but he had to be sure. "Is he on the island?"

"My Daddy's dead!"

God forbid, he hadn't wanted or expected to hear those words.

"I'm sorry."

"I heard Mommy tell my Aunt Evie that the man who killed him went to hell."

"A more fitting place was never created for murderers." 'Twas just the place he wanted to send Thomas Low.

Slowly he raised a hand and touched his index finger to the broad side of the blade, but Casey held the sword firmly in place.

"Is it your belief that I should be in hell, too?" he asked.

"Are you a murderer?"

"What do you think?"

"You don't look too mean."

"Ah, but looks are often deceiving. After all, who would ever expect a pretty little girl like you to take me captive? Why, even *I* find it difficult to believe that you could have stolen my cutlass while I slept."

"It was easy. You were snoring."

"I have been accused of much in my life, but never that. I did not wake your mother, did I?"

"Casey!"

The child jumped as her mother's voice rang through the air, and the tip of the blade grazed his skin.

He gritted his teeth at the sudden pain. Only a scratch, he assured himself. He'd experienced much worse, but he could still feel the sting of the open wound, could feel a trickle of blood running down his neck.

Tears sprang from the child's eyes as she gaped at the cut. "I didn't mean to hurt you," she cried, shaking her head right along with the cutlass. "I'm sorry. I'm sorry."

"Give me the cutlass, Casey," he said softly but firmly, stretching out his hand.

"But you'll go away."

"Nay," he said, with more calm than he felt. "I give you my word. I will not go anywhere without you and your mother."

"Promise?"

"Promise."

Reluctantly Casey stepped back, and Black Heart pushed up from the ground, taking the jeweled hilt from the child's hands.

"Casey!"

In the span of a heartbeat, Black Heart watched the woman emerge from behind a wall of cypress and palm and saw her eyes widen in fear, then narrow in rage. She streaked across the sand and dived into his chest with the full force of her body, knocking both of them to the ground.

The cutlass slid from his fingers as the woman threw a fist toward his face. He turned his head just in time to keep her from connecting with his nose, but felt her knuckles slam into his temple, the same place he'd taken the blow on *Satan's Revenge.*

What godforsaken thing have I done to deserve the wrath of the child, and now the woman? he wondered. Bloody hell, he should have left without them, but he'd let an ounce of long-forgotten compassion work its way out of his stone-cold heart.

Somehow he found the strength to fight back,

but it was difficult, given the fact that the woman had straddled his stomach and was alternately beating his chest and slapping his face. If she wasn't such a firebrand, he might take pleasure in admiring the view of her breasts swaying with each stroke to his body.

There was no time for admiration, though—not while she had the upper hand. He had to gain control. In one swift move he wrapped an arm around her slender waist and rolled her to the sand, laughing at the anger in her flaming green eyes.

"Take your hands off of me or I'll . . . I'll. . . ."

He never saw her move, never felt the jerk of her knee until it hit his groin, not quite on center, but close enough. Pain ripped through him, and another bout of godforsaken nausea, but still he kept his hold on her arms and pressed the length of his body against hers so she couldn't move again.

"Damnation, woman!" he groaned through gritted teeth. "Do you mean to unman me?"

"I mean to *kill* you," she spat out, the force and truth of her words hitting him square in the face.

"What did you do to my daughter?"

"I have done nothing to the child."

"You were pointing a sword at her. She was crying."

The woman struggled, but he was twice her size, making it impossible for her to escape. He refused to let her go until she saw reason—or at least, realized that the blood from his neck was dripping onto her chest.

"Get off me," she moaned, but all he did was move closer, looking at her eye to eye.

"Give me one good reason."

The child screamed, and that was reason enough.

Black Heart spun around to see Casey holding the cutlass again, and his only thought was that she'd injured herself on the blade.

Dear God, let her be unharmed, he silently prayed.

Shoving away from the hellish woman, he quickly, carefully retrieved the cutlass from Casey's hands and stuck it into its scabbard.

The girl screamed again, and giant tears flowed from her big, bright blue eyes.

Bloody hell!

"Stop crying!" he demanded in frustration, then swept the child up into his arms and smoothed a curly strand of hair from her tear-dampened cheek.

Half a moment later, the she-devil lunged at his back. "Get your filthy hands off my daughter!"

She clawed his skin, and he could feel her nails through his coat and the linen of his shirt.

"Stop it, woman," he yelled, holding onto the girl with one arm, trying to pull the mother's fingers from his neck with the other. " 'Tis not my intention to harm the child."

"Then let her go."

He could see the child's lips puckering as she

looked at her mother over his shoulder. "Mommy, I hurt . . . I hurt. . . ."

"Let her go, damn you!" the woman screamed, striking him once more in the temple.

"Blast it, wench! 'Tis me who is injured, not the child."

He whipped around quickly, unbalancing the woman as he moved. Her hands ripped free from his clothes, and he watched with a grin as she stumbled backward and landed on her backside in the sand.

"Damn you!" she sputtered, scrambling up from the ground.

Without thought, he drew his cutlass and held her off. "Stand back, woman. I mean the child no harm. And if you will keep your infernal hands off me, I'll not harm you, either."

"You've already hurt her. She's bleeding, can't you see?"

" 'Tis me who's bleeding!" he bellowed, wondering when his words would penetrate her skull. "She sliced my throat, and I do believe she came damn near to cutting off my head."

"I'm sorry, Mommy. I was only playing," Casey cried. "You have to fix the cut. Please."

The woman stared at him for the longest time with pursed lips and angry eyes. Her gaze traveled to his neck, to the child, and to the blade he was holding between them.

Slowly he sheathed the cutlass. He'd never drawn a blade on a woman before. But he'd never met a woman from whom he'd had to protect himself.

She stepped forward, yanked Casey from his arms, and set the child firmly on the ground, then moved protectively in front of her. He could see her fists clench at her sides. Her stern face was frozen like the figurehead on one of Her Majesty's ships. God, but she was beautiful—in spite of her anger.

"Were you planning to steal my boat?"

"The thought had crossed my mind."

"I suppose you were going to steal my daughter, too?"

"I beg your pardon, madam, but I'm here because I mistakenly thought you might need my help. As for your daughter, she accosted me, not the other way around. Now, if you'll stop blustering like a sea hag, we can get off this blasted island."

"You can stay on this *blasted* island. We're leaving."

"I thought you might tend to my wound."

"I'd rather see you dead."

"You and a hundred others, madam. Perhaps you'll get your wish if I continue to bleed."

"My wishes rarely come true, so I doubt you'll die."

Without taking her eyes off him, she picked up the child, then stormed away from the clearing, like the hurricane that had whipped across the island yesterday.

What an impertinent, infuriating woman, think-

ing she could just walk away and leave him behind.

He followed in her wake, taking full advantage
of the view before him. She had shapely legs, not
too long, not too short, nicely rounded hips, trim
waist, and from what he remembered, she had a
bosom that would pleasantly fill both his hands.

She was carrying the child through the water
when he reached shore. He would have carried
them both had she waited, but she was in too big
a hurry to get away from him.

Without so much as a thank-you for staying behind or for getting her vessel back into the sea,
she waded bosom deep, until they reached the
ladder suspended over the side and climbed into
the boat after her daughter.

He stood on the beach, legs spread wide, his
arms folded across his chest. "Is it your intention
to leave without me?" he called out over the gently rolling waves.

"You got here of your own accord. I suggest
you find your own way off the island."

"Would you leave me here to starve?"

"I don't give a damn what happens to you. You
tried to kidnap my daughter."

"Must I argue that point yet again?"

"Mommy." He heard the child's soft wail. "You
can't leave him here. He might die, and I'm the
one who hurt him."

The woman looked briefly at his neck—a cause
of little concern to her, he was sure. She frowned
at the weapons he had tucked into his belt, and

then her eyes traveled to the scar on his face, the patch on his eye.

The girl tugged on her mother's arm. "Please, Mommy."

"I don't want that man anywhere near us," she muttered to the child. The woman ignored him completely and set about hauling in the anchor.

It had taken him a year to get off the island the first time he'd been marooned there, and he'd be damned if he'd let her leave him stranded again.

Invitation or not, he was getting on that boat.

Wading quickly through the water, he hoisted himself up the ladder and onto the vessel before the woman had raised the sail.

She jerked around and glared at him. "Get off my boat."

He folded his arms over his chest and shook his head, an action that seemed to anger her more than mere words.

She lunged, striking his stomach with her shoulder, and before he could push her away, she'd wrested his dagger from his belt and pointed it at his belly.

"Get off my boat."

"I will go nowhere, madam, lest I go with you. Argue and sputter as you wish, but it will serve no purpose other than to fuel your anger and strain your throat."

Her blessed bosom rose and fell with the deepness of her sigh.

"Well, you're not staying on this boat as long as you've got that arsenal strapped around you."

She held out the hand that wasn't holding the dagger to his middle. "Give me the rest of your weapons."

"I will not."

He grinned.

Her jaw tightened.

"All right," she said, through clenched teeth. "You can ride back to St. Augustine with us. But so help me, if you put one hand on my daughter or me, I'll run you through with your very own blade."

He laughed, stuck a finger against the flat edge of the dagger, and pushed it away from his stomach.

Settling against the cabin, he folded his arms across his chest and winked at the scowling lady.

"Sail away, madam. 'Tis a most pleasant and entertaining voyage I am looking forward to."

Chapter 4

Once more upon the waters! Yet once more!
And the waves bound beneath me as a steed
That knows his rider. Welcome to their roar!
Swift be their guidance, wheresoe'er it lead!

LORD BYRON
CHILDE HAROLD'S PILGRIMAGE: CANTO III

Kate shielded her eyes from the glaring sun, looking out across the glassy sea for some sign of land, but St. Augustine was nowhere in sight. The trip that should have taken just under two hours had now stretched into three, and for the first time she wished Joe had spent more money on the sailboat, buying one equipped with an engine so it could go faster on days, like today, when the wind was too weak to billow the sails.

Below deck, Casey slept, cuddled up safe and snug on one of the berths, far from the steady gaze of their unwelcome passenger. She herself wasn't so lucky.

With nothing else to do and nowhere else to go, Casey's pirate silently watched her every move, his eyes much too often roaming to the broad-bladed dagger she clenched in her fist.

"I assure you, madam," he'd said, when they'd first set sail, "you have no need for protection from me."

Ted Bundy might have said something quite similar to the women he'd murdered, but she wasn't a fool and she wasn't taking any chances, not with her life, and definitely not with Casey's.

He'd said nothing more after those first few words. Instead, he'd stood quietly, watching the ocean one moment, the sails another, moving only to accommodate the tack of the boat. He seemed intrigued by the way she handled the main sail and jib, but he never smiled, never sat. He just stood steadfastly, booted feet planted wide on the deck, arms folded across his chest. It seemed as if sailing on the open sea was something he'd been born to, as if his body were perfectly in tune with the gentle roll of the water.

He'd be an interesting man to study, to learn more about, if he didn't look so frightful.

He was tall. Six-one, six-two, she imagined, and the heavy heels on his boots added at least an inch to his height. His shoulders were broad, his hips narrow, and as far as she could tell through his disheveled clothes, there was not an ounce of fat anywhere on his body.

Coarse black whiskers coated his cheeks and chin, making him look like a fiend—half-man, half-beast. But Casey was wrong about the scar. It wasn't red and ugly, it was thin and white, and it swept from the edge of his patch down to his lip. A well-deserved disfigurement, she imagined.

"Does the scar intrigue you, madam?"

Kate's focus was drawn from the corner of his mouth to his eyes—the azure blue one that seemed to be laughing at her, and then the one covered with black satin.

"I'm only curious about how you got it," she said, her gaze never once leaving the smirk on his face. "Did you irritate someone?"

"On the contrary, he irritated me. Unfortunately, he had a crew of over eighty men standing behind him and I had but myself. My hands and legs were bound, and. . . ."

The laughter disappeared from his eye as he turned away and looked at the calm surface of the water. "My face was used to test the sharpness of my enemy's dagger," he said coldly, and when he looked back, she saw only emptiness in his stare. "He wanted me to know that he was my master, that he could do anything he bloody well pleased—to me or anyone else."

Kate swallowed, half believing the horrid story, half not. "And your eye?" she asked. "He didn't . . . cut it out, did he?"

Laughter burst from his throat, a devilish laugh that raised goosebumps on her arms. "Aye, madam. Would you care to see?" He reached toward the patch.

"No!" Kate blurted out. "I was just curious, that's all."

She turned away, suddenly more interested in studying the water than making note of his features, but the tone of his voice, his English accent and manner of speech, stayed with her. He sounded too refined to look so disreputable. Dressed in pirate costume the way he was, she could only assume he was an actor, a British actor, who someone had gotten fed up with and dumped overboard.

She'd dump him overboard if she could. The sooner he was out of sight, the better. She didn't like the manner in which he stared at her. You'd think she was naked, like a marble statue in a museum, the way he analyzed every inch of her.

"How'd you get on the island?" she asked, tired of the quiet that had enveloped them.

"I blew in with the storm."

Obviously he wasn't a man of many words.

She studied the finely crafted dagger in her hand, the pistol shoved under his belt, and the jeweled hilt of his cutlass.

"Why do you need so many weapons?"

"Protection from women like you."

Well, asking questions was useless. His answers were less than civil and just as far-fetched as the one he'd told about his scar. A barroom brawl seemed a more logical explanation for that.

God, but she wished they'd reach St. Augustine.

The sun was high in the sky now, beating down on them in all its glory. She could feel a trickle of perspiration slowly making its way down her chest, leaving a dark blue streak at the center of her bright blue suit. Another trickle followed, and the man standing before her watched its descent, from the hollow of her throat to the crevice between her breasts. He raised his eye, but he didn't smile. Instead, his steady gaze seemed to burn through her, hotter than the blaze of sun.

"Please don't watch me like that."

"I am a man, madam, and you have chosen to flaunt your godgiven charms in front of me. 'Tis better that I watch you than ease the agony your appearance has caused me since first we met."

Without much thought, she raised the dagger threateningly in front of her. "Touch Casey, touch me, and I'll make sure you're incapable of easing your agony ever again."

That damnable laugh of his rang out once more. "I do not rape, madam. When I want a woman, I make love to her. I do not do it in front of a child, I do not do it without consent. I do it when the woman's cravings are equally as strong as mine—if not more so."

With his egotistical speech completed, he began to remove the wide leather belt about his waist.

"What are you doing?"

He did not answer. Instead, he unbuttoned the front of his coat, and slowly revealed the white linen of his shirt, damp with perspiration and clinging to a very muscular, very hard chest. If he got too close, she'd use the knife, but she had the feeling it would bend if she tried shoving it through his heart.

In spite of the knot growing larger in her throat, she maintained an outward calm. She'd be damned if she'd let him get the better of her. "Have you already forgotten what you said about raping a woman?"

He moved the short distance toward her and held out the coat. "The sun will burn your skin if it is not properly covered. Lest you confuse my concern for your welfare with lust, madam, I will allow you to drape it over yourself."

He was maddening, with his condescending tone and his brief attempt at gentlemanly ways. She knew she should thank him for his kindness, but being polite didn't seem necessary at the moment, not when he continued to glare and smirk and make her wish she could jump overboard rather than suffer his stares.

She toyed with the coat, thinking about returning it to its owner, but she found herself studying the intricate stitching at the seams—hand sewn rather than machine made, like the delicate white lace christening gown she'd created while waiting for Casey's birth. *How did he come to own such a coat?* she wondered. Garments as carefully sewn as this hadn't been fashioned since at least the nineteenth century, or they cost a fortune if you could find a tailor with the skills to do such work.

Perhaps he'd stolen it, along with the rest of his

costume. That seemed as likely an explanation as the barroom brawl was for the scar.

She found herself stealing a glance at Casey's pirate, but quickly turning her eyes back to the coat when she met his intense, burning stare. Once more she concentrated on the garment. Etched brass buttons bearing the imprint of crossed swords ran the length of the jacket, and swirls of gold braiding decorated cuffs and pockets. The fabric was royal blue velvet, but what should have been soft was rough, a consequence of soaking too long a time in water and then baking dry in the sun.

The coarse fabric scratched her skin when she drew it about her shoulders, but it blocked the unmerciful sun, for which she was thankful. It smelled of brine and the distinctly masculine scent of the man who'd lent it to her, but wrapped inside it, she felt cool, almost comfortable.

Again she looked at him, at the scar on his face, the patch on his eye, and the scabbed-over cut at his throat. Damn! Her own daughter had been responsible for almost killing the man. He hadn't threatened to sue. He hadn't struck back. What he'd done was show concern when he thought Casey might have been hurt. He'd also gotten her sailboat back into the water when she hadn't been able to do it herself, and he'd given her the coat off his back.

As much as she hated to admit it, a nice man—a gentleman, perhaps—lurked behind the scar, the beard, and the patch.

Reluctantly she smiled. "Thank you for the coat. I suppose I should thank you for getting the boat back in the water, too. I never could have done it on my own."

"You're quite welcome madam."

"Must you continually call me that?"

"What, pray tell, should I call you?"

"Kate. Kate Cameron." She imagined the polite thing to do was ask his name in return. "And you?"

"Morgan Farrell."

Kate fought back her grin when he swept a courtly bow.

"Why are you dressed like a pirate, Mr. Farrell? Are you an actor?"

"Actor?" he asked indignantly. "Do I look as though I spend my days frolicking on a stage?"

"What other explanation is there for parading around in pirate costume?"

He cocked one dark eyebrow. "Would you prefer that I parade around naked, as you are doing?"

"I don't give a damn how you dress, I just think it's rather strange. . . ." She let the thought trail away, finding it useless to argue with the man, and a waste of energy to explode over his insensitive and immature comment. Instead, she tugged at the coat that was slipping over her shoulder and put her mind back on sailing to St. Augustine. The sooner she got there, the sooner she could rid herself of Morgan Farrell.

He settled once more against the cabin and easily fell into his routine of staring at her. She glared right back, but she kept her focus away from his eyes and concentrated on the wide shoulders and broad chest hidden behind the voluminous white shirt. It laced up the front, with ruffles at the wrists, and was neatly tucked into smoke gray trousers that fit snugly over thighs she could only imagine were as well muscled as the rest of him. The black leather boots were cuffed just above his knees, and she followed the length of them all the way down to his toes, then made a slow journey up again. His jaw was strong and square, and his nose, although straight and well proportioned for the rest of his face, had a slight bump at the bridge. Broken at least once in a fight, she imagined.

His skin was tanned a swarthy bronze, and there were narrow white creases at the side of each eye, as if he'd squinted too much in the sun. Hastily she skimmed over his one azure eye that twinkled because, damn it, he knew she was studying him.

There was little else to do when the wind refused to cooperate. And he was intriguing, after all, especially his brownish-black hair that glinted in the sunlight as it spilled over his shoulders and halfway down his back. Thick, glorious hair, the kind many women paid a fortune to possess, the kind many women had probably run their fingers through, the kind many women would probably love to have feathering their body in the midst of making love.

Damn! Why was she thinking such thoughts?

Had the incessant sun given her some type of heat stroke? Surely she was losing her mind, to find such a vile, nefarious-looking man . . . handsome. She'd never cared for men like him. She liked men clean cut and blond—like Joe—and despised the ones who walked around with a gold stud in their ear. And this man had hoops the size of quarters dangling from each.

Definitely not her type. But since she wasn't in the market for another man, it didn't really matter. Knowing what possessed him to dress like the men who'd sailed the seas over two hundred years ago was no concern of hers, either.

"Your face contorts with much confusion, madam. Is there something else you would know of me?"

"I know your name. . . ."

Her words trailed off when she saw the unmistakable black and white stripes of the lighthouse not too far in the distance. They were almost home, thank God.

"I don't need to know anything more about you, Mr. Farrell, especially since we'll be parting company as soon as we reach the harbor."

"Perhaps I choose to know more of you."

"Look. I gave you a ride home, and I have no intention of giving you anything else. When we get to the marina, you're going in one direction, and Casey and I are going in the other."

"I beg to differ with you, madam—"

"Kate," she interrupted. "My name's Kate, not madam, and you can disagree all you want, but I want no further association with you."

"I will see you home," he said adamantly. "A woman—especially one dressed in only a corset— has no business walking on the streets alone."

Kate frowned at his words. *Corset?* What was he talking about? "This is a *swimsuit*, Mr. Farrell, and no one will look twice at me when I walk home."

"Then they are fools. I would look more than twice—*Kate*."

"You're wasting your flattery on me. I'm not interested in men like you."

He grinned. "That is not the truth, madam. Your eyes betray you."

Kate laughed. "You'll soon know just how honest I am, Mr. Farrell. We'll be in the harbor in a few minutes, and then Casey and I will turn our backs on you and walk away. It will be quite easy to leave you, and even easier to forget you."

The grin touched his face again. "Mark my words, madam. You will find I am not an easy man to forget."

Chapter 5

He stood a stranger in this breathing world,
An erring spirit from another hurl'd . . .

LORD BYRON, LARA: CANTO I

What the bloody hell? This was not St. Augustine! The woman, in spite of her obvious skill at sailing, must know nothing of navigation, for surely she'd set her course in the wrong direction.

The curve of the shoreline and the breadth of the inlet to the bay looked just as they had the last time he'd entered the city. But the church spires were new, as were the masses of houses and buildings littering the waterfront. And who the bloody hell had constructed the monstrous round lighthouse, circled with black and white stripes, that jutted into the sky like some vainglorious god's tribute to his manhood? Was not a simple gray stone structure enough?

Nay, this was not St. Augustine, nor any other
city he'd traveled to.

Yet . . . he shoved his fingers through his hair,
confused by the familiar sight of Castillo de San
Marcos standing guard at the edge of the city. The
high stone walls, the parapets and towers had the
same line and curve as he remembered, but they
appeared older now. Worn. Battered, not unlike
his own fortress.

How could this possibly be St. Augustine?

What had happened in the short year he'd been
gone?

Morgan's head snapped to the left when a
strange, exotic vessel breezed across the water, followed shortly by many others that looked nearly
identical. They were small boats like the one he
stood on now, and their orange, yellow, blue, and
green sails turned the bay into a rainbow of colors.

God forbid! He had never seen sights like these,
and he felt he must surely look the fool, the way
Kate stared at his obvious puzzlement.

He could not let her know that he found the
city odd, that he almost believed a mighty magician must have cast a spell over the town. She
would surely call the authorities and have him
carted off to an asylum for the mad.

Nay, he must remain calm. He must appear
strong, in control of his wits, even though he was
beginning to believe he'd lost his mind.

Another vessel screamed past him, its sound almost deafening, its speed quaking the water and
leaving behind a wake nearly as high and strong

as a storm-tossed wave. The boat had no sails, there were no men bearing oars, and he wondered how it could move so swiftly across the water. Surely this was something his tired mind had conjured.

He hadn't conjured the strange objects inside Kate's vessel, though, like the one she'd held to her mouth many a time during their voyage. The woman's mannerisms had been quite odd, the way she'd attempted to talk to the thing. Naturally, no one had answered, and then she'd sworn. "Damn it!" seemed to be her favorite choice of words.

He'd like to swear, too, but he could not let her see his frustration. She stared at him as if he were an odd creature from a foreign land, when he was the one who should be staring with mouth agape. But he stayed calm, even though the world about him appeared to be spinning out of control.

It was a blessing that the dark blue waters of the bay hadn't changed, but he longed to see galleons laden with riches from ports around the world, and heavily armed warships, teeming with men, whose masts reached high into the heavens. Where had they gone?

Where the gleaming white sands had once run directly into the harbor, there now were great stone walls to separate the sea from shore. The vegetation that had grown wild had been cultivated and now came closer to resembling his grandfather's estate in Kent than the untamed land he remembered.

There was much to marvel at and admire, yet it all caused him great consternation. Not only was it mentally impossible to fathom these changes, it was physically impossible to perform such a transformation in the span of one short year.

Of course, what other explanation was there?

He ducked as the woman tacked without warning and the boom nearly knocked him from the boat. "Bloody hell, woman! Do you intend to send me overboard?"

She grinned. "I wouldn't think of it."

'Twas a lie, of course. She wanted him gone and had made that obvious from the moment they'd met. He'd have to keep a watchful eye on the woman—a task he'd find none too difficult. She was a beauty, a woman a man would never forget.

He braced his feet on the deck, contemplating the wildness of her hair, the brightness of her eyes, the angry set of her lips. Nay, he would not forget this woman. In fact, he planned to know her better, and when he did, he'd ask her to explain what the devil had transformed the world he'd known.

He surveyed more of his odd surroundings, like the people standing on green lawns that circled the castillo, looking out across the waterway, and, by God!, the massive bridge spanning the channel.

He closed his eye tightly, opened it again, then rubbed it. Who could have built such a bridge in a matter of months? And . . . bloody hell! What were those bright and shining objects moving swiftly over the top? They weren't carriages or wagons, yet he could faintly see the shapes of men, women, and children inside. They traveled rapidly, almost soundlessly, over the gray stone structure, without the aid of horses or oxen.

Deep in his chest he could feel the beat of his heart pick up momentum. A tightness wrapped around his throat as if he were being strangled, and a fear that he'd never known before overwhelmed him.

What was happening? Was he caught in the middle of a dream? He considered himself a learned man, a reader of books, a man greatly interested in what could be, if mankind had the power to imagine great things. But even his own imaginings had never conjured something so wondrous as this.

He turned toward the woman, who was readying the craft to tack. She seemed not the least confused by what was going on around them. Wind blew through her hair, the ship glided easily over the water, and when Casey climbed from the cabin, Kate pulled her daughter close and allowed her to assist in sailing the ship.

"Do you know how to sail?" the child asked, looking toward him.

"Aye."

"Mommy's teaching me. I want to be a pirate someday, and pirates have to be really good sailors."

"Aye. That they do."

Suddenly Morgan realized that this could not

possibly be a dream. He had to have gone to heaven, in spite of his hell-bent life, because he never would have dreamt of guardian angels, and surely that's what he was seeing now.

But guardian angels didn't carve a man's neck with his very own blade, nor did they come at him with claws, or knees swiftly aimed at his balls.

This was surely not a dream. Perhaps he'd gone to hell, after all.

"Where have you taken me?" he asked, no longer caring if he appeared the fool. He had to know the truth.

The celestial creature with eyes the color of emeralds glared at him as if he'd gone mad. Of course, he'd expected nothing less. "St. Augustine," she said.

" 'Tis not as I recall."

"Maybe you were drunk the last time you were here."

"I do not imbibe to the point of oblivion, madam. Nor do I mistake one city for another. I have sailed to nearly every major port in this world, and I know the intricacies of all those cities. This place may bear a striking resemblance to St. Augustine, but I assure you, it is not."

"Yes, it is," the child said, making him feel even more the fool. "I was born here. Six years ago."

He shook his head slowly, trying desperately to understand what was going on around him. "When last I was here, Spanish warships blockaded the harbor to keep the British away. Houses had been destroyed by cannon fire, and there was no bloody bridge across the river."

"That *bloody* bridge has been here for a good seventy years, and it's been centuries since there were any Spanish *or* British warships in the harbor. You know what I think, Mr. Farrell? I think you've damn well lost your mind, because I seriously doubt you were here in the eighteenth century."

"I was here in the year of our Lord seventeen hundred and two—"

"Yes, of course you were," she interrupted. "And I'm the Queen of England."

"You are no Queen Anne, I can assure you of that, madam."

"Knock it off, will you? Your accent's convincing. You look crude enough to be a pirate, but I'm not falling for your pathetic little act."

She took a deep breath, working up the energy to lecture him more, he assumed. "Once we're docked and I make sure you're off the boat, you can argue the progression of St. Augustine history with someone else."

"Aren't we going to take him home with us?" Casey asked.

"No, Case. We won't be seeing Mr. Farrell again."

"Your mother and I have differing opinions on that subject," he said, kneeling before the child. He reached out to brush a strand of hair from her lips, but Kate slapped his hand away.

"Don't touch her."

"He won't hurt me, Mommy."

"I don't want him near us."

Morgan winked at the little girl whose lower lip had jutted out, then rose to his full height, towering over the woman as he moved close to her side.

"Are you afraid of me?" he asked.

Kate looked up. Her pretty pink lips were pursed tightly, her green eyes squinted into a frown. He had the oddest feeling she was contemplating aiming her knee at his groin once more.

What a damnable woman she was, but he admired her spirit.

She nudged him out of the way as she tacked again. "I'm not afraid of you or anyone else."

"That's not entirely true, madam. Your entire body bristles whenever I near you. Either you're afraid of me, or some other emotion—desire, perhaps—makes you shiver."

"You're a smug bastard, aren't you?"

"Mommy! That's a nasty word."

"The child's correct. I daresay, one might mistake you for a barroom wench when you continually use such language."

"And it's quite obvious you've known a lot of barroom wenches."

"I've known a few. I choose to know no more. They may have the same devil in their tongue that you possess, but they have not the same fire in their eyes. You may wish to be free of me once we've docked, my dearest Kate, but I do not wish to be free of you."

"What are you, some kind of lunatic?"

He looked at his unfamiliar surroundings, at the harbor filled with small sailboats, at the beautiful woman and heavenly child who'd appeared in his life when he least needed them. "I am not mad, madam. I am merely a man who finds himself in unfamiliar surroundings, a man who would greatly benefit from your continuing generosity."

"I've already given you enough, Mr. Farrell."

"That is not possible, madam. There is much, much more I would have from you."

With Casey's hand held tightly in hers, Kate rushed away from the boat, away from the marina, and away from Morgan Farrell and his blasted eyes and hair and innuendoes. Damn, but he unnerved her.

"Please, Mommy," Casey begged, trying to tug out of Kate's grasp. "Don't leave him alone."

"He's crazy, Case. We don't need someone like that in our lives."

"He's not crazy," Casey said adamantly. "He's a pirate. If Daddy was here, he'd ask him to go home with us."

"Your father invited home every homeless person he came in contact with. I didn't mind it when he was around, but I don't feel comfortable having strangers in the house when just you and I are there."

"He won't hurt us."

"We don't know that, Case. Please, let's not talk about this anymore. We've got to get home. I'm sure Evalena's worried sick about us by now."

Casey stopped dead in her tracks, stubborn yet again, and Kate rapidly counted to ten. Patience wasn't a virtue she possessed, and counting had been a habit since childhood.

"I think he's scared, Mommy," Casey said, looking toward the marina.

Kate didn't want to look back, but she couldn't help herself. Casey's pirate stood like a stalwart statue at the edge of the docks, his arms folded mightily over his chest. He was wearing his blue velvet coat now, even though he'd expressed his desire that she keep it. "To protect your honor, madam," he'd said. Ha! He sure knew how to play the gentleman, but he was anything but. That was obvious by the way he tucked his cutlass, his dagger, and his pistol under the wide leather belt he wore.

"Please, Mommy. Let's go back and help him."

"He's a grown man, Case. I'm sure he can take care of himself."

The proof of her words stared her in the face. The usual throng of summer tourists flocked around him, flashing cameras, asking him questions, and he just stood there, as if he owned the world and was afraid of nothing.

He ignored the people around him, interested in something else entirely, something a good distance away.

Her.

Across the heads of women, men, and children, over the occasional car that passed on the street between them, he stared, and she could feel the radiating heat of his one azure eye.

Her heart beat rapidly. A lump caught in her throat, and she found it difficult to breathe.

What was he doing to her? *Get away*, she told herself. *Leave. Fast, before his incredibly gifted skills as an actor fool you into believing there's a nice guy under that scruffy beard and ugly scar.*

"Come on, Case," she said, the tone of her voice offering no room for argument as she tugged Casey up the street. "We're going home. Mr. Farrell will be perfectly fine now that he's back in his element. He's an actor, not a pirate, and right now he's doing what he does best—entertaining the crowds."

The whole lot of them were mad, inspecting his clothing, his hair, the patch on his eye and the scar down his face.

"Where's your parrot, huh?" some nasty street urchin wearing short ragged trousers chortled. "Did you leave him on Treasure Island?"

"Look over here," a woman called out, as she stuck a black box in front of her face. "Smile."

Bloody hell! He would not smile, not for her, not for any of these people milling about. They were strangers, and he was in a world as unfamiliar to him as Queen Anne's court.

"Be gone, all of you," he bellowed, but the men, women, and children only laughed, as if he were a jester there for their entertainment. An actor— that's what Kate had called him. Well, he refused to act or be the amusement for anyone. He was Morgan Farrell, and for the past six years he'd been commonly known as Black Heart—hero to some, enemy to many.

He shouldered his way through the crowd, running now in an attempt to catch up with Kate and Casey. In the past he would have made his way to a public house when he had first entered port. He'd order up a rum and spend the night in some accommodating wench's bed. But that's not what he wanted now.

He wanted to know more about this strange city of St. Augustine, how it had changed and why. And he wanted to learn these things from the guardian angel who spoke with all the fire of hell.

He had to find her.

The streets were teeming with people, and many of those hellish contraptions he'd seen on the bridge rolled past him so quickly they seemed little more than a blur, like the slash of a blade, and he imagined stepping in front of one would be just as deadly.

If not for the heat of the sun on his face, the jabs of shoulders and elbows as he brushed through the crowds, he might believe he was trapped in a nightmare. But the thick, humid air was something he knew quite well, and the scents of seafood and pastries wafting out of unfamiliar shops made him remember his hunger, the gnawing in his belly that was nearly as strong as the now re-turned pain in his head.

But still he pressed on.

He should have caught up with Casey and Kate, but too many sights and sounds got in the way. Fascinating things that made his head spin, like the great winged object flying high over his head. It tore his attention from everything else as it sailed like a silver phantom across the sky, then disappeared behind the clouds.

Other things caught his eye, too, like the glowing signs at street corners directing people when to walk and when not to, as if they had not the intelligence to know.

'Twas all most amazing.

A woman breezed past him clothed in tight blue trousers, another rushed by in little more than a thin chemise. Backing against a wall, he wondered at their propriety, while admiring their charms, and decided that there was much to appreciate in this odd and wondrous city.

Again he stepped out into the throngs, stopping abruptly when a heavy wooden door opened directly in front of his face. A man and woman exited, arm in arm, but he paid them little attention. Instead, he concentrated on the sign posted on the door that clearly read, "Established 1790."

Impossible! It was 1702, and he refused to believe anything different. His mind screamed at him to believe the truth—St. Augustine had changed far too dramatically for only one short year to have elapsed.

But how could ninety years have gone by?

'Twas impossible.

And frightening.

He stumbled on, twisting and turning in an effort to take in every curious and astonishing sight.

He'd once read the theories of great men like Galileo and Newton who talked of the stars and motion and time. He had conversed with scholars at Oxford who'd spent hour upon hour discussing the philosophies of astronomers and academics. They had claimed time travel was possible, but no one had claimed to know how such a miraculous event could be accomplished, and they refused to espouse their thoughts to the world for fear they'd be laughed at. Of course, daVinci's theories about flying machines had been scoffed at, and now he'd seen one for himself. He'd also seen the amazing material that made up the hull and mast of Kate's sailboat, not to mention the carriages that moved rapidly along the streets, seemingly of their own accord.

Perhaps time travel was possible, after all.

"Watch it, mister," a red-faced, overfed man barked, when Morgan bumped into him head on.

"My apologies, sir." Morgan stared directly into the man's eyes, wondering if the human anatomy might also have changed over the years, but he saw nothing new or different. What he did see was anger.

"Do you mind moving out of my way?" the man bellowed.

"Could you answer one question for me first?" Morgan asked, only to be met with the roll of the man's eyes.

"I'm in a hurry."

"This will take but a moment, sir. Tell me, please ... what year are we living in?"

"Is this a joke or something?" the man asked, laughter making his ample belly bounce beneath the thin shirt he wore close to his skin. "Am I on *Candid Camera*?"

"I do not know what you speak of, sir. I merely need to know the year."

The man shrugged. "Nineteen ninety-eight. Now, do I get a prize or something?"

Morgan could only stare as he repeated the year over and over in his head.

Nineteen ninety-eight.

"Are you okay?" the man asked.

Morgan met the man's concerned eyes. "I am not quite sure. But I thank you for your assistance, sir."

In a fog of thought, Morgan walked up the street, the man's words, the date, swirling through his mind.

Nineteen ninety-eight.

He stepped out of the throng of people, walked to the middle of an empty street, and looked at all the amazing things around him.

He couldn't help but smile at what he saw, what he felt.

Bloody hell! It was nearly three hundred years since he'd been knocked over the side of *Satan's Revenge*. He did not know how it had happened or why; all he knew was that he needed to share this miraculous occurrence with someone, and the only two people he knew were Kate and her daughter.

The woman had thought he was mad before. 'Twould be more than a bit interesting to see and hear her reaction when he told her he'd traveled through time.

Chapter 6

He had (if 'twere not nature's boon) an art
Of fixing memory on another's heart:
It was not love perchance—nor hate—nor aught
That words can image to express the thought;
But they who saw him did not see in vain,
And once beheld, would ask of him again . . .

LORD BYRON, LARA: CANTO I

"Oh, my precious ones. I've been worried half out of my mind about you."

Kate and Casey flew into Evalena's ample arms and the elderly woman nearly smothered them in her girth, pressing kisses to cheeks and eyes and hair, anything she could reach.

"My goodness gracious, where on earth have you been? You can't imagine how many people asked me about you at church this morning, and there was absolutely nothing I could say to them.

It's just so unlike you, Katharine, not to tell me what you're up to."

"I'm sorry, Evie," Kate offered. "We went to the island."

"Treasure hunting?" Evalena asked, eyebrows raised exceedingly high, even for her.

"Just a picnic," Kate fibbed, hoping to avoid Evalena's criticism. "And then we got hit by a hurricane. If we'd known there was going to be a storm we never would have gone, but it came up all of a sudden, out of nowhere."

Evalena pushed Kate out to arm's length and inspected her eyes.

"You haven't been drinking, have you?"

"Of course not. What makes you think that?"

"There's been no hurricane, and I've heard nothing about one on the news. Peaceful and quiet it's been here."

"Well, it was anything but peaceful and quiet on the island, or on the trip home. God, we never should have gone."

"It was a big storm, Aunt Evie," Casey added. "Biggest one I've ever seen. Trees were flying everywhere. Even our sailboat flew—right onto the beach. If it hadn't been for my pirate, we might never have gotten home."

Evalena's eyes narrowed as she looked from Kate to Casey then back again. "I suppose I can accept a hurricane out on that island of yours, although for the life of me, I don't know why I haven't heard about it. But a pirate?"

"He was big and ugly," Casey answered.

"Oh, dear, we can't have that now, can we?" Evalena asked, circling Kate, eyeing her up and down.

"Mommy doesn't like him," Casey said, following behind her aunt.

Evalena stopped directly in front of Kate and raised both white eyebrows. "I'm waiting for an explanation, Katharine."

Kate wove the fingers of both hands through her hair, wishing she'd gone straight home instead of going to Evie's. She was tired, dirty, and hungry, and in no mood for one of Evalena's interrogations. She loved the woman dearly, but Evie made it a point of knowing everything that was going on in the lives of both family and friends, and if nothing was happening, she made an attempt to set something in motion.

"It was nothing. Honest," Kate said, crossing the elaborate Victorian drawing room and collapsing in a red and gold brocade loveseat. The blue lovebirds in the cage next to her squawked, ruffled their feathers in unison to let her know they didn't appreciate the disturbance, then tucked their heads together and ignored the rest of the world. Kate wanted to do exactly the same thing right now, but that wasn't going to happen.

When Evalena lifted Casey on to her hip and ambled across the room, Kate knew what was coming. It wasn't the first time she'd been through her matchmaking aunt's routine.

"You know how much I despise being told nothing's the matter, or nothing's up, or having anyone use a phrase with the word 'nothing' in it. There's always something, and if you really did meet a pirate, I want all the details."

Kate rested her head on the back of the loveseat, looked up at the intricately carved ceiling, and began to count the plaster cupids that circled the room.

From the corner of her eye, she could see her aunt wiggle into the other half of the S-shaped sofa, and with Casey still in her arms, she leaned her head back and stared at the ceiling, too.

"There are still twenty-two cupids, twenty-two bows, and twenty-two arrows," Evalena reminded her. "I long ago grew wise to your attempts to ignore my questions."

"I'm not ignoring you, Evie, I'm counting."

"That's what she does when she's mad about something," Casey added.

"Oh, I know full well about her counting. Your mother has a temper, and she's stubborn as well. She certainly didn't get that from me. But as I was saying, Katharine, I want to know more about this pirate."

"I don't want to talk about him."

"It's high time you start talking about someone. I imagine a pirate's just as good as any other man, especially when you've been without one for two and a half years."

Kate continued to stare at the cupids, and each one was beginning to look like Evalena. "I'm not interested in settling down again, and I'm definitely not interested in Morgan Farrell."

"Ah, a good Irish name."

"Irish . . . English, it doesn't really matter." She finally turned to face her aunt's inquisitive stare. "Would you believe the man actually had a hoop in each ear, a scar down his face, and wore a patch over one eye?"

"How very intriguing. When are you going to see him again?"

"Never," Casey stated. "She told him to drop dead."

Evalena's eyes narrowed. "That's the same thing you said to that nice Mr. Andrews who asked you out on New Year's Eve, and remember what happened to him? Died in his sleep that very same night. You've got to be careful who you tell to drop dead, Katharine."

Kate faced the cupids again, counted the first ten, then turned back to her aunt. "Mr. Andrews was eighty-three years old. On top of that, he didn't ask me out, he asked himself in, then pulled a handful of condoms out of his pocket."

"What's a condom, Mommy?"

"One of those things you're not ready to know about. Why don't you go outside and play."

"I'd rather listen to you and Aunt Evie."

Evalena pushed herself up in the chair, and Casey slid off her lap. "You know, sweetie, you're the best PB and J maker in the entire city of St. Augustine, and I'm dying for a double. Why don't you scoot on into the kitchen and make one for each of us?"

"Okay," Casey chirped, always eager to please

her aunt. "But don't talk about anything good while I'm gone."

When Casey disappeared from the drawing room, Kate moved from the loveseat to the window that faced her home across the street, the run-down Queen Anne she loved, the home she'd shared with Joe.

She heard Evalena's slippered feet crossing the hardwood floor, and felt a light, comforting hand on her shoulder. "Joe's been gone for over two years," she said softly. "Casey needs a father and you need a husband."

"We're doing fine on our own."

"You're in debt up to your ears."

"It won't last forever."

"You should sell some of Joseph's things, especially that island. He was a saint, bless his soul, but he was much too frivolous with his money, and now you're suffering. Give some of it up, Katharine."

"I can't. There's a little bit of Joe in that island, and in everything in the house. If I sell something, I'd feel like I was getting rid of part of him."

"He's tucked away in your heart, right where he ought to be," Evalena said. "No matter what you do now, that's not going to change. You're alive, Katharine. Joseph isn't, and he's never going to be ever again. That's why it's high time you let him go and find another man."

Kate turned, lovingly brushing a hint of confectioner's sugar from Evalena's cheek, as she allowed a faint smile to touch her face. "I'm not in the mood for another man and I doubt I ever will be. But if the mood strikes, I want to find him all on my own."

"Okay, so what did you like about this pirate? Was he tall, dark, and handsome like Errol Flynn, or did he look more like Blackbeard, with lighted candles sticking out of a mangy growth on his face? What about his voice? Was it sensuous or dull?"

Kate laughed. Evalena would never give up where the love lives of men and women were concerned. Draping an arm around her aunt's shoulders, she leaned close and whispered in her ear. "He had only one eye, but it was the color of a cloudless sky, and . . . and I didn't see him without his shirt, but I'm absolutely positive his entire body rippled with muscle."

"Oh, my." Evalena clapped a hand to her chest. "You have got to find this pirate of yours and take back every word you said about dying."

"I didn't tell you everything," Kate added. "He may have the body of Michelangelo's David, but he prefaces most every sentence with 'Bloody hell!' "

"And you use 'damn,' " Evalena quickly reminded her. "Go on, what other qualities do the two of you share?"

"None that I know of." Kate plopped down in the loveseat again. "He's not my type, Evie."

"Well, when you decide to go looking for a hero, Katharine, you'll have to open your heart to all possibilities."

*   *   *

The night was quiet except for the soft brush of palm fronds on the shingles and the voice of Perry Como seeping through the open window in Aunt Evalena's bedroom across the street. From where she sat on the second-floor balcony, Kate could almost hear Evalena's rhythmic snores, keeping time with the music she loved. She'd gone to bed with Perry Como every night since her husband had gone off to war in 1943. Harry Beecher had never returned from the shores of Iwo Jima, and Perry had become Evie's constant companion. Oh, there'd been other men. How could a practicing matchmaker insist that others marry if she herself stayed single?

There'd been three more husbands: Lou, Jim, and Bill, and according to Evalena, if they didn't love Perry, they didn't get to love her. So Como had played on the old hi-fi every night, and Evalena, so she said, wore Lou out, then Jim, then Bill. But Perry never wore out. Like her, he just grew better and better with time.

Kate wished she'd found it so simple to shift her love from Joe to another man. She'd idolized him as a child, as a teenager, as a young woman. In her eyes he could do nothing wrong. She'd wanted to marry him—and she had, not too long after graduating from high school. She'd never dated anyone else. She'd never wanted to.

Now she wondered if her love for Joe might have faded with time. It didn't seem possible, but she'd grown up a lot in the last few years, and she wanted more from life than a constant treasure hunt. She wanted stability, and although she wasn't the least bit interested in marrying again, she knew if she did, she'd want someone more interested in chasing her than in chasing dreams.

The warm summer breeze wove through her hair as she listened to Perry's slow, sultry voice. Closing her eyes, she began to hum with the music, to lyrics about being alone, about being lured on by a smile, and the words wrapped around her like strong, warm arms.

Damn it, she *was* lonely ... *desperately* lonely, and Joe's memory wasn't the best of company any longer. She hardly remembered the sound of his voice, his laughing eyes, his gentle smile. It was wrong to forget him, wrong to allow someone else into her thoughts.

Like a one-eyed pirate.

A man as different from Joe as night and day.

But temptation, just like the title of Perry's song, was leading her on. She was lonely and vulnerable, and Casey's pirate intrigued her.

He definitely hadn't lied when he'd said he wasn't an easy man to forget.

How could she dismiss him from her mind when he'd looked at her with that one powerful azure eye that had nearly burned a hole through her? How could she concentrate on important matters when all evening long his unforgettable, seductive smile kept creeping into her mind, when every enticing word he'd spoken in that lush English accent rang through her ears?

Forget about him, she told herself. *Just forget him.*

"Good evening, madam."

Oh, God!

Kate leaned forward in the old wicker rocker and peered over the balcony to the lawn below. Morgan Farrell rested a shoulder casually against a palm, arms folded, as always. His now familiar smile softened the hardness of his face. But she wasn't falling for his attempt at charm.

"Go away."

"I cannot do that. I have walked all over your fair city looking for you. I am tired, I am hungry, and although I hate to admit it, I'm too weak to look for shelter or sustenance elsewhere. It was my fondest hope that—"

"Hell would have to freeze over before I'd allow you into my home."

The laugh she'd grown accustomed to on their journey home from the island rang out. "You have a frozen heart, madam. I would gladly accept that as the closest thing to hell freezing over."

"Go away!"

"That is an impossibility. 'Tis only the palm that supports me, and were I to leave, I daresay I would fall. Is it. . . ." His words trailed off, and his shoulder slipped across the palm before he grabbed onto the prickly trunk. "Is it your wish to have a dead man on your lawn?"

One leg collapsed beneath him, but again he steadied himself. Slowly he looked up, his face as pale as the moon. "I am much in need of food, madam." With a shaky hand he drew his cutlass from its scabbard and dropped it to the ground. His pistol and dagger followed. "The jewels on the cutlass are worth at least two fortunes. They are yours, Kate. All I ask. . . ." He drew in a deep breath, swayed dizzily, and rested his cheek against the palm.

Damn! She didn't want to help him. She didn't want him any closer than he was right now.

Again he looked up at her. The smile was gone from his face, and she could almost hear his silent prayer for help.

Oh, hell!

"Don't move," she hollered.

Pushing through the French doors, she ran across her bedroom and down the hall, and took the stairs two at a time in her rush to get to him. She threw open the etched glass front door, jumped off the edge of the porch, and wrapped her arms around his waist as his body inched its way down to the ground.

"If you're going to pass out," she said, struggling to keep him on his feet, "could you wait and do it inside?"

A touch of laughter rushed from Casey's pirate in a pain-filled gasp. Kate could tell he was trying to smile. She could also tell he was suffering as she ducked under his arm to give him support. God, but he was heavy. Still, she maneuvered him across the lawn and up the stairs, and somehow led him to the couch—and dropped him.

His breathing was raspy, his skin hot and dry, and his one azure eye was now a cloudy blue,

ringed with red. She couldn't just dump him on
the sofa, then sit on the stairs with the cutlass held
between them until he got better. Someone needed
to take care of him, and she didn't see any vol-
unteers lining up for the job.

She let out a deep sigh, knowing what she had
to do. "I hate to tell you this, Mr. Farrell, but you
need to be in bed, not on the sofa."

Again he smiled, very faintly. "You are most
generous, madam."

"Don't get too accustomed to my hospitality. As
soon as you're well, you're out of here."

Sliding her arms under his, she pulled him from
the couch. "Don't pass out, okay? We've got at
least fifteen steps to climb."

He didn't say a word, but she could hear his
deep gasp for air, could feel the heavy rise and
fall of his chest as he struggled up each stair. She
didn't think twice about putting him in the room
that had been Joe's as a boy—the room she'd once
hoped to decorate for a second child.

Holding him close, she led him to the small
twin bed and somehow managed to rip back the
covers before her strength gave out and together
they fell on the cool white sheets. She expected
some kind of suggestive retort. Instead, his hand
slid from her arm, his breathing grew deep and
heavy, and his unpatched eye closed in exhausted
sleep.

Quietly, Kate lifted his legs on to the bed and
removed his boots. She would have removed his
socks, but he was wearing stockings that ended

somewhere above his knees, somewhere she wasn't quite yet ready to explore.

Sliding one arm under his shoulders, she managed to lift him just enough so she could slip off his coat. They were close now, her chest against his. His breathing, although heavy in sleep, was even, not raspy any longer. His heartbeat was steady, not too fast, not too slow. She had no medical background, but from all outward signs, she knew he wasn't going to die. He just needed to sleep, and she needed to bring down his fever.

The jacket came off easily enough, but the white linen shirt had to be pulled over his head after she unlaced the front and loosened the buttons at the ruffled cuffs. She tried not to look as she removed the shirt, but his shoulders were so broad and muscular, his chest covered with so much dark curling hair, and his stomach muscles so hard and flat that she couldn't stop herself. No one could fault her for looking. Her motives were innocent. She was nursing a man back to health, not lusting after his body.

Nestled in the hair on his chest was a small gold cross studded with what appeared to be dark red rubies. It was beautiful, a work of art. The gold had been intricately carved in the shape of tiny vines which swirled around at least a dozen small round jewels. The gold chain was just as intricate, and both it and the cross seemed much too delicate to be worn by a man—especially one as virile as Morgan Farrell.

She wondered why he was wearing it. He

didn't look rich, and he definitely didn't act religious. Maybe he'd found it on the island, just as she'd found the emerald ring—and the broken chain that looked so similar to the one he wore around his neck.

He shivered, drawing her attention from his chest to the fluttering of his eyelids, to the frown that wrinkled his brow. And then he whispered, "Melody." His lips quivered for just an instant, then tilted into the slightest of smiles.

Melody. He'd spoken the word so softly that Kate wondered if the woman was his lover—or maybe even his wife.

Such a strange man, Kate thought, as she reached for the sheet and dragged it over his chest. She held it high for just a moment as she gazed at the muscles in his arms, the hard planes of his stomach. God, but he had a beautiful physique.

And it had been so long since she'd had the leisure to look.

A tremor of long-forgotten desire rippled through her, and heat rushed up her neck to her cheeks. The sheet slipped through her fingers and floated down over his chest.

He shivered again. The natural thing would be to cover him with blankets, but she knew she had to cool him down.

She quickly went to the bathroom, soaking two washcloths in cold water and ringing them out. She went back to the bed, sitting down easily beside him. Carefully she lifted his head from the pillow and slipped one cool cloth beneath his hair, so it rested against his neck. The other washcloth she pressed to his feverish forehead.

He was hot, so very, very hot, and just as she did when Casey had a fever, she gently smoothed damp hair away from his face, wondering what had caused the fever, wondering why he'd come to her instead of going home, wondering why he was dressed like Captain Hook.

She turned the washcloth behind his neck and her fingers brushed over a raised stretch of skin. Moving closer, she lifted his shoulders from the bed, and a chill raced down her spine.

His back was crisscrossed with long, thick scars, fifteen or twenty, at least. Wicked things that slashed from waist to shoulder. Immediately she thought of the story he'd told about the scar on his face. "My hands and legs were bound ... he wanted me to know that he was my master. . . ." The scene played out vividly in her mind, sickening her as she saw someone cut his face, then apply a whip to his back. And the whole time she watched the image, she saw his eyes—open, alert, wracked with pain, yet he didn't utter a sound. No scream. No begging for mercy.

She saw only hatred.

She shut off the thought, not wanting to see any more. And then, without thinking, she kissed her fingertips and pressed them softly against one of the scars, swallowing back the heavy knot of compassion that had welled inside her throat.

Gently she lowered Mr. Farrell's shoulders to the bed and sat down beside him, cleansing his sleeping face with the cloth she'd placed on his forehead, lightly stroking the rapidly warming terrycloth over his whiskered cheeks, the small cut Casey had left at his throat, his temples.

He winced, jerking slightly when her fingers neared his scalp, then drifted once more deeply into sleep. Carefully she parted his hair, nearly sickened by the swollen, blood-crusted gash grazing his head.

Dear God. What else had this man suffered?

She should wake him if he had a concussion, but he was sleeping so soundly she didn't have the heart to rouse him. She should probably call a doctor, but she couldn't afford to pay for his care and she was sure he couldn't either.

Maybe those were excuses to keep him right where he was?

She laughed at herself. Why should she want him around? A man with a multitude of scars and only one eye?

Surely she'd lost her mind.

She rushed down the hall to her own bathroom, peeking in on Casey for a moment to make sure she was sleeping soundly. Rifling through the medicine chest, she gathered up cotton balls, alcohol, and gauze, dumping them into a small plastic pan she could fill with water.

Joe's old razor sat on the glass shelf in the medicine cabinet. Like so many other things, she should have thrown it away long ago, but she hadn't. She started to put it with the rest of the items, then stopped, looking at the blade, wondering if there were any traces of the dark blond whiskers that had covered Joe's cheeks.

But there were none. She looked into the mirror, hoping she'd see the face she'd loved so well standing before it, shaving as he'd done every morning. But the only face she saw was her own, and in her mind she saw the dark brown whiskers covering Morgan Farrell's feverish face.

She dumped the razor into the pan along with her own can of shaving cream.

Casey's pirate might be burning up. He might be suffering from a severe wound to his head and possibly a concussion, but he was going to lie there close to death with a cleanly shaven face.

Sitting beside him once more, she swabbed the wound with alcohol, jumping each time he winced. It seemed as though hours had gone by before she'd cleaned the gash, but she smiled at her accomplishments when she sat back and studied the now sterile cut that looked as if it had already begun to heal. Thank goodness there was no need to cover it with a bandage, because she didn't have the heart to shave away any of the hair that flowed so gloriously over his shoulders.

His face was another matter entirely.

Applying cool compresses once more to the back of his neck and forehead, she leaned over her patient and whispered close to his ear. "Mr. Farrell."

He didn't move a muscle.

Shaking the can of shaving cream, she applied a dollop on the tips of her fingers and gently smoothed it over his cheek, applying even more to his chin and neck, lightly swirling it over the heavy coat of whiskers.

She'd never shaved a man before, and her fingers shook as she held the razor close to the base of his neck, remembering how in old western movies the barber always began there, dragging the razor upward.

She took one light stroke, leaving behind too many whiskers. Again she shaved that very same spot, then ran her fingers over the stripe of soft, bronze skin. She shivered. It had been so long since she'd touched a man. She'd nearly forgotten the wondrous feel of a freshly shaved face.

Wiping the blade on a towel, she worked up the courage to rid his face of the rest of his beard. His neck was the simplest, long and strong, and it looked so much better once the whiskers had been shaved away. Carefully she ran the razor over his square jaw and up his left cheek, trying to keep her mind on what she was doing, rather than on the fluttering behind his eyelid.

Was he dreaming? she wondered. *Was he ready to wake? How would he feel, knowing that she'd shaved his face?* Maybe he'd been growing the beard for a reason, possibly for a movie role? Well, it was too late now. She couldn't stop halfway through.

Lightly sweeping his hair behind his ear, she allowed her fingers to admire the texture, the silkiness of the waves. It seemed odd, almost sinful, to be touching a man's hair this way, especially when he was asleep. Especially when he was little more than a stranger.

Touching him made her feel . . . made her feel things she hadn't felt in a long time, stirrings in her heart, quivering in her stomach. And it made her realize just how lonely she'd been.

His head rolled on the pillow, fully exposing his right cheek—and the scar. She'd wanted to ignore that cheek, afraid of disfiguring his face any further. She'd also wanted to ignore that side of his face because it reminded her that he was dangerous, that she shouldn't have allowed him in her house, near her, near Casey. But it was that side of his face that intrigued her the most.

She took a deep breath, rested the razor near his hairline just above his ear, and slowly dragged it downward, easing it over the scar, until she'd scraped away the last remnants of beard.

She took the razor back to the bathroom and returned with a warm washcloth. Sitting beside him again, she gently bathed his face and throat. She applied fresh, cool compresses to his forehead and neck, studying his face as she worked.

Long black eyelashes curled upward instead of resting on his skin, and dimples at both corners of his mouth softened a face made dangerous looking by the scar. She knew better than to think it, but he really did look like a pirate—a handsome one, now that he was shaved.

The patch over his eye fascinated her nearly as much as the scar. How he must have suffered, if he'd indeed told the truth about someone carving out his eye. She couldn't begin to imagine the pain, couldn't imagine someone doing something so horrid in this day and age, but the thing she wondered most was if someone had cared for him afterward. If anyone had comforted him. Slowly, she smoothed her fingers over his cheek, lightly caressing the length his scar. It was raised only the slightest bit. Smooth, oh so very smooth, like the rest of his cheek.

Her fingers accidentally brushed the bottom of his patch, and lingered. What would it hurt to take a quick peek? He was asleep; he'd never know.

Swallowing hard, she slid her index finger just under the edge of the patch. Her heart thumped heavily in her chest, and a lump grew wild in her throat. *Don't do it, Kate. Don't do it.* But she'd gotten this close; she couldn't stop now. Besides, it was just a little patch, and so easy to lift.

She expected to see a gaping hole, skin that was thickened and scarred. Instead she saw an eyelid, and curling lashes. She hadn't given any thought to the fact that with his eyelids closed he'd look like a normal man, that the scarring would be hidden from view.

What she was doing was crazy. She didn't need to see any more of his scars, but curiosity pushed her on. Gently she touched his lashes, his eyelid.

It will only take a second, Kate, she told herself. *Just one second, then you can put the patch down again.*

She took a deep breath and started to lift the

lid. Suddenly it jerked open, and the azure eye beneath it twinkled.

Morgan Farrell winked.

"Damn you!" she sputtered, as a grin slanted across his face. "You are the biggest liar I've ever met, and I want you out of my house. *Now!*"

The grin faded to a softened smile. His eyes closed, and he drew in a deep breath. "I have barely the energy to speak, madam, let alone leave this bed."

"But you lied! You told me your eye had been cut out!"

"And you said you didn't want me anywhere near, yet you've cleaned my wound and shaved my face. Who's the liar, madam?"

"Don't call me that."

"Ah, Katie." His hand inched out from under the covers, and he reached toward her cheek. She pushed away from the bed and walked to the window, not wanting to know his touch, not wanting to get any closer to him than she'd already allowed herself. She crossed her arms over her chest and looked back at him.

His smile had drained away. His Adam's apple rose and fell, and he took a deep breath before he spoke. "I apologize for the ruse. 'Tis difficult to tell the truth when one has lived a lie for many years."

"What other lies have you told me?"

"Most of my life has been a fabrication, but one of my own design. Now my life has taken another turn. You would not believe the truth if I told you, for I scarce believe it myself."

"Try me."

"Come close, Katie. I fear you cannot hear me from such a distance."

"I have perfect hearing. What's your story?"

"I've come here from another time—long before you were born." He took a deep breath; his eyes fluttered closed, then opened again. "There was a storm at sea. The waves were frightening, and my ship—*Satan's Revenge*—was being ripped apart. Suddenly I was struck by lightning and tossed overboard. By the time I washed up on the island, nearly three hundred years had passed."

"You mean to tell me you traveled through time?"

"Aye. As difficult as it is to believe."

"Oh, it's quite difficult to believe."

Again he gasped for breath, and through the sheet Kate could see the rapid rise and fall of his chest. He was feverish. He was ill. No wonder he was telling such tales.

"Why don't you go back to sleep, Mr. Farrell? You'll feel better when you wake up. Maybe then you'll remember what really happened to you."

"I know quite well, Kate. I was born in the year of our Lord sixteen hundred and seventy-three. It was seventeen hundred and two when my ship and I were separated, and just today I was informed that it's nearly the year two thousand."

"And I suppose you're a real pirate, too?"

"Aye, madam, although I was once a gentle-man."

His eyes closed, and she stood by the window, waiting, watching, hoping he'd go back to sleep. When his breathing had steadied and the set of his jaw had relaxed, she moved quietly toward him. She untied the unnecessary patch and tucked it into the pocket of her shorts, wrung out another cool washcloth, and replaced the warm one on his forehead.

"I would have you believe me, Katie," he whispered.

She couldn't help but smile, and on unconscious impulse, she caressed her palm over his cheek.

"Sleep, Mr. Farrell. Just sleep."

Chapter 7

Though thy slumber may be deep,
Yet thy spirit shall not sleep . . .

LORD BYRON, MANFRED: ACT I

For long hours he tossed and turned, his body aching, shivering with a chill so deep in his bones he believed he was sailing on the godforsaken North Atlantic, and that he'd never know warmth again.

Somewhere near, he heard the chirp of birds, the distinctive rustle of wind through the shaggy-headed palms, and the unmistakable bliss of children's laughter.

And then something teased his nose, a pleasant memory of a sweet-smelling woman with long and wild honey-colored hair and eyes that sparkled like the rarest of emeralds.

Comforting hands spread over his chest, his stomach, pulling back the bed coverings before deft fingers loosened the buttons on his trousers, spreading a heat through his loins that he had not the strength to enjoy. Opening his eyes, he saw Kate hovering above him like a celestial spirit encircled in gold.

"I didn't mean to wake you, Mr. Farrell. I just want to make you more comfortable. Please. Go back to sleep."

He managed to smile, lifting a weak, almost useless hand to her cheek. So soft. So smooth. "Lie down with me, Katie. 'Tis cold I am. So very cold."

Gentle laughter rang through his ears. She stepped back, letting his hand fall heavily to his chest.

"I'd rather run you through with your cutlass," she stated flatly, tugging not too gently on the ends of his trousers. "Now, go back to sleep."

Ah, but the fire in her words soothed his pain and warmed his soul. He would sleep peacefully knowing she was near.

But the peace he sought would not come so easily.

"Please, Morgan, please. Don't let him hurt me."

He jerked at the chains, twisting and turning, but the bonds at his arms and legs were far too strong, and he could not get to the frightened little girl running from Thomas Low.

"She is mine," Low hissed. "Your efforts to keep her from me have been in vain. I always win, Mr. Farrell. Always."

He wanted to strangle the bastard, wanted to feel the

shudder of his last dying breath, but he could not escape. "I'll see you dead," Morgan shouted.

"Not today, Mr. Farrell. Not today."

Melody had scrambled to the top of the railing around the quarterdeck, linking her arms through the rigging. Tears streamed down her cheeks. "Help me, Morgan," she cried. "Please."

The chains cut into his wrists. Blood welled up from the shredded skin, but that pain was nothing compared to the ache in his heart for the sister he could not help, for his parents, who'd been sent to their watery grave just moments before.

Low stood at arm's length from his sister, hands clasped behind his back. "Come down, child," he coaxed. "I will not harm you."

Morgan saw the quiver in Melody's lips as she looked to him for help. "Dear God," he prayed silently. "I know not what to do. Give me guidance. Please."

"Morgan!" she screamed.

Low moved closer, teasing Melody with his advances.

"Jump." Morgan shouted. He hated the sound of his words, hated himself for what he was asking of his sister, but there was no other choice. "Jump," he cried. "Please."

"But I'm afraid."

"Say your prayers," he whispered, swallowing down a lump of fear. "Say your prayers—and jump."

Melody looked at him one last time, trust and faith mixed with terror in her sweet childish face.

"I love you, Melody. I love you."

She smiled faintly. Then she disappeared over the side.

"I love you," he whispered, and as if his little sister had heard his words, a soft hand touched his cheek.

"Melody?" he asked, but she did not answer, and even in his sleep, he knew she never would. She was gone—forever. Unconsciously he reached for the cross he'd taken from her lifeless body, for his mother's ring that he'd retrieved from Thomas Low.

He grasped the delicate piece made of rubies and gold, but the heavy wedding band did not fill his hand.

His eyes flew open. Kate sat beside him.

"Good afternoon, Mr. Farrell."

"What have you done with my possessions?"

She raised an eyebrow at his abruptness. "For your information, I have washed your clothes, I have locked away that blasted arsenal you carry around, and I've spent nearly two days taking care of your worthless hide."

He didn't care about anything she'd done for him. All he could think of was his mother's wedding band.

"Where's my ring?"

"You weren't wearing one."

"It was around my neck."

"Well, it's not there now, and if you don't stop yelling at me, the only thing you'll have around your neck are my hands."

If not for her anger, for the redness rising in her

cheeks, he might have continued to bellow, might have gone on questioning her until doomsday. Losing his mother's ring was something he could not abide, but being rude to a woman did not set well, either.

"I do believe you *would* strangle me, madam."

"I would," she stated, pacing across the room, then back again to the side of the bed. "Of course, killing you would be a pretty stupid thing to do after I've nursed you back to health."

"Aye. 'Twould have been smarter to let me die on your lawn."

"I should have thought of that earlier," she said, a smile softening the anger in her face. "I made you some chicken soup. Can you sit up?"

He'd found the strength to get upset about the loss of his mother's ring, but in spite of his efforts to lift his shoulders and arms, he hadn't the energy to rise from the bed.

Kate sighed, something he was learning was as commonplace as her quick-tempered passion and her seemingly unwilling generosity.

She unfolded the stiff arms that she'd clasped over her chest, leaned over, and slipped a hand beneath his head. He savored the softness of her breasts against his cheek, the sweetness of her perfume, and the steady beat of her heart as she propped him up with extra pillows. A man could easily leave the sea behind if he were to have a comfort like this woman in his home.

Sitting beside him, she lifted a bowl from the

bedside table. "I suppose you don't have the strength to feed yourself, either?"

He answered her with a smile, and gave a silent prayer of thanks when she placed the warm spoon against his lips and let the salty brew slide over his tongue and down his throat. Again and again she ladled the soup into his mouth, the only sustenance he'd had in God knows how many days.

"Who is Melody?" she asked cautiously, her eyes intent on the spoon and his mouth.

"My sister, God rest her soul. Why do you ask?"

"You called her name while you slept. I thought she might have been your wife."

"I have no wife, no children that I know of, nor do I have any other family. I have only you now. And Casey."

Those words made her look up. "You're taking a lot for granted, aren't you?"

"I have told you . . . I have nowhere else to go."

"You can't stay here forever."

"Rest assured, madam, that that is not my desire. I have but to regain my strength, and then I shall try to find my way back home."

"And where is that?"

"I have told you already."

Pushing up from the bed, she set the bowl back on the table and moved about the room, opening a window to let in the slightest of breezes that rustled the lacy white curtains. She stared out at the gathering clouds. "I thought it might be best if you stayed in bed the rest of the day, and maybe tried coming downstairs this evening."

"I believe you do not wish to acknowledge where I have come from."

She turned, shaking her head. "You make a pretty convincing pirate, Mr. Farrell, but I don't believe you traveled through time."

A more stubborn wench he'd never met. 'Twould be difficult to make her believe.

Walking slowly across the room, she lifted the tray from the bedside table. "The bathroom's over there," she said, pointing to the door across the room. "If you have the strength later, you might want to take a shower, or soak in the tub."

"Have you a servant to carry the hot water?"

She laughed cynically. "The pipes carry the hot water, Mr. Farrell. In case you've forgotten, you just turn a knob and water flows right out of the tap."

An ingenious idea, he decided. One he longed to investigate. Knowledge of such things would benefit him well when he returned to his own time.

"And what of my other bodily needs?" he asked.

She rolled her eyes. "Figure it out on your own, Mr. Farrell. I'm in no mood to humor you."

Kate crept into Joe's office, the place where she'd slept the first few months after his death. She'd felt closer to him there. At times she'd imagined him sitting at his desk, polishing a pistol, a sword, or one of his other special "finds." In the past six months, she hadn't seen him there at all. She no longer smelled his aftershave, no longer heard the sound of his footstep on the hardwood floor, or the stories he'd so often told Casey.

Joe was gone.

If time travel truly were possible, she'd go back and. . . . She laughed to herself. Time travel wasn't possible, and she couldn't change history.

Going to the bookshelves, she pulled down a few of Joe's favorite volumes on pirates. She carried them to the desk and sat, flipping one open to the index. Running her finger down the alphabetical listing, she stopped next to the name *Black Heart*. She started to thumb to the proper place, then hesitated, turning one more page until she found the F's. *Falcon, Fame, Fancy, Farquhar, Farrell*. Her hands began to shake as she turned back one page and compared the numbers with those under *Black Heart*.

Identical. Every one the same.

She flipped to page 43. There were no pictures, but she read the text.

The early life of Morgan Farrell, more often called Black Heart, is as mysterious as his disappearance in 1702. Some say he had been a gentleman from Kent, England, a scholar, and a man admired by women, but the truth was never known. His life as a pirate was no less puzzling. Reputed to be a bloodthirsty beast of imposing stature, he terrorized the American Colonies and the shipping trades throughout the West Indies. Other stories

abound concerning his gentleness with children,
and more than one thankful wench and starving
family were heard to praise his generosity.

Kate flipped back to the index, having learned
nothing she didn't already know, except that the
names *Morgan Farrell and Black Heart* were syn-
onymous. What she hoped to see was a picture.

She tried page 81 and page 115, and finally, on
page 147, she found it. The work was rough and
dark, the colors faded, but Kate could easily see a
scar sweeping down the right side of the man's
face, and a patch over his eye. The lips were too
thin, the nose too straight, and the jaw a little too
weak to resemble the man lying in her extra bedroom. Still, the hair in the painting was the
darkest of browns, and it rippled over the man's
shoulders, stopping halfway down his chest—so
much like Morgan Farrell's hair, which she'd nervously touched and admired. Rings hung from
both ears—just like the earrings Morgan Farrell
wore, and tucked under a wide leather belt were
a pistol, a dagger, and a sword with a jeweled hilt.

Kate twisted around in the oak swivel chair and
looked at the weapons she'd locked away in Joe's
display cabinet. The cutlass Morgan had given
her, the one he'd said was worth a fortune, looked
identical to the one in the painting.

Not for the first time since Morgan Farrell entered her life, her heart thundered in her chest.
The man in the next room being the same man
who had lived three hundred years ago seemed

too impossible to believe, yet the proof she should trust was in the book before her.

She read the caption beneath the painting.

Artist Josiah Lansdown sailed with the infamous Black Heart for only one year, serving as his cabin boy until the pirate established him with a wealthy family in England. At the insistence of Black Heart, the boy was tutored in the arts. This painting, one of only six completed before his untimely death at the age of twenty-one, was accomplished from memory, and inscribed "Black Heart—generous benefactor; beloved friend."

Could the man she'd nursed and the man in the picture be one and the same?

No, it was impossible. He was delusional. He'd been injured, he wasn't thinking straight. He couldn't have traveled through time.

Maybe he was interested in pirates, just as Joe had been. Maybe he was a collector of pirate memorabilia and owned Black Heart's sword. Maybe he knew the history of Black Heart and liked acting out the part. Maybe there was some resemblance between him and the man in the picture, but she found it difficult to imagine the man in the next room as a generous benefactor, or even a beloved friend.

Yet she remembered well the tear sliding down his cheek while he slept, the way he'd lovingly called out his sister's name, the way he'd reached for the cross at his neck, and the ring that had disappeared. Men without heart, without compassion, wouldn't do those things.

Sliding open the desk drawer, she removed the velvet box where she'd put the emerald ring she'd found on the island—the ring that might belong to Morgan Farrell. It was the most beautiful ring she'd ever seen, and she wanted very much to call it her own.

As she slipped it on her barren wedding ring finger, the odd feeling that it belonged there overcame her. She held up her hand, wiggling her fingers, and watched the way the sun's rays glinted off the diamonds and emerald, splashing a kaleidoscope of light about the room.

She sighed, feeling a moment of guilt for not having asked Morgan more about the ring he'd lost. If he brought it up again, she'd try to find out if this one really belonged to him. Until then, she might as well hang onto it for safekeeping.

She dropped the ring back into the box and closed it away in the desk drawer.

Taking one more look at the picture of Black Heart the pirate, she shook her head. She didn't want to believe he could be the same man who'd mysteriously appeared in her life any more than she wanted to believe the emerald ring belonged to him, but the coincidences were startling—and too darn confounding.

Quietly closing the door to Joe's office behind her, she walked down the hall, taking a moment to peek over the landing to see Aunt Evalena playing contentedly with the day care children she herself should have been watching yesterday and today. What would she do without that woman? Evie was always there when Kate needed her. Of course, she'd been dishing out a fair amount of guidance about the "man upstairs."

"What more could you possibly ask for, Katharine? He's a rather delightful looking man, he's helpless at the moment, and if you just bat your eyes a few times, I'm sure he'll fall right into your arms."

That was the last thing she wanted. Although, for the first time since Joe's death, she hadn't felt lonely.

She laughed to herself. Morgan Farrell had long hair, rings in his ears, a scar on his face, and those horrendous scars on his back. He wasn't the kind of man she could be interested in—if she *ever* wanted to be interested in a man.

Down the hall she heard Casey's giggles. She'd told her to stay downstairs, told her in no uncertain terms that she was not to go anywhere near Morgan Farrell unless an adult was around, but her words had apparently fallen on deaf ears.

Kate stopped outside the bedroom, and listened to Casey and her pirate.

"Do you have telephones where you come from?" Casey asked.

" 'Tis not a word I'm familiar with."

"Well, this is a telephone," Casey said, and Kate could easily picture Casey showing Mr. Farrell the phone that sat on the nightstand, lifting the receiver and punching the buttons. "Here, I'll call Aunt Evie."

"The woman is downstairs. Would it not be simpler to go into the hallway and call down to her?"

"Well, yeah, but I'm not really calling her. I'm calling her phone. In her house across the street."

"And what is the reason for doing that?"

Kate could hear the exasperation in Casey's voice. "So you can hear what a ringing phone sounds like."

There was silence then, and a moment later, Casey said, "Here, listen."

Kate peeked around the door and watched Mr. Farrell's brow furrow into a frown as Casey held the phone to his ear. "If your aunt was in her home across the street, she would pick up an object like this and talk into it?"

"Uh huh."

"And you could speak with her?"

"Yeah, I do it all the time."

" 'Tis a marvelous machine, Casey."

"Definitely better than the toilet I showed you. Yuck!" Casey wrinkled her nose and picked up the picture book of *Treasure Island* that Joe had given her on her fourth birthday.

"Can I tell you some more of the story now?"

"Aye."

Before Casey began, she plumped the pillow behind Mr. Farrell's head; then, climbing to the foot of the bed, she sat down cross-legged and began to mesmerize her listener.

"The old sea-dog was an awful man who did nothing but sit around the Admiral Benbow Inn drinking rum. Poor Jim Hawkins. It was his job to serve the captain his food, to help him up and down the stairs when he was too drunk to walk on his own. Most of the time, though, the old sea-dog just sat at the table telling stories, and running his finger up and down the big ugly cut on the side of his face." Casey leaned forward and studied her pirate's face. "Robert Louis Stevenson didn't say what the cut looked like, but I figure it was just like yours."

"Many a pirate had scars," he told her, lightly drawing a finger over the curving one on his cheek. "Some were visible to everyone, but most were hidden deep inside," he said, putting a hand over his heart.

"Do you have scars there?" Casey asked. Kate saw the deep sadness on his face, the same look of sorrow she'd seen when he'd mentioned his sister Melody.

"Aye," he said softly, allowing a smile to return to his face. "But let us not talk of wounds that can't be healed. Tell me more of this Treasure Island."

"Well," Casey said, flipping to a page in the book she knew by heart, and continuing the story in her own words. "The old sea-dog wasn't a pretty sight, and he was awfully mean. People were scared of him because he yelled all the time, and because he talked about pirates and treasure, and about one-legged men who would run you through without blinking an eye. But Jim Hawkins wasn't scared."

Kate had been so intent on watching Casey while she'd told her tale that she hadn't noticed Mr. Farrell's eyes closing, until Casey crawled toward him and prodded his arm with tiny fingers. "Are you awake, Mr. Farrell?"

His eyes opened. "Aye."

He smiled warmly, and that odd gentleness that didn't seem to match his outward appearance melted a little more of the animosity Kate felt toward him.

"You look like an old sea-dog," Casey said, "but I'm not afraid of you."

"I thank you, Mistress Casey," he said, gently running a hand over her curls before it dropped weakly to his side.

"My Mommy's afraid of you. My Aunt Evie says that Mommy's scared of all men."

"And why is that?"

"Because she's afraid of falling in love again. Aunt Evie says that's absolute nonsense. Do you think it's nonsense?"

Morgan Farrell tilted his head, looking directly at Kate, as if he'd known she'd been standing there all along. He didn't smile. He didn't frown. He just stared, and his gaze burned through her, warming her insides, making her tingle like an intoxicating drink of hot mulled wine.

He grasped the cross resting on his chest, and faced Casey again. "I do not believe it's nonsense. 'Tis painful to lose someone you love, far worse than having your face carved with a knife."

Casey leaned forward and innocently ran her finger lightly down his scar. "Did it hurt a lot?"

"Aye, Casey," he said, and Kate knew he was thinking of his sister, not the injury to his face. " 'Twas the greatest pain I've ever known."

Chapter 8

But there are wanderers o'er Eternity
Whose bark drives on and on,
and anchor'd ne'er shall be.

LORD BYRON
CHILDE HAROLD'S PILGRIMAGE: CANTO III

Kate sipped hot cocoa at the kitchen table, wishing she had someone to keep her company, but Evalena had spirited Casey off for an evening of fun and one of her midsummer slumber parties. Kate remembered them well—the food, the music, the dancing and games.

When she was lonely, she often remembered her first night with Evie, that summer in 1980 when, at the tender age of eight, the social worker had dropped her off at Evalena's door. She'd already lived in five other foster homes, and the moment she saw the fat old lady in fuzzy slippers and a brightly colored muumuu, she decided there'd be at least one or two more. There was no way she was going to get stuck with a grandma type.

That afternoon they'd had a staring contest, Kate on one side of the drawing room, Evalena on the other. By evening Kate had relegated herself to one half of the crazy-looking loveseat, where she counted cupids while Evalena talked incessantly about her many husbands, her matchmaking abilities, and the absolutely luscious wedding cakes she made for all the people whose marriages she'd arranged.

At midnight, Evalena put a Perry Como record on the turntable, dragged a kicking kid into her roly-poly arms, and danced her around the room, hugging her tightly as she hummed with the music.

In the morning Evalena taught Kate how to make Mickey Mouse pancakes. By ten they were finger-painting on the kitchen floor. At noon they were making royal frosting roses to go on a four-tiered wedding cake, and by two Kate had decided Aunt Evie was worth her weight in gold, and that had to amount to close to a billion dollars.

Her worth had increased tenfold since then. She'd been Kate's mother, her sister, and her friend, and Casey's doting grandmother, and since Joe had died, Evie had easily recognized those moments when Kate needed time alone.

But she'd goofed tonight. Kate didn't want to be alone—not with Casey's pirate.

Directly above the kitchen, in the room where Morgan Farrell slept, the floorboards creaked and Kate heard the distinct sound of someone moving slowly across the floor. A moment later she heard water running down the pipes in the walls. It flowed for a good minute, then stopped. Again it rushed through the old copper tubing. And stopped.

After that, the toilet flushed. Not once, not twice, but three times.

She could hear the tub filling with water, the slippery sound of feet climbing into the ancient cast iron clawfoot, and the slosh of water.

Mentally she made a note to put more insulation in the walls and between the floors, then scratched it off her list. She couldn't afford the extravagance. The house needed a fresh coat of paint more than she needed the quiet.

Taking another sip of cocoa, she listened to the sound of a slick body rubbing against the tub, and couldn't help but imagine Morgan's wet, thoroughly naked physique filling the clawfoot. She saw his muscular chest and shoulders rising above the water like the mighty god Poseidon, rivulets of bath water dripping from his hair, over his pecs, over his small, hard nipples, and into the water, sending ripples across the surface.

Through the miniscule waves she could see his belly, firm and flat, the gathering of dark hair at his groin, and . . . she imagined other things that she dared not think of. Things she'd tried not to look at when she'd removed his clothes, like the scar on his left hip, and—

"Good evening, madam."

Kate jumped, startled by the sound of Morgan's voice. Cocoa sloshed out of her cup and onto the table, and she twisted around to see him standing in the doorway, his body naked except for the white towel clinging to his hips. His long hair was wet and little streams of water trickled down his chest—just as she'd envisioned, only the real thing was so much better.

She swallowed hard, drawing her cup close to her face to hide her sudden embarrassment.

"Pardon me, madam, but I seem to have misplaced my clothes."

"I . . . I washed and ironed them," she stammered, feeling like a schoolgirl who'd never seen a half-naked man. She took a deep breath, trying to regain her composure, and went to the room just off the kitchen to retrieve the stack of folded laundry.

"You look like you're feeling better," she said nonchalantly, placing the clothes in his outstretched hands. "I imagine you're hungry. It's been days since you've had any real food."

"Aye. It has been long since I had a woman for company, too." He smiled, and the dimples at each side of his lips deepened. "You *will* keep me company, won't you, Kate?"

Absently her gaze traveled the length of his body, resting much too long on the damp towel. She nodded, slowly turning her attention to his sparkling eyes. "Casey's at Evalena's for the night. I wouldn't mind someone to talk to." Again her gaze drifted momentarily to the towel. "You'll get dressed first, won't you?"

"Aye." He grinned, and without another word, strolled from the kitchen.

Kate leaned against the doorjamb, watching the play of muscles across his back, the tightness of every inch of his body, and for just one moment, she wished the towel would slip away. But it stayed in place, and all too soon he disappeared up the stairs.

Grabbing a damp rag from the sink, she wiped up the chocolate she'd spilled on the table and thought about spending the evening with Morgan Farrell. It had been two and a half years since she'd spent any time at all with a man. What would they talk about? What would they do?

She laughed to herself. They definitely wouldn't leave the house—not with him dressed as a pirate.

Pulling a plate of cold roast beef and a head of lettuce from the refrigerator, she stood at the kitchen counter fixing a thick sandwich. Her stomach growled, but at the moment she was too nervous to think about eating.

Nervous! Like a girl getting ready for her very first date, instead of a woman who'd been married and had a six-year-old daughter. Evalena would chuckle if she knew all the things going through her mind right now, like would he try to kiss her? Would he want more from her than polite conversation? Would he. . . .

Damn! This wasn't a date.

She tossed the rag into the sink and wiped her hands on her cutoffs. Ripped cutoffs! Ones with a nearly threadbare bottom. And her white cotton blouse had a splotch of spaghetti sauce on it, a definite reminder of a toddler's pudgy hand pressed close to her breast.

She couldn't spend the evening like this.

Racing from the kitchen to her bedroom, she tossed clothes everywhere as she rapidly looked for something to wear in her meager wardrobe. At the back of the closet she found a green silk shift. It was plain and simple. A little too short, maybe, and possibly a little too low in the front. But it was summertime in Florida. It was hot, humid, and . . . hell! She didn't need to make excuses.

She slid it over her head, shoved her feet into a pair of sandals, and hoped she could get back to the kitchen before Morgan did.

Throwing open her bedroom door, she rushed into the hall and collided with Casey's pirate.

Strong fingers wrapped around her upper arms, and she tilted her head to meet his smile.

"You look lovely, Kate."

A flash of heat rushed to her cheeks. "Thank you."

He leisurely took in the length of her body, from her eyes to her pink polished toenails, all the way back to her face, and she couldn't help but do the same to him.

His billowing white shirt laced only partially up

his chest with the ruby cross and bright gold chain shining against a backdrop of curly dark hair. Freshly washed and pressed gray trousers hugged his hips and thighs. Boots that glistened from several coats of black leather wax she'd applied embraced his legs and knees.

His face was cleanly shaven, his thick dark brown hair had been tied back at the nape of his neck, and his lips curved into a smile that filled her insides with sensations she knew she shouldn't be feeling—not with a near stranger.

A stranger who was the most handsome man she'd ever seen—and nothing at all like any man she'd ever desired.

She backed away from his hold and drew in a deep breath before nervously brushing past him. She had to get far away from her bedroom and back to the kitchen, which seemed a better place to hold a conversation with Morgan Farrell. He was too masculine for her own good.

"I made you a sandwich," she said. "And my aunt brought over an apple pie."

Again she felt his powerful hand seize her arm, and the squeeze of gentle fingers pulled her to a stop before she was halfway down the stairs. "Have I frightened you?" he asked, his voice, his touch, commanding her to turn around and look at him.

"No," she said softly. "I'm just not used to having a man around—sick *or* healthy."

"Your husband has been gone for some time, then?"

"Too long," Kate admitted. "I've almost forgotten what to say or do when I keep a man company."

"Be yourself, Kate. 'Tis your ability to say and do the first thing that comes into your head that I admire about you."

She laughed. "I've always been a little impulsive. You could ask my aunt, even my sister-in-law, Nikki, and they'll tell you I have a tendency to rush into things."

" 'Tis my good fortune, then. I imagine if you'd given my situation any thought, I wouldn't be here now."

"Probably not." She smiled and continued down the stairs.

He followed her to the kitchen, ignoring the chair she pulled out for him. Instead, he lifted the sandwich from the plate and took a bite while walking around the room running his fingers over the glistening white refrigerator, the burners on the stove, and the blue tile countertop, as if he'd never seen such things before.

He turned the water on and off in the sink, and watched it slowly swirl down the drain. "There are many wondrous inventions in this home of yours," he said. "I was particularly intrigued by the chamberpot that you call a toilet, and the levers on the walls that make light appear and disappear."

"You aren't going to tell me you don't know about indoor plumbing or light fixtures, are you?"

"In my day we burned oil for light. Privies were

usually outside, or in a small closet in the bedroom. I much prefer this toilet of yours."

She turned away, quickly taking a glass from a cupboard so he couldn't see her grin. Did he really believe he was from 1702?

"You must tell me more about the marvels of your century. I must know about the carriages that roll along the roads without horses to pull them, and the ships with wings I have seen flying through the sky."

Flying ships? Carriages without horses? How long would he keep up this charade?

"What about TV?" she asked, setting down the empty glass. "I imagine that's new to you, too." She flipped on the small television that sat on the counter, then watched the way Morgan frowned, totally intrigued by the flickering screen and the way it brightened when two people appeared before him.

"Bloody hell!"

Setting his unfinished sandwich on the counter, he crossed the kitchen in two long strides and touched the glass on the front of the TV, jerking his hand away when static snapped at his fingers. Cautiously he again reached for the glass, tracing a finger over the image of the female newscaster on the screen.

"Miniature people," he whispered, moving so close that his nose nearly touched the television. He swept a hand over the top of the TV, around the sides. He peeked at the back, running his fingers along the cords that trailed from the set to the antenna and electrical outlets on the wall.

How easy it would be to believe he'd never seen a television before, or a stove, or refrigerator, or running water.

Impossible, she told herself. *Absolutely impossible*.

Again he stood in front of the television, then he turned to Kate, his blue eyes filled with confusion. "Can they see me?"

"No. They're miles away from here."

"Then how do I see them? How do they get inside the box?"

"It's a television," she said, pushing the channel selector, watching the bewilderment in his face as the picture continually changed. "You must have seen one before."

"We did not have such a thing in my time," he said flatly. He nudged her hand aside, putting his finger where hers had been. "What is this?"

She laughed. "A button. That one changes the channels. The ones beside it raise and lower the volume."

He tested them all, jerking back when the sudden loudness nearly blasted them both from the room. His expression changed from a smile to a grin, and to amazement as the pictures changed from bathing beauties running on the beach to a couple kissing passionately to a high-speed car chase up and down the hills of San Francisco.

"Explain this television to me."

"It's quite simple," she lied. "A cameraman takes pictures of the actors, and then *poof!* They disintegrate into a zillion pieces that float through the sky and suddenly appear on the TV screen."

His smile disappeared. She could see the flex of muscle in his jaw as he gritted his teeth in annoyance. "I am not a child, Kate. I am a grown man who is quite capable of understanding the concepts of your time were I to be given a civil answer. Do you think I would ridicule you if you'd been sent to the past and found yourself confused by all you saw?"

She wasn't ridiculing him. Well, maybe a little, but how could he expect her to believe he'd never seen a television before? As for her going back in time, she didn't see where that would be a problem.

"There'd be nothing odd if I went to the past," she answered. "I'd know how everything works."

"Would you know how to turn tallow into candles to light the rooms of your home?"

"No."

"Of course you wouldn't, because you have been spoiled by the inventions of your time. In the past you would not have had the luxury of hot bath water just by turning a knob. And, my dearest Kate, the chamberpot would not clean itself. If you did not have servants, you would have to carry it outside at least once a day. You could not light the rooms of your home simply by flipping a switch, and if you were far away from your loved ones, you could not speak with them on this marvelous telephone Casey has shown me."

He leaned against the refrigerator and crossed his arms resolutely over his chest. "I wonder, Kate

. . . would you want to scream when no one believed that you'd traveled through time?"

"Time travel's impossible."

"But what if it were not? How would you react?"

She shook her head. "I don't know."

"Then I will tell you. You would find yourself amazed that something so incredible could happen. You would marvel at the differences between your time and the one you find yourself in. And then you would long for the things familiar to you. You would want, with all of your heart, for someone to believe you were telling the truth."

For the longest time she stared over his shoulder at one of Casey's pictures stuck to the refrigerator, unable to meet his eyes. Her brain screamed at her not to believe in time travel, but her heart told her he was telling the truth. Finally she looked at him and tried to smile. "If I did believe you, what would you need from me?"

"I only wish to know more of your time. I need to know what happened between seventeen-oh-two and now. I need to know how I can go back."

"Do you really want to leave?"

"My life is in the past, not here. If I can go back to my own time, I can teach others about the wondrous things here and now. Perhaps I could change what happened before."

"And take the chance of altering the future?" she asked. "Not that I believe any of this is possible, but if you were to change things that happened three hundred years ago, today might end up being different."

"Have you considered the possibility that me coming forward in time has already altered what was to be?"

"I haven't thought about it at all. I don't want to think about it, either." She turned to the window and stared out at the cloudy early evening sky. "I'd rather believe that you've had the sense knocked out of you, and that pretty soon you'll remember who you are."

She heard his footsteps behind her. Felt him moving close. Could sense the heat of his body through the silk of her dress. "I am a pirate, Kate." He moved to her side, and the ties at the front of his shirt brushed against her arm, sending an unexpected quiver through her stomach.

Tilting her head, she looked up into his intense blue eyes.

"I have taken lives," he said. "I have burned villages, captured ships, and stolen precious gold and jewels." He looked out the window, his gaze far away, as if he were seeing into the past. "At one time I was a gentleman. I was destined to be a landowner, a grower of sugar cane in the West Indies, but that life ended abruptly—and savagely."

Again he looked at her. "I do not belong in your world, and I want to go back to mine. That is the truth, Kate, whether you choose to believe it or not."

She sighed, concentrating on the intricate cross

resting on his chest, on the laces of his shirt, on the silver buckle on his belt. All his possessions looked as if they belonged in a museum, and he himself looked and acted like no modern man. With every passing moment, she was finding his far-fetched tale a little easier to believe.

"Okay, what do you want to know about first?" she asked. "The Revolutionary War? The Civil War? World Wars I and II?"

"Wars are nothing new to me and are of little interest at the moment. 'Tis your vehicle and the others I have seen that interest me now."

Kate looked nonchalantly out the window at the faded green '57 Chevy parked in the garage. "It's just a car."

"I know nothing of these *cars* except that they have no sails to catch the wind or horses to pull them. I would know how they move along the roads."

"It's complicated, and I'm the last one on earth who could explain something so technical to you."

"Then show me. Take me for a ride." Morgan tugged on her hand, pulling her toward the kitchen door.

"You can't go out in public," Kate exclaimed, coming to a dead stop at the threshold.

"And why not?"

"You're dressed like a pirate. People will stare."

" 'Tis no concern of mine what other people do."

"Well, I care. I know too many people in this

town, and if they see me with you, they'll think I've lost my mind."

His infectious laughter rumbled through the room. "Let them think what they will, Kate." His hand tightened around hers as he pushed open the screen door.

"Wait a minute," she said, tugging against his pull. "We can't go anywhere without keys, and I need my driver's license, and some money, and—"

He put a silencing finger to her lips, and a burning tingle raced through her insides. "You make too many excuses, Kate. Get your keys and the license you speak of, then meet me at the vehicle. There is much I want to see and do, and you are the only one I want to see and do these things with."

His finger brushed lightly over her mouth, and just as abruptly as he'd stilled her words of protest, he drew his hand away and strolled from the house, letting the screen slam behind him.

Kate touched her lips, the place that still burned from his caress, and watched his resolute and powerful walk as he headed for the garage. She liked the movement of his long muscular legs, the power radiating from the wide set of his shoulders, and his hair, so thick and lustrous, hanging down his back.

A smile tugged at her mouth as she plucked her key ring from the rack mounted near the door. Being lonely was a far worse fate than spending the evening with a gorgeous, although possibly deranged, pirate.

Morgan was sitting behind the big green steering wheel, tracing the glass-fronted speedometer and the temperature and fuel gauges when Kate entered the garage. His eyes were bright with wonder, like a little boy with a brand new toy. " 'Tis a beautiful vehicle," he said. "I am most eager to drive it."

"Oh, no. You're not driving it anywhere."

"I'll have you know, madam, that I have captained the finest sailing vessels in the world, and until that blasted storm, I'd had nary a mishap. I have—"

"Move over," she said adamantly. "This isn't a ship and it isn't a carriage. It's a car. You've never driven one, you don't have a license, and I'm not about to go anywhere with you behind the wheel."

He raised an eyebrow, looking as if he was going to argue.

"Move!" she ordered.

His devilish laughter echoed through the garage. "Aye, madam. As you wish."

He slid to the passenger seat and Kate took his place behind the wheel. Turning the key in the ignition, she watched the play of emotions on Morgan's face when the souped-up engine roared. Worry lines formed between his eyes. His chest rose and fell heavily, and he gripped the edge of the seat as if the car was a ship bucking on a turbulent sea.

Unconsciously she reached across the empty space between them and put her hand over his. "There's no reason to be afraid."

"Afraid?" he said incredulously. "Nay, madam, you mistake my excitement for fear. I have ridden the fastest of horses, driven carriages over rutted English roads, but I have never been in a vehicle such as this. 'Tis fascinating . . . and daunting."

She smiled softly, remembering her own fear-filled excitement the first time she'd driven a car. "When I was twelve, Joe—my husband—let me sit beside him and turn the steering wheel while he drove to the beach. I thought it was the most thrilling thing in the world. Would you like to try?"

"Aye."

Morgan seemed to relax as he moved to the center of the seat, and without any instruction, he put his hands close to hers on the wheel, his arm brushing lightly against her breast. She sucked in a deep breath as a tingling sensation rippled through her chest and down to the center of her being. She'd nearly forgotten how good it felt to have a man touch her breast, even accidentally, and for one brief moment, she wondered how good it would feel if Morgan Farrell touched her on purpose.

Don't think about it, she told herself. *Concentrate on the fact that you're giving him his first driving lesson, not getting swept up in foreplay.*

"See where my right foot is?" she asked. He looked down, his gaze skimming the length of her body before it rested on her foot. "The brake's on the left," she told him, swallowing back the nervousness she felt with his powerful body pressing against her arm, her hip, her thigh. "The gas pedal—the one that makes the car go—is on the right. You have to touch them easily or else the car will jerk."

He crossed one leg over the other and settled his right foot close to hers on the brake.

"Now what?" he asked, and when he tilted his head she could feel the warmth of his breath whispering over her cheek.

"You have to shift the car into reverse," she said, and his strong, long-fingered hand followed hers, warmly closing over her knuckles as she touched the stick. She fought for control of her senses while she explained about park, reverse, neutral, drive, and low. Absently he drew lazy circles over the back of her hand, his callused thumb feeling more like velvet than sandpaper.

Hoping he couldn't feel the trembling in her fingers, she finished her explanation, and then he squeezed her hand. " 'Tis a simple concept," he said, shifting nonchalantly into reverse, as if the emotion-packed interlude had meant nothing to him. "Now, do I put my foot on the gas pedal?"

She nodded, laughing inwardly at letting herself get caught up in the moment, and lifted her foot from the brake as he moved his boot to the gas. He touched the pedal lightly and the car rolled back an inch or two. A grin crossed his face. He drew in a deep breath, just like a first-time driver, and confidently pressed the pedal again.

The car shot backward, screeching out of the garage onto the crushed shell–and-gravel drive.

"Bloody hell!"

His foot flew off the pedal and Kate trounced on the brake, bringing them to an abrupt and jarring halt.

"I said you had to do it easily!"

"That was my intention, madam."

"Well, you didn't succeed! Now, try it again."

She watched the hard set of his jaw as his teeth ground together in determination. Again he touched the gas pedal, his fingers tightened on the wheel, and he backed slowly and skillfully to the end of the driveway, moving his foot to the brake, and pressing it slowly when they neared the road.

Kate looked at him and smiled. "Are you sure you haven't done this before?"

"Never. What do I do now?"

"Look both ways, and if there are no other cars coming, or people or animals or anything else in the street, you back *slowly* onto the road, turning the wheel as you go."

"Which way do I turn the wheel?"

"I'll show you."

He twisted, his hair brushing lightly over her bare arm as he looked into the darkened street. Again, she was conscious of every move he made, every touch of his body against hers, every breath he took. She was being silly. Morgan Farrell was more interested in her car than he was in her. She supposed that was the way it ought to remain, especially since he would be leaving soon.

Especially since she wasn't interested in getting romantically involved with another man—even though Morgan Farrell was causing her to have second thoughts on the matter.

Pressing a foot on the gas, he backed onto the road, and Kate guided his hands as they turned the wheel.

"Now stop," she instructed, and he braked the car gently.

"Put it in drive."

He followed all her directions, and in a few moments they were moving along St. George, heading toward the center of town. They crawled at a speed of about five miles an hour, and Morgan's eyes were in constant motion as he watched for other cars. He braked easily at stop signs, looked both ways, and crept like a tortoise across the intersections. She couldn't help but smile. It was like teaching Casey how to ride a bicycle or thread a needle—things that were new, different, and simple, but always a thrill the very first time.

"Where would you like to go?" Kate asked, guiding the steering wheel a bit to the left when Morgan veered too close to a parked car.

"I saw much of your city that first day I was here. I walked past cathedrals, taverns, and many a shop in my search for you. 'Twas all new and different, yet I saw these things through my eyes only. 'Twould be good to see them through yours, to know what you feel when you look at places that are familiar."

"I never get tired of this city," she told him. "I've lived here all my life, and even though everything's familiar, I have special memories about most every place."

"Tell me about them," he said, easing away from the steering wheel and letting Kate take over the driving. He leaned casually against the passenger door where the wind blew through the open window, ruffling his shirt and hair. Breathing came easier for Kate with him sitting further away.

She parked in front of Flagler College, pointing out the fountain, the stained glass windows, the places where she'd hidden when she and other children had played hide-and-seek. She told him how she'd wanted to go to school there, to someday be a teacher, but that she'd gotten married right out of high school instead.

"All I wanted to do was be around children," she said. "Lots of them. Joe and I had always hoped to have more."

"Perhaps you will have others one day."

"I don't think about it much anymore. What I wanted was all part of another life, and that ended."

He nodded, understanding evident in his far-away smile.

As they wove through the narrow streets, she told him about her childhood, about being taken in by Evalena, finding it easy to tell him about the rejection she'd felt when her mother and father abandoned her. "I don't think my parents realized that love was more important than money or material possessions."

"Perhaps they wanted you to have both."

"I got more love than anything else from Evalena. She didn't have any children of her own, but she knew what I needed. I wanted to be just like her when I grew up, and I wanted to give that same kind of love and attention to a bunch of my own kids."

"Is that why you take care of other people's children?"

"They brighten my day. I need the money, too," she admitted. "I don't need a lot of material things, but I need to make a living, and taking care of children is what I do best."

Kate pulled into the parking lot near Castillo de San Marcos and stopped so the car was facing the lighted fortress. "I used to come here for picnics with my aunt, or to play pirates with Joe and his sister. He was fascinated with pirates—good ones, bad ones, it didn't really matter. I guess he found them romantic."

"And you?" he asked, smiling his warm and dangerous smile.

Heat rushed to her cheeks as she contemplated his question. "I liked anything Joe liked, but I'd never really understood his fascination—until now."

Morgan's smile deepened, and without saying a word, he climbed from the car, then came around to the driver's side, opened Kate's door, and took hold of her hand. "Walk with me," he said, his voice low, almost hypnotic.

She slid out of the car and strolled at his side across the sweeping lawn that surrounded the centuries-old fort. "St. Augustine was much different in my time," he said, walking slowly, his hands folded behind his back. "There were houses, of course. Many lined the streets as they do now. I remember wandering around the city at night, staying out of sight of the Spanish soldiers, and looking through windows to see and hear families laughing together over the evening meal. 'Twas the life I longed for but could not have."

"Why?"

"I was a wanted man. My mother, father, and sister had died, and my family in England had disowned me. 'Twas not surprising. My grandfather had raised honorable sons, and my uncle could not abide what I had become."

"Why did you become a pirate?"

He laughed, taking hold of her hand and squeezing it tightly, even when she tried to pull away. "You believe me, then?"

"It's hard not to."

"Then believe me when I tell you I had good reason to become a pirate."

"That's all you're going to tell me?"

" 'Tis all you need to know."

They stood near one of the swaying palms that lined the bank between the fortress and the bay. "The sea never changes," Morgan said, as they looked at the moonlight shining on the waves lapping against the shore. "I sailed many times from Dover to Calais, but I was in my early twenties when I first crossed the Atlantic. I had never been at the helm of a ship before. I'd always been a passenger, but the first time I raised a sail and felt my hands around the wheel, I knew I'd found my home."

His hand slid around her waist, and he pulled her close to his side, but his eyes didn't leave the dark line of the ocean on the horizon. "I must find a way to go back, Kate. 'Tis where I belong."

Chapter 9

⚔

Farewell! a word that must be, and hath been—
A sound which makes us linger;—yet—farewell!

LORD BYRON
CHILDE HAROLD'S PILGRIMAGE: CANTO IV

He'd wanted to kiss her. All the way home, as she'd driven the car and stared straight ahead, speaking nary a word, he'd wanted to kiss her. When they'd stood outside her bedroom door, he'd wanted to sweep his fingers over her creamy-smooth cheek and wind them through her hair. He'd wanted to draw her face close to his and capture her velvety lips.

But Kate was not a barroom wench whose affections could easily be trifled with. She was a lady of the first order, a woman of compassion, who stirred his senses as none other had ever done.

And he'd hardly touched her.

Morgan folded his arms behind his head and stared at the dark ceiling. In the room next door he could hear Kate stir, could hear the faint crackle of a wooden bed frame and the creak of a floorboard as she walked across the room.

Rising from the small bed that barely fit his body, he went to the window and looked to the balcony where he'd seen her sitting the night he'd arrived at her home.

She was curled up in a chair, her knees drawn up to her chest. He leaned against the wall and watched her in silence.

The moon shone on her honey-colored hair, where it hung about her shoulders and curled at the crest of her soft, lush breasts. A thin white gown edged in lace scarcely skimmed her body. Her legs were bare, and he wanted to touch them, to draw his fingers up their silky length and drive her to madness.

His loins ached at the thought.

But he would not touch her. Nay. He could not take her to his bed, love her thoroughly, and then walk away. 'Twould be too difficult to leave this woman—a woman who warmed his heart and enflamed his soul—were he to taste everything she could give him. 'Twould be wrong to ask her to give herself completely, to make her think he would stay.

A true gentlemen—even one who had turned to piracy—would not tamper with a woman's heart, especially if it would shatter his own.

* * *

Kate watched the sway of the pines silhouetted against the dark clouds floating across a blue-black sky. She wished that sleep had come, but her thoughts had been too full of Morgan Farrell, and she'd tossed and turned trying to drive him from her mind.

She didn't want someone taking Joe's place. She didn't like the idea of comparing a confessed thief, murderer, and scoundrel with her beloved Joe.

Resting her forehead on her knees, she closed her eyes and concentrated on thoughts of her husband, but the pictures that came to her mind were of a young boy playing pirate and making her walk the gangplank he'd rigged up in the backyard, a teenager giving her her first chaste kiss, and a young man with a childlike face asking her to be his wife, telling her about all the fun they could have.

And then Morgan's face came into her mind. Worldly. Rugged. Scarred by a cruel life that she imagined had been anything but fun. An older face. A wiser face.

With lips that she'd wanted to kiss.

Behind her, she heard the whine of a floorboard and turned. Morgan was standing in her doorway, the breeze wafting through his hair. His shirt was loose, hanging over his gray trousers. His feet were bare. His eyes were warm, and they searched hers, as if trying to know what she was thinking at this very moment.

But she didn't even know herself. Confusion was all she felt.

"I could not sleep," he said, leaning against the doorframe. "I saw you sitting alone. I hope you don't mind me joining you."

She shook her head. "I often sit out here at night. Sometimes I read, sometimes I just wait till everything's quiet so I can hear the waves hitting the beach."

"If I were in my own time, I would stand at the helm of *Satan's Revenge*, watch the stars, and plan my course for another voyage."

"Was planning your next voyage what kept you from sleeping tonight?"

"Aye." He walked to the edge of the balcony and gripped the railing. He looked across the street at Evalena's darkened house, and farther still, toward the Atlantic. "I long to be on the ocean again, back in a time that is familiar to me. But try as I might, I do not know how to go home."

"I've thought a lot about it."

He turned, a slight frown narrowing his eyes. "Do you know something I am not aware of?"

"I wish I did know something, but I don't. It just seems that if you could go back, you'd have to do it the same way you came."

He laughed. "I would rather forgo another hurricane, and I do not believe even my hard head could weather another blow from a falling mast." He turned again to the railing. "Besides, I no longer have a ship to take me back out on the ocean."

"You could take my sailboat."

She'd allowed the words to slip quickly from her lips. If she'd given herself time to think, she never would have offered. Doing so made it much too easy for him to leave, and she wasn't sure that was what she wanted.

"You are most generous, Kate." He spoke without looking at her, and for one moment she wondered if he was as torn about returning to his own time as she was about him going. He was silent for far too long, and then he slowly faced her. A warm smile shone in his eyes and on his lips. "I will sleep on your offer." He bowed his head in his ever-so-proper manner. "Good night, Kate."

And then he was gone—far, far too soon.

Kate yawned. Morning had come too early, awakening her from sweet dreams of sailing on placid waters, beneath a bright full moon. She wandered down the hallway and peeked into Morgan's room. It was empty, and her heart sank. She stepped through the door and looked around for any hint that he might return, but his coat was no longer draped over the chair, and the bed was made. There were no outward signs that he'd ever been in her home.

If it weren't for the strange loneliness she now felt, she might have believed she'd dreamed the past few days. They'd been real, though—very, very real—and Morgan's smile, his scar, the intensity of his eyes overwhelmed her every thought.

"Good morning, madam."

She jerked around at the sound of his voice.

"I have startled you. I apologize."

"I thought you'd gone."

"On the contrary. I have been downstairs, eating breakfast with Casey and your aunt. Something quite tasty called Mickey Mouse pancakes."

Kate pushed her hair behind her ears and tried not to look as relieved as she felt. "Casey should have woken me up. I've got kids coming any minute."

"You were sleeping soundly. We did not have the heart to disturb you."

"You came into my bedroom again?"

"Aye, madam. With your daughter." He smiled. "You are quite beautiful—awake and asleep."

She ignored his comment, tilting her head to look at the toes of his boots rather than meet his eyes. Then she changed the subject. "Did you think any more about taking my boat?"

"Aye."

She raised her head slowly and met his smile. She swallowed the lump of dread that had formed in her throat. "So, are you going to leave?"

"Nay. Not on your boat. 'Tis a vessel I would be proud to sail, but in my heart I do not believe it will take me home."

"Why?"

"As you suggested last night, I imagine I will be able to go home only if the circumstances that brought me here are repeated."

"Then you're going to stay?"

"Casey talked of making breakfast for me tomorrow morning, and the next day, too. 'Twould be hard to break her heart."

Kate couldn't help but smile. "There's so much to think about if you're going to stay. You'll need a job. You'll need identification. You'll need—"

"I'll need to search for a ship," he interrupted. "I'll need to do everything in my power to re-create the events that brought me here."

The finality of his words slammed against her chest. She didn't want him to leave, but . . . but maybe his leaving would be for the best, she rationalized. He was a pirate, after all, a man not suited to the kind of life she led, a man who'd never be happy tied to one place. A man with a past that would be far too hard to ignore.

"I would appreciate your assistance, Kate."

She bit the inside of her lip. "Sure," she said, not knowing what else she could possibly say. "What would you like me to help you with?"

"I need books to read. I need to know everything that happened between my time and yours."

The doorbell rang downstairs, helping her to forget about him leaving, pulling her back to reality. "That's Bubba and his mom. I've got to go."

Morgan's fingers circled her arm and kept her from rushing away. "I need a place where I can be alone. A place where I can think—and plan."

"You can use my husband's office," she said, surprised at her own words. Everything in that room was personal, private. That room had been Joe's own special place, yet she hadn't hesitated a moment in allowing Morgan to use it.

She moved quickly down the hall and opened the door. She'd expected to see the image of Joe looking up at her from behind his desk. She'd expected to see his smile. But Joe was gone, and when Morgan walked into the room lined with bookshelves filled with volumes about the history of his time, and glass display cabinets holding artifacts that seemed old and unfamiliar to her but were so much a part of his life, it seemed as if he belonged there.

The doorbell rang again.

"I've got to go," she said, quickly scanning the length of him from the scar on his face to his boots, and back again to the rings in his ears. "You'd better stay up here all day." She smiled faintly when he raised a questioning brow. "You might frighten the children."

He laughed. "Run along, Kate. There is much here to occupy my time," he said, looking about the room. "I give you my word that I will stay away from the children—and you, at least until this evening."

A nervous smile touched her lips. For a moment he thought he saw them quiver. God, but he wanted to kiss them.

He watched her run down the stairs when the bell rang at the door yet again. He watched the way she lovingly slipped her arm around a little boy and took him from his mother's arms, and saw the look of delight on the child's face as his fingers wound through Kate's hair.

He longed to touch her hair, too, to bury his face in her mass of honey-colored waves, to hold her close.

He took a deep, calming breath.

You have to go home, he reminded himself. Far away from Kate and this life that you were never meant to be a part of.

Slowly he closed the door, and concentrated on his need to return to 1702.

He wandered about the room, a chamber paneled in dark wood that reminded him of his cabin on board *Satan's Revenge.* He swept his hand over the large desk, studying the picture of a man in uniform that sat off to one side. Handsome, young. A broad smile brightened his face. He looked to be the kind of man anyone would be proud to call friend.

Several worn but inviting chairs were scattered about the room. Glass cases sat against one wall, filled with sabers, muskets, daggers, and pistols, weapons that looked as if they'd weathered the storms of many centuries. Resting on one shelf was his own jewel-hilted cutlass, his dagger, and his pistol, locked away for safekeeping.

But it was the books that interested him most. Volume upon volume stood upright on the shelves lining two walls, and he scanned the titles, pulling down one on the history of North America, one on piracy in the Caribbean, another chronicling maritime activities in the seventeenth and eighteenth centuries.

Taking them to the desk, he sat down and

opened the history book, and immediately began skimming pages. The Revolutionary War intrigued him. More than likely he would have been long dead by the time that conflict took place, but he imagined he would have sided with the Colonies. Freedom was something he cherished, and he longed for the days when he could again walk the streets without hiding from soldiers or those who wanted the bounty on his head.

As he browsed, he realized that war was the turning point for most everything that had occurred in this country, not unlike the history of any other land.

He read about the development of the railroads, the motorcar, and the airplane, an invention that captured his imagination. 'Twould be a marvel to fly through the clouds, far above the earth, and look down at the vast and beautiful oceans and land.

There was space travel, too, and he thought about putting his foot down in the dust on the moon, exploring a place far different from an uncharted tropical island, and gazing thousands of miles away at the small planet known as earth.

These were things that he could never do. They were unheard of, almost undreamed of, in his own time, a time he must return to. 'Twould be enough, though, to know of the future, to tell others of what was to be, although they would think him mad.

He laughed, and his voice echoed through the room.

Rising from the chair, he stretched, then went to the window and looked out to the grassy lawn where Kate played with Casey, the boy he'd seen earlier, and four other little ones.

As a young man, before his life had taken its disastrous turn, he'd thought of having a wife and children, and he'd pictured scenes such as this taking place on the grounds of his own home.

A woman like Kate would have made the perfect wife for him, but he'd never looked for anyone like her because a woman in his life—a good woman—would only complicate his existence.

Watching Kate and the children was the closest he would ever come to the life he'd once longed for.

The littlest boy crawled toward Kate, and she swept him up into her arms. She held him close and kissed the top of his head.

A woman like Kate should have a dozen children of her own. He imagined he should have had that many, too, but life had sent them both on different courses.

As if she knew he was there, Kate tilted her head and looked up to the window. She smiled softly, then turned her attention back to the children, and his heart ached for all that he had missed, and would continue to miss, in his life.

Morgan was asleep in the easy chair when Kate walked into the room. The children had gone home and Casey had gone to Evalena's for yet another evening. Kate knew her daughter and

aunt were conspiring. They wanted her to be
alone with Morgan. Tonight, unlike last night, she
didn't seem to mind. She liked his company and
wanted to take advantage of it as long as possible.

He looked vulnerable and peaceful with his
eyes closed in sleep. He'd removed his jacket and
the ties were loosened on his shirt. One leg was
slung over the arm of the overstuffed recliner, an
open book rested in his lap, and one arm hung
lifelessly over the other side of the chair.

He looked like he belonged in that comfortable
old seat, in this room.

She picked up the now empty plate she'd
brought up to him at lunchtime. Two photo al-
bums sat on the desk, one opened to a page filled
with newspaper clippings about Joe's death, about
Nikki shooting Joe's killer, about Joe's funeral.

She closed the book, not wanting to remember
the worst time of her life.

From the corner of her eye she saw Morgan stir,
saw the look of concern on his face. " 'Tis sorry I
am about your husband."

She smiled, accepting his sympathies just as she
had accepted those of so many others, then she
leaned against the desk and looked at the pile of
books stacked beside the recliner. "So, what do
you think about everything that's happened in the
past three hundred years?"

" 'Tis overwhelming when you attempt to di-
gest all the information in one day." He rose from
the chair, moving slowly toward her. "Is it pos-

sible for me to leave the room now? I feel as if I've been locked away forever."

"Was it all that bad?"

"Nay. I learned much."

"Did you find anything on time travel, anything that might help you go home?"

He leaned beside her on the edge of the desk. His sleeve brushed against her shoulder as he folded his arms over his chest. His hip touched hers, and she moved away, afraid of letting him get too close, afraid of letting her feelings get caught up in something that couldn't last.

His gaze followed her across the room. "I learned very little about my ship, and nothing about my crew." His jaw tightened. "From all I read, I fear that only one man survived the storm—the man who had been my prisoner."

Kate stepped behind the chair where Morgan had been sleeping, and rested her hands on the leather. "At least one person survived."

" 'Twas he who should have died."

"Why? Who was he?"

"The bastard who murdered my family." He paced across the room, staring out the window. "My crew perished in that storm. I was hurled through time. But that bastard lived a good long life. He should have died at the end of my sword instead of peacefully in his bed in Dover."

"He's dead. Does it matter now how he died?"

"Aye. It matters greatly." Morgan turned, stalking back to the desk. He picked up one of the books and flipped it open to a page he'd marked.

"He told many a tale about his imprisonment on *Satan's Revenge* and his torture at the hands of Black Heart." Morgan shook his head. "I gave the bastard bread and water, which was far more than he deserved. He was chained, but I did not hang him from the yardarm, as I'd wanted, nor did I cut his skin away inch by inch. I made the mistake of allowing him to live until he could be tried by a court of law, and because of my foolishness, the blackguard lived a long, rich life."

Kate moved toward him and touched his arm, hoping to give him comfort. "I'm sorry."

Morgan slammed the book shut. "At least he wasn't able to claim *Satan's Revenge* as his own. He'd wanted her—just as much as he'd wanted everything else that I loved. But she disappeared." A satisfied grin touched his mouth. "My ship had a mind of her own. Like any good woman, she'd never willingly give herself to someone low and disgusting."

"Do the books say what happened to her?"

"She disappeared in a flash of light ... glimmered like a ghostly figure, or so the story went. There was no fire. She didn't sink. She just vanished, and at that very same moment, the storm cleared and the sky turned blue." His eyes settled on hers, hatred mixed with thoughtfulness turning their azure color to a stormy blue. " 'Tis only a guess, but I strongly believe *Satan's Revenge* traveled through time, as I did."

*   *   *

He wanted to go home.

He wanted to find Thomas Low.

He also wanted to stay.

Standing in the kitchen, watching Kate prepare the evening meal, brought back images of the life Morgan had once known. Servants had prepared the food and he'd rarely gone into the kitchen, but as his family sat around the dining table, they'd talked of the day's events, of travels they had taken, of trips that were on the horizon. After dinner, his mother would play the harpsichord and sing, his father would puff on his pipe and read books on agriculture, and his sister would dance, or sit on his lap and listen to fairy stories.

He smiled wistfully. Those had been the grandest of times.

And he was able to recapture some of that closeness and warmth here in Kate's home.

"Kennedy Space Center isn't too far from here," Kate told him, as she slid a plate loaded with Evalena's apple pie and the deliciously cold treat called ice cream in front of him. "We could drive there this weekend, maybe. You, me, and Casey. You could see the launching pads, some of the spacecraft, and even a moon rock."

He smiled, listening to the sweetness of her chatter, talk that sounded as if she believed he'd be there forever. They'd talked briefly about the disappearance of *Satan's Revenge*. She'd insisted it had been hit by lightning; he contended that he'd see his ship again. She talked of the future; he thought only of today.

He could not stay, no matter how much he wanted to. And he could not allow her to believe that he would.

She sat down across from him and folded her arms on the table. "You're awfully quiet."

"I cannot stay, Kate. I must go home."

She bit her lip, and her gaze focused on his plate. "I know, but you should take advantage of every moment you're here. There's so much to see and do."

"And you wish to be my guide?" he asked, far too cruelly. "You wish to spend every spare minute with me, knowing I could leave at any time? 'Tis rather foolish, Kate."

She pushed up from the table and went to the kitchen sink, where she stared out the window into the darkness. "If you're worried I might fall in love with you, you're wrong. There's no chance in hell of that happening."

" 'Tis glad I am that that matter is settled. I am not the kind of man a woman should love."

"No," she said. "No, you're not."

She turned on the television, allowing the noise of other people to fill the silence of the room, then busied herself by cleaning the dishes.

Morgan stared at the stiffness of her back for the longest time. 'Twas better that she remain angry with him. 'Twould be good for him to leave— the sooner, the better.

A flicker on the television caught his attention, and he turned to see a dark-haired woman standing before the silhouette of a ship. "They say seeing is believing," the woman behind the glass said, "but I'm still not sure if this is real or a magician's illusion."

Morgan pushed up from the chair, knocking it over in his rush to the TV.

"Just after sundown this evening," the woman continued, "what appears to be an eighteenth-century sailing ship washed up on the beach near the St. Augustine lighthouse. From all outward indications, the ship is in good condition, except for a missing mast. Whether it is a replica—or, unbelievable as it might sound, the real thing—has not yet been determined. Police have boarded the vessel. . . ."

Kate's shoulder brushed lightly against his arm as the woman disappeared from the picture and *Satan's Revenge* came into view. "Oh, my God," she whispered. "Please tell me that isn't your ship."

"I cannot."

The voices on the television became nothing more than a loud hum as he looked at Kate. "I must go."

"But the police are there. You'll never be able to get on board, and how on earth do you think you can sail her away from here?"

" 'Tis something I will deal with when the time comes."

He cupped her cheek, fighting the urge to kiss her. "You will tell Casey good-bye for me?"

"What about the pancakes she wanted to fix for you tomorrow and the next day?"

"I cannot stay, Kate. I have told you this already."

"Do you think you're just going to walk on that ship and *presto*, you're back in seventeen-oh-two?" she blurted out. "Do you really think leaving is going to be that easy?"

'Twould be as difficult as leaving her behind.

He searched her eyes, seeing her hurt displayed by the mere hint of tears pooling at their corners.

His throat tightened, but he swallowed the torment that ripped through him. "I do not know what will happen. I only know that I must try to go home."

One tear spilled from her eye. "Fine! Go!"

Her frustrated anger warmed his heart. It had been many a year since anyone had cared enough to be angry when he left.

"May I have my weapons?"

"Sure, why not?"

She pulled away from his touch, running from the room and up the stairs. He followed, much more slowly, and entered the office, where he'd felt strangely at home.

Shrugging into his coat, he'd fastened each button by the time she had unlocked the cabinets and withdrew his dagger, sword, and pistol.

He shoved the cutlass into its scabbard and the other weapons under his belt, and then he looked again at the sadness in Kate's eyes.

"I will miss you," he said.

"No, you won't. You'll be too preoccupied fighting off the police and getting your ship back out to sea. The second you leave this house you'll forget all about me and Casey."

"Nay, I will not forget."

She shrugged, obviously not believing his words, which was for the best, and then she went to her husband's desk and opened the drawer. Taking a box from the back, she opened the lid and dumped the contents into her hand.

His mother's ring rested in the softness of her palm.

"Does this belong to you?" she asked.

"Aye. 'Twas my mother's wedding band."

"I found it on the island," she said, her lips trembling as she smiled. "I wasn't sure it belonged to you at first. Now I know." She let the ring and chain slide into his outstretched hand.

His fingers closed around hers. They were cold, but the teary gleam in her eyes warmed his heart.

"I wish I could give you something in payment for all you've done for me."

"You don't owe me anything."

"Ah, but I do, Katie. I owe you more than mere money. I would give you this ring if I could, but 'tis the only remembrance I have of my mother's."

"All I want is for you to be careful," she said. "The next time I'm browsing through those history books, I hope to read that you were pardoned by the queen, and that you lived a long and happy life, instead of disappearing in seventeen-oh-two."

"Thank you." He managed a faint smile. "I will think of you often."

"Me, too."

He squeezed her hand, then let go of its warmth. "Farewell, Kate," he whispered, and without another word, without the kiss he'd wanted to taste, without wiping away her tears that would haunt him forever, he walked down the stairs and out into the night.

Suddenly the world felt empty, void of life, and the loneliness he'd known for seven long years wrapped around him once again.

Chapter 10

By Heaven! It is a splendid sight to see . . .

LORD BYRON
CHILDE HAROLD'S PILGRIMAGE: CANTO I

For long hours Morgan stood in the dark, hidden amid the buildings lining the waterway, waiting for an opportunity to board *Satan's Revenge*. He'd found her resting regally against wooden moorings, while men and women—some in uniform, some not—rushed about her chaotically, waving sticks with shining light beaming from them, and stringing yellow ribbon from one end of her hull to the other, as if that would keep out a man determined to get on board.

In the distance he could see moonlight shining on the *castillo*, the pointed spires of cathedrals, and the bridge he'd run across in his hurry to get to his ship. Further off, somewhere in the town that twinkled with a thousand lights, slept Kate. He drew in a deep breath, willing himself to forget her, and turned once more to look at his vessel.

Earlier, her decks had been littered with men, her holds searched and her hull inspected above and below water, but as the hours passed, most of the curious disappeared, as did those who had a reason to be there. Still, there were far too many around for him to easily slip on board.

So he waited, longing to stand at her helm, listening to her unfurled sails rustle in the wind as she effortlessly breezed over the water. Her mainmast had been destroyed, but her foremast and mizzen stood tall and firm. Once he got to her, once he drew in her anchor, he would take her out to the open sea, and if God would give him another chance, he'd find a way home—crew or no crew.

Night droned on, the moon sailing slowly across the sky, and when Morgan saw the first sign of pink and orange peeking over the horizon, he noticed the quiet, and the changing of the guard. One by one the vehicles left, until only two remained. He could not wait any longer, hoping for a better time.

Dashing through the shadows that morning light had not yet touched, he eased his way close to the ship. He neared her stern, touching the well-remembered wooden planking, finding at last the wooden slats that climbed her side. They were simple enough to scale. Reaching the top, he peered over the railings, then slipped quietly onto the deck and crept toward the hatch, down to his cabin.

Home at last. He sucked in the scents of cedar paneling, lamp oil, the faint traces of smoke, and the ever-present and longed-for brininess of the sea. He smoothed his fingers over the table where he kept his charts, over the bottle of ink set in its own carved-out niche in the mahogany that kept it from tipping with the roll of the ocean. For just one moment he tested the massive bed where he'd slept but an hour or two at a time, and remembered the comfort of another bed in another room, where an emerald-eyed woman with honeyed hair and the spirit of a fiery angel had cared for him.

That's another life, he told himself. *Your place is on the sea, in another time.*

And Kate will never be with you.

Opening a floor-length cabinet recessed into the wall, he moved aside his sextant, telescope, and journal, and removed a flask of the finest rum he'd ever tasted. He filled a crystal goblet with the liquor and felt its burn as it slid down his throat. God, but it tasted good. Enough of this and he'd wipe away the memories of the past few days, and the nagging thoughts that he might prefer staying here to going back to his empty home.

Taking another swig of the potent rum, he drew out his dagger and pried loose the cedar panel at the back of the cabinet, pulled away the wool batting he'd shoved inside to keep the secret compartment from sounding hollow, and withdrew a small black velvet pouch. In it were opals, rubies, emeralds, and diamonds, a fortune in precious jewels he'd taken in just one raid on a Portuguese East Indiaman. He'd never seen such a prize, nor had his crew, and they'd divided it equally. Now, most of it rested at the bottom of the sea with his men.

Morgan retrieved another pouch from the cabinet, and tested the weight of gold doubloons and silver pieces of eight in the palm of his hand. The contents of that pouch alone would more than pay for a new mast, for a new crew of wanderers, cutthroats, and fugitives from Her Majesty's ships, and for information that would help him recapture Low.

It would also pay for a bevy of women to help take his mind from the beautiful lady he was leaving behind.

Above him he heard the lift of a hatch, unfamiliar voices, and footsteps on the stairs leading to his cabin. There was no time to stow away his treasure, no time to rid the room of evidence that someone had been there. He had to hide.

He tossed down the remaining drops of rum, shoved a pouch into each boot, and shook them down to his ankles.

Voices grew louder. Footsteps neared.

The only means of escape that he could readily see was the window, a tight fit for a smaller man than he. Still, he saw no other way to leave. Loosening the latch, he pressed against the wood frame. Again he pushed, harder this time, until at last it gave, and swung open on rusted hinges.

He hoisted himself up and thrust both boots through the narrow passage, pushing hard to squeeze all the way through. Expelling his breath so his chest cavity would shrink, he wiggled the rest of his body out the window and sucked in a quick gasp of air before turning, one hand gripping the ledge, the other closing the window until it rested on his knuckles, his fingertips barely over the sill.

He hung on the side of the boat, knowing he could drop down to the water and escape, but his plan was to stay on board *Satan's Revenge* and eventually sail away. Nay, he'd hold on tight—and wait.

Voices filled his cabin. A man's laughter. A woman's giggle.

Lovers?

Suddenly all was quiet, and Morgan could sense the first kiss, then heard the faint sound of the woman's moan, low, deep, and full of passion.

He'd had a devil of a time getting on board, yet two people with nothing more on their minds than a romantic liaison had managed to find their way down to his cabin. Why couldn't they have gone somewhere else?

The woman laughed. "Stop it, Jack. I knew I shouldn't have brought you with me, not when I'm on duty."

"You wouldn't be on duty if you hadn't been paged. You'd still be in bed, and we'd be making love right about now."

"Two more weeks and there won't be any pages in the middle of the night."

"You mean you're actually going to go off duty while we're on our honeymoon? No playing cop for a while?"

"I'll be your subservient little wife. I promise. Until then," the woman continued, her voice turning serious, "I've got to make sure no one sneaks on this ship."

"No one's going to sail her away, not with that hole in her side."

Bloody hell!

"It's not someone sailing her away that's got the mayor's office and mine worried, it's vandals. Just look at the stuff around here. There's a fortune in antiques."

"Several fortunes." Morgan could hear the distinct sound of the man walking about the cabin, could easily imagine him trailing his fingers over the desk, the tables, the bed. "I've seen old ships before, but nothing like this."

"It's a replica."

"I don't think so," the man said, "although I don't understand why it looks so new. I'm going to bring someone from the museum back with me later today so we can authenticate a few things. Then I hope to get in to see the mayor."

"Why?"

"The museum could use a ship like this in its collection."

"If I know you, you'd rather sail it around the

world while you look for a bunch of other old stuff."

"Now there's a thought. Would you go with me?"

"If I didn't like my job so much, I might consider it."

The man laughed. "You're too dedicated, Nikki. Someday I hope to change your mind."

"You could try."

Morgan heard the kiss again. He adjusted his fingerhold, wondering how much longer they would keep up their leisurely lovemaking and their infernal prattle. He wanted to get back on the ship, hole or no hole. With the riches on board and the obvious concern for the welfare of *Satan's Revenge*, he imagined the damage would be repaired within a matter of days. All he'd have to do is wait.

And he didn't want to do that hanging from the window.

"Are we still on for dinner tonight?" the man asked.

"I don't know. We've had all those reports about a fully armed pirate roaming the streets. Last night this ship turns up, and then I get called out about a murder. I may be working overtime for a while. You'll forgive me, won't you?"

"This time," the man said, and Morgan could hear the deep warmth in his voice.

"I love you," the woman said softly.

"Me, too."

Silence again. Finally Morgan heard the man's

footsteps moving toward the door. "Call me when you get home."

"I will."

He left the cabin, but the woman remained.

She paced the room, opening map drawers in the table, rifling through the storage compartments below Morgan's bunk, and then he heard the clink of the rum bottle against a crystal goblet.

Again he heard her pace, then stop beside the window.

He heard the tapping of glass against glass.

"Hey, you out there."

Bloody hell! She was talking to him.

"Did you enjoy the liquor? If I were prone to drinking on duty, I might have some myself. Hell, I might even invite you in to share some with me."

Morgan looked down at the water below. *Drop, you fool,* he told himself, but he waited, hoping against hope that she'd tire of the game and leave.

He heard the window creak open. "It's a long way down to the water," she said, and he saw and felt clammy hands latching onto his wrists. "If I find out you haven't taken anything, I'll let you go."

He'd taken a pouch of jewels and one of gold and silver doubloons. She wouldn't let him go and he couldn't be caught.

When he saw blond hair poke through the window, a forehead, and then two wide blue eyes, he gave the hull one swift kick. He pushed away from the ship, from her grasp, from her sight—he hoped—and in less than a heartbeat, he landed on his back in the water and sank deep below the surface.

The jewels, his clothing, the gold and silver weighted him down, kept him close to the murky bottom as he twisted about and swam for the dock, for the piers he could see buried into the sand. Slowly he pulled himself to the top, sucked in air, then went under again, swimming away from his ship, away from the dock, until, once more, he needed to breathe.

He'd reached a sandy stretch of beach. Far behind him he could see *Satan's Revenge*, and hear the shouting of a guard. Crouching low to the ground, he rushed to a stand of trees, to a cluster of buildings that stood not far from shore. Water sloshed in his boots; the jewels, gold and silver, had slipped under his feet, filling each step with pain, but still he ran until he reached a narrow alley filled with empty crates and barrels spilling with garbage.

Squeezing between two stacks of wooden boxes, he squatted out of sight, catching his breath, watching and waiting until he knew it would be safe to walk out in the open.

The morning was just coming to life. He heard the sounds of many vehicles in the distance, doors opening and closing in the buildings around him, and the sound of footsteps not too far away.

Had the woman found his hiding place?

He moved further back into the shadows until the unmistakable sound of boots died away.

He could hear the sound of an engine, and peered around the boxes. A car drove by much too slowly—and stopped. The blond woman he'd seen through the ship's window sat behind the wheel, staring into the passageway.

Once again it seemed he was a wanted man, yet this time he'd done nothing wrong. He'd merely taken what rightfully belonged to him.

But a pirate had been spotted in town, and a man had been murdered. Morgan laughed to himself. He had been accused of many things in the past six years simply because he bore the name "Black Heart." It did not matter that most of the wrong doings had occurred when he was hundreds of miles away. He was a pirate. That in itself has been enough evidence to prove him guilty.

That could be enough to prove him guilty again.

The car drove away at last. He hadn't been seen—and he had to keep it that way.

Easing down to the pavement, he pulled off his boots and dumped out the water. He shoved the bags of jewels and doubloons into his coat pocket, then rested his head against the cool wall of the building.

He'd have to hide again, at least until his ship was repaired. Maybe he should consider purchasing other attire so he wouldn't continually stand out in a crowd.

Maybe he should go back to Kate.

That thought brought a smile to his lips.

Ah, Katie. I believe our paths are destined to cross again.

*   *   *

A pair of dark eyes looked out across the beach, to the ship he'd sailed into harbor on, to the cluster of buildings not far away. Pearly white teeth shone when he smiled. He liked the changes he saw in this new century he'd been miraculously thrust into. There was so much to offer a man such as himself, a tall, slender, and handsome fellow with freshly trimmed beard and hair, not to mention his newfound attire.

He turned to the glass-fronted shop he stood before and examined his reflection. The boots fitted him well. He rather liked the style, the way the black and white snakeskin hugged his feet and ankles and gleamed in the moonlight. 'Twas a stroke of good fortune to find a man of nearly the same exceptional stature, a man with the same impeccable taste.

A man with a wedding ring that, to his misfortune, he no longer needed.

Holding out his left hand, he admired the diamonds that glistened in the light from the street lamp. "What a perfect morning," he whispered. "Absolutely perfect."

Polishing his new ring on the sleeve of his just acquired shirt, he stared further up the beach to the place where he'd seen his old enemy hide.

Well, well, Black Heart. Our paths have crossed again. But this time, you will not see me. You will not know I am near. I'll be watching you, though. Baiting you, and when you least expect it, 'tis then I will strike.

The thrill is in the hunt, Mr. Farrell.
So let the chase begin.

Kate had slept fitfully—once she'd gone to bed.
She'd spent part of the night rocking in the wicker
chair on her balcony, listening to Perry Como,
watching the silhouettes of Casey and Evalena
dancing in the parlor. When they'd retired for the
night, she had, too.

But she'd tossed and turned, and finally gone
back to her rocker.

Morgan Farrell had given her a headache. She
supposed she deserved it for letting him inch under her skin. She'd sworn she'd never allow another man to do that, but he'd accomplished the
impossible.

Not only had he traveled through time, but he'd
brought havoc to her peaceful if lonely existence.

And then he'd walked away.

Damn him!

Leaning back into the rocker, she closed her
eyes and massaged her temples, hoping most of
the pain would go away before Mrs. Ash dropped
Bubba off at 6:45, before the other children dribbled in.

Somehow she'd go through the motions of
greeting each parent, of sweeping each child up
into her arms for their first hug of the day. Somehow she'd serve milk, juice, and cereal, play
games, read stories, and change half a dozen di-
apers. If she was lucky, she might get all five children, not counting one of her own, down for a

nap at the same time, then maybe she'd be so exhausted she'd drop off to sleep.

This wasn't her usual routine. Normally she looked forward to having her house filled with the sweet voices of children. But her organized life had been thrown completely off balance.

And it was all Morgan Farrell's fault.

Damn him!

"Yoo-hoo. Katharine."

Popping open one eye and allowing the other to open a little more slowly, she peered over the balcony to the porch across the street. Evalena stood there in her fuzzy slippers and old flowered houserobe, an immense glass bowl clasped between an arm and her breasts, a wooden spoon waving right along with her hand.

"Hi, Mommy!" Casey cried out. "We're making Mickey Mouse pancakes and there's going to be enough for everyone."

At least she didn't have to deal with cereal this morning, Kate thought with relief.

"Sounds yummy," she answered back, standing finally, pressing her hands against the curve of her back as she stretched her spine. "Make an extra for Bubba, okay? And stick a few extra chocolate chips on one for me."

"What about Mr. Farrell?" Casey asked. "How many do you think he's going to want?"

Kate pushed her fingers through her hair, wishing she had an easy answer, but knowing she had to come right out and tell her daughter the truth.

"He's gone, Case."

Even from this distance she could see Casey's smile fade away. "Did you tell him to go?" she asked.

Kate shook her head slowly. "He had to go home."

"But it's too far away. He won't be able to come and see me."

"He asked me to tell you good-bye. He wanted to do it himself, Case, but he was in a hurry."

"I thought he was my friend," Casey said, her lower lip jutting out. "I wanted him to stay. I wanted him to be my daddy."

Kate could feel the tremble of her lips, the tightness in her throat, as Casey rushed into Evalena's house and let the screen door slam behind her. She hadn't known Casey wanted another father. She thought the memory of Joe was enough, just as she'd wanted it to be enough for her.

But she was wrong. So very wrong.

"Don't let her words upset you," Evalena said, shuffling down the steps, across the lawn to the narrow strip of road.

"You look awful, Katharine. Nothing a good night's sleep or a good man can't cure. Tell you what: why don't you let me watch the children again today?"

Kate looked down at her aunt, laughing lightly. "I'd rather have the distraction."

"The best distraction is a man, but it appears you've run another one off."

"That's not true. I halfway asked him to stay."

"Next time, ask all the way."

"There isn't going to be a next time. Is that understood?"

"Well, of course," Evalena answered, but Kate knew Evie would never let her out of her matchmaking clutches, and she even imagined Evalena had someone in mind when she scuffled across the street, right underneath the balcony, and looked up at Kate.

"I almost forgot," Evie said, as her hand rapidly beat the wooden spoon through the bowl of batter she held against her chest. "You've heard the news, haven't you? The town's all abuzz with it."

"You mean about the ship that turned up on the beach?"

"Oh, no, Katharine. That's old news. I'm talking about the dead body they found in an alleyway downtown."

Kate thought for sure her heart would stop. She had no details, but she couldn't help but imagine the worst. "What body?"

"Well, they didn't give too many details on TV, but they said he was a big guy."

Kate's trembling fingers gripped the balcony rail. "Is that all they said?"

"Seems to me they said someone sliced his throat. Can you imagine? And not only that, but they stripped him naked. It's terrible. Just terrible."

"Do the police know who it was?"

"No one seemed to recognize him. Of course, this time of year there are tourists everywhere."

Evalena stopped stirring, and frowned. "Are

you okay, Katharine? You're white as a ghost."

"The man that they found—he didn't have dark hair, did he?"

"Why, yes, as a matter of fact. It *was* dark and ... and. ... oh dear. It was long." Worry pinched Evalena's face, but she quickly forced a smile.

"It couldn't possibly be Mr. Farrell, Katharine. It's impossible. Don't even think it."

Whatever Evalena said after that swept right past Kate. She barely saw the VW bug pull up to the curb, or Bubba's mother climbing out of the car.

Somehow she stumbled into the house and down the stairs to begin her day. But something tight and terrible had twisted around her heart, something that wouldn't go away, not until she knew the truth.

Morgan Farrell couldn't be dead. He just couldn't.

Chapter 11

*He was the mildest manner'd man
That ever scuttled ship or cut a throat.*

LORD BYRON, *DON JUAN: CANTO* III

Standing at the window, Kate slid a finger along her temple to wipe away the beads of perspiration that even the air conditioning couldn't keep from forming. She'd lived in St. Augustine her entire life. She'd spent twenty-six summers in the heat and stifling humidity, but it seemed more oppressive today.

Outside, the gray sky rolled and pitched, like smoke billowing out of a burning building. The almost steady thunder shook the hardwood floor beneath her feet, and lightning crackled as it slashed through the late afternoon clouds.

It seemed a fitting day for her desolate mood.

For two long hours she'd made phone calls, trying to learn more about the dead man, hoping to alleviate her fears. But no one at the police station had wanted to talk, until she'd gotten in touch with Nikki.

"Good God, Kate! You don't know the guy, do you?" Nikki had asked over the phone.

"I don't know," Kate had said almost frantically. "That's what I'm trying to find out. All I know is, he's tall, with long dark hair."

And then Nikki had laughed. "Where'd you hear that?"

"From Evalena. From TV. Damn it, Nikki, tell me if the guy had a scar on his face."

"Big? Little? What?"

"Forget the one on his face. Did he have scars all over his back?"

"No, Kate. He didn't have long dark hair, either. It was short and red. Damn reporters."

She'd almost cried, but there hadn't been time. The kids were making her life hell, and in the brief moments of calm, like now, she thought of Morgan, wondering if he was somewhere out there in the storm. Or if he'd made it home—to the year 1702. . . .

To a place where she could never go.

To a place where she'd never see him again.

Oh, hell! He wasn't dead. Nothing else mattered.

But the fear lingered. What if he hadn't made it back? What if something awful had happened to him somewhere between the present and the past?

She would never know.

And she'd always wonder and worry.

Behind her she heard the triplets giggling almost identically, the crash of toy trucks into toy trains, the topple of building blocks, and Sara singing something from *The Little Mermaid* to the big floppy doll that rarely left her side. It was free-for-all time, one hour of controlled mayhem that Kate lived through every afternoon from 3 o'clock until 4, even today, when her head felt as if cannons were exploding inside.

At 4 they'd have quiet time, she'd read to them, and by 5:30 they'd all be gone. Then she'd curl up somewhere cool, someplace where the breeze would flit across her cheeks, and go to sleep.

And dream pleasant dreams—if she could.

Chubby fingers clasped her leg, inching their way up to the hem of her shorts. Without even looking, she knew it was Bubba, begging to be held. In a movement that seemed second nature to her, she swept the toddler up into her arms and cradled him on her hip. At eighteen months he still preferred crawling to walking, he weighed nearly as much as the three-year-old triplets, and if she could have another child, she'd want one exactly like him.

Pressing a kiss to his pudgy pink cheek, she raised her eyes and caught the flash of anger on Casey's face. "She'll get over the jealousy," the doctor had told her. "Give her time. She's lost her father, she's not used to sharing you with other children, and don't forget, Kate, she has the same temperament you had as a child. She'll grow out of it. Trust me on this."

When she was Casey's age her own mother and father gave her up to the county because they had too many other mouths to feed, and because they couldn't put up with her tantrums. She'd never seen them again after they'd stuck her, kicking and screaming, into the social worker's arms. She hadn't cared—at least, that's what she'd proclaimed. But she *had* cared, and she'd hurt—until Evalena and Joe had come into her life.

It had taken her twelve long hours to fall in love with Evalena, but it had taken less than a minute to fall in love with Joe. He'd knocked on Evalena's door about two minutes after the baseball had burst through the plate glass window, apologized profusely, looked down at her, the scrubby little girl who'd just moved in with Evalena the day before, and asked her if she wanted to play ball with the rest of the kids on the street.

She'd been hooked. He was twelve, she was eight, and from that day forth, she'd followed him everywhere, whether he wanted her to or not. Her jealousy had flared every time she'd seen Joe with another girl, just as Casey's flared now, when she was with the other children. But Joe had rightfully deserved, and needed, someone closer to his own age at the time, just as she'd needed to care for these children now. It was her job. It was the only thing she really knew how to do, and it was the only thing she'd wanted to do for a living.

She only hoped that someday Casey would understand.

But now—she didn't. She'd come out of hiding

nearly an hour ago, and had sat glumly on the stairs ever since, tossing a small rubber ball from one hand to the other. Kate had hoped Casey's frustration with her would melt away after spending most of the day in the dark closet beneath the staircase, but it hadn't.

Now probably wasn't the time to talk to her, but she couldn't stand to spend the entire evening looking at a pouting face. The doctor told her to ignore the tantrums, but she herself had been ignored far too much before Evalena had come into the picture. No, she wouldn't ignore the daughter who meant more to her than anything else in the entire world.

She walked across the room, with Bubba still in her arms, and sat beside her daughter, scooting her bottom as close as possible to Casey's. "Something troubling you?" she asked nonchalantly, even though she already knew the answers she'd receive.

"Yeah. You."

"I see. Does this have anything to do with Mr. Farrell?"

"You made him leave, didn't you?"

"He went of his own free will, Case. He had to go home, and I don't think I could have kept him from leaving even if I'd wanted to."

"But you told him to drop dead. Now he probably has."

"He's not dead. He's just gone."

"Then he has to come back," Casey said, her eyes reddening as tears threatened to spill. "He *has* to. I want a daddy like everyone else."

Bubba began to wail, and Kate hugged him against her, rocking him back and forth, wishing Casey was little again so she could carry her around on her hip and hug her this way, calming her fears, her anxiety, with nothing more than a tender squeeze.

She stroked away a tear from Casey's cheek. "You have a daddy, Case. A daddy who loved you very much."

"He's dead!" she yelled, running down the stairs, stopping only when she reached the circle where the other four children were playing. "*They* have daddies," she said, pointing to the triplets. "Sara has a daddy, and so does he," she said, throwing the ball toward Bubba.

In one swift move, Kate reached up and caught the ball, her heart aching for her daughter, wishing there were something she could do or say to make Casey understand that she had to hold onto Joe's memory, because he was the only father she'd ever have.

"It's not fair that everyone else has a daddy when my daddy's dead." Tears poured down her cheeks, and her lips trembled as Kate stood with Bubba pressing his little head to her neck. "And it's not fair that you're kissing and holding *him*."

Bubba wailed louder, Sara began to sob, and so did the triplets, as Kate rushed down the stairs and through the chaos and tried to reach Casey, who was running for the door.

She tromped on a tiny metal car, and nearly lost

her balance when Casey threw open the front door, and ran smack into a pair of black leather boots.

"It sounds as if you have a mutiny on your hands, madam."

Morgan scooped Casey up into the strongest, most needed pair of arms Kate had ever seen. He ran a soothing palm over Casey's cheek and through her mop of curly hair, all the while looking at Kate with warm blue eyes that sparked with a mixture of humor and concern.

"I thought you were gone—maybe dead," she said, wishing she'd muttered something nice like, "I'm glad you're back," or, "I've missed you." But the words she'd wanted to say were trapped inside, eating away at her heart, churning in her stomach.

"I only look dead," he said, drawing her attention to his rumpled and stained clothing, the dull black boots, that had looked neat and well cared for yesterday morning. "A few obstacles got in the way of my returning home, like a hole in my ship. It might be awhile before I leave again."

Casey pushed back in his arms, alarm in her frowning eyes. "You can't go. Ever."

"Ah, Casey," he said, drying her tears with the pad of his thumb. " 'Tis not a decision I make lightly. My home is far from here, and I long to return. 'Tis the same as you would feel if you were to be separated from your mother for too long a time."

When Casey twisted in Morgan's arms, Kate

could see the first trace of a smile, and she knew everything would be okay—until he left again.

"I guess this means you'll want to stay with us a little longer?" Kate asked.

"Aye."

Morgan slid Casey gently from his arms, and for the first time she noticed the black and white bag he held in his hand.

"Have you been shopping?"

"A change of clothes. I have noticed, madam, that I do not fit in with St. Augustine society." Holding the bag out to Casey, he slipped it into her outstretched hand. "Would you take this upstairs for me? I have something to give your mother."

Casey skipped across the room and dashed up the stairs, running past the triplets, who sat wide-eyed and open-mouthed in the middle of a scatter of toys, staring up at Morgan. During the commotion, Sara had dropped her doll and now cowered behind Kate's legs, peeking out every now and then to look at the pirate in their midst. And Bubba, sweet, precious Bubba, ceased his crying and sucked his thumb.

"I have no need of these at the moment," Morgan said, drawing his pistol from under his belt.

Sara screamed, loud and piercing, and another cannon went off in Kate's aching head. On instinct, Kate shifted Bubba back to her hip and in an easy, fluid motion, she lifted two-year-old Sara to her other hip.

"Hush, now," she whispered, carrying both

children across the room, rocking them gently as she walked, humming softly to calm Sara's fears.

Over Sara's head, she watched Morgan remove his weapons and hide them away, high atop a china-filled buffet. Slowly he came toward her, mesmerizing her with the warmth of azure eyes she suddenly realized she'd been afraid she'd never see again.

With the same tenderness he'd shown Casey, he caressed away a damp strand of pale brown hair from Sara's face, sweeping his fingers lightly over her cheek and chin, before cupping her tiny face in a hand as gentle as a whisper.

"May I hold her?" he asked, directing his question to Kate, although his gaze never left Sara's spellbound eyes.

"If she'll go to you." Kate loosened her hold as Sara squirmed from her arms and snuggled comfortably against Morgan's chest, her little hand finding its way into his hair, twisting it about her fingers.

"I had a sister once," he said softly to the child as he carried her to the window. "When she was not much older than you, storms like this one frightened her in much the same way my pistol—and my presence—frightened you. When she was scared like that, I'd take her in my arms and sing the song my dear mother sang to me when I was a wee one. Would you like to hear it?"

Sara nodded, and Morgan looked out at the blackened sky. In the glass Kate could see the reflection of his face and his smile when he began to sing, his voice the purest of tenors, telling, in song, the story of a butterfly spreading its wings for the very first time, and even though it was frightened, how it flew away from its cocoon.

Casey had crept down the stairs, and she wrapped her arms around Morgan's waist, her head tilted upward as she listened to his words. Bubba no longer squirmed. Instead, his eyes closed peacefully in sleep, and the triplets never moved a muscle. They just watched and listened. How could they do anything else when Morgan had hypnotized them—and her—with his voice?

Slipping from playtime to quiet time had never happened so easily, and by the time Morgan finished his song, Kate's headache had gone, and only sore, tense muscles remained.

He turned slowly, looking at ease with Sara in his arms, and in his wonderful English accent, he whispered, "What would you have me do now, madam?"

"Do you tell stories as well as you sing?"

"Aye. And I know many."

Smiling came easily. Liking him was even easier, but knowing he was going to leave again cast a whole new light on her feelings. She couldn't allow herself to fall in love with him. She'd hurt far too much when he'd left last night. She didn't want to hurt even more the next time.

"Should he sit in the storyteller's chair, Mommy?" Casey asked, interrupting her thoughts as she dragged Morgan across the room.

Kate nodded, and Casey looked at the man who

towered high above her. "You have to sit in this chair, and the rest of us sit around you."

"And what of your mother?"

"That's easy. She sits in my usual spot."

Oh, no. Kate didn't like the sound of that at all, but Casey took her hand and tugged her across the room, between the triplets, who'd already taken their place facing the storyteller's chair that Morgan had eased himself into.

"Sit there," Casey ordered, pointing to the empty space on the floor between Morgan's wide-spread boots.

"But where will you sit?" Kate asked.

"In Morgan's lap, of course."

Casey urged Kate down to the floor, then scrambled onto Morgan's empty thigh. "Okay, we're ready whenever you are."

Embarrassed, Kate pulled a still sleeping Bubba close, and refused to look up at the storyteller. Instead, she concentrated on the toes of his scuffed black boots, which inched ever closer to her bare knees as she sat cross-legged on a braided carpet.

" 'Twas a foul and blustering night when my story begins," he said, his voice low, hushed, the way Joe's had always been when he began one of his favorite pirate tales. "Lightning shot through the sky, and the thunder sounded like a thousand banshees beating their drums. A lone horseman rode through the stormy night, frightened by the trees that hovered over him like giant skeletons. He needed a place to rest, he needed to find some-one who would give him food and shelter, because he was tired, scared, and very much alone. But instead of friendly faces, he saw anger, and snarls of fear, and doors were slammed and bolted in his face.

"When he had barely the strength to hold onto his horse's reins, a shooting star fell through a hole in the blackened clouds and burst into flame on the ground before him, brightening the earth with a golden light. At first he was frightened, but the warmth of the fire wrapped around him like a fine velvet cloak, and out of the blaze stepped an angel with emerald eyes and hair the color of honey."

The triplets were on their stomachs now, their heads propped on their arms, their wide eyes transfixed by the storyteller's words. Kate, too, was drawn in, anxious for him to go on every time he paused.

Closing her eyes, she rolled her aching neck as she listened intently to Morgan's tale of fairies and trolls, of a handsome prince and the guardian angel who made him see good in a world that to him had been filled with nothing but evil.

She'd expected to hear a dastardly yarn about pirates of old, of buried treasure, murder and greed, but he appeared more at ease telling a fairy tale that seemed more real than fiction, a story she found easy to believe.

"Did the prince marry the angel?" Casey asked, and just like the triplets, whose eyes widened, Kate waited eagerly to hear his answer.

" 'Twould not be fair to spoil the story, Casey.

You must listen, and wait, for the greatest of treasures appear when you least expect them."

Kate doubted that Casey or the other children understood those words any more than she did, but Morgan made falling under his spell so very easy, and Kate had the feeling that once you were hypnotized, he could say anything and you'd believe it.

Bubba yawned, nestling his cheek against her breast. She could sense Casey and Sara stirring in Morgan's lap, and he continued his story as rain pounded against the windows and wind howled through the trees.

Kate jumped when warm fingers touched her neck, and for the first time since he'd begun his story, she twisted around to look at him. Casey was wedged between the chair and Morgan's side, and Sara was cuddled in her lap, both with their eyes closed. Morgan smiled, drew one hand from Kate's shoulder, and put a silencing finger to his lips. Without skipping a beat in his story, he swirled one thumb lightly around the curve of her neck, then the other thumb joined in.

She lowered her head, letting it fall lazily forward, as his fingers worked the same magic on her aching muscles that his story worked on her mind. Drawing in a deep breath, she closed her eyes, and lulled by his soft English accent, the warmth of his voice, the comfort of his hands, she dozed, in and out of a dream world where she'd never been, a world inhabited by honey-haired angels, and a tall, dark, and handsome prince, with a scar racing down the side of his face.

The doorbell rang, loud and obtrusive, and Morgan's knee banged into her side as he abruptly pushed up from the chair, thrusting Sara into her lap, and Casey to the floor.

Kate scrambled up, groggy from her dream-filled nap, and the doorbell rang again.

"It must be Sara's father," she said in a rush of words, knowing how impatient the man was, how he was always in a hurry to drop Sara off in the morning and to leave at night.

Morgan's face bore a heavy frown, and worry filled his eyes. Again he put a finger to his lips. Without a word, he rushed up the stairs, taking them three at a time, and disappeared from sight.

The magic of the fairy tale had come to a sudden and much too abrupt end, and a new fear pulsed through Kate. Morgan Farrell had reason to hide when he was in the eighteenth century. But what reason did he have for hiding now?

Chapter 12

Too oft is a smile
But the hypocrite's wile,
To mask detestation, or fear;
Give me the soft sigh,
Whilst the soultelling eye
Is dimm'd, for a time, with a Tear . . .

LORD BYRON, *THE TEAR*

Kate stood on the front porch, waving good-bye to Bubba and his mother as the battered VW bug sputtered away from the curb. Wrapping an arm around a newel post, she breathed in the sweet fragrance of gardenia and jasmine, of fresh-mown lawn and damp earth, and was overcome by the sudden and unexpected feeling that something good, something special, was going to happen tonight.

Behind her the screen door slammed, and Casey skipped out to the porch, tucking her hand into her mom's. "Do you think Mr. Farrell's going to stay this time?" she asked, looking up at Kate with wide blue eyes that were the very picture of Joe's.

"I don't know, Case," she answered truthfully, wishing she could offer a positive answer. She looked away from her daughter to the faint gray puffs dotting the sky, where a mere fifteen minutes before there'd been only swirling sheets of black, thunder, lightning, and rain. Dark blue sky peeked out from behind the clouds, and one lone star twinkled, a sure sign that night was on its way.

"There's a wishing star way over there," Kate said, and Casey's eyes followed the direction of Kate's pointed finger. "Why don't you make a wish?"

"I wish . . . I wish . . ." Casey giggled, bringing a smile to Kate's face. "I wish Mr. Farrell was my daddy."

The smile faded, as Kate knelt down beside her little girl and pulled her close. "I'm not in love with Mr. Farrell, Case."

"But I am."

"I know you are, but that's a different kind of love. I'd have to marry Mr. Farrell for him to be your daddy, and people should be in love—really, truly in love—when they get married."

"The way you loved my daddy?"

Kate nodded, a hint of sadness squeezing lightly at her heart. "That's right. The way I loved your daddy."

Across the street Kate heard the squeak of a
wooden plank on Evalena's porch, and her aunt's
high-pitched voice. *"Yoo-hoo!"*

Evalena bustled down the stairs, her slippers
scuffling across the walk and over the wet asphalt
road. Her muumuu fluttered around her, an
empty basket swung at her side, and she was red-
faced and winded by the time she reached Kate's
house. "I have the most wonderful news," Evalena said, clapping a hand to her breast and taking
a deep breath. "I've met a new man. The most
devilishly handsome thing to ever wander up St.
George Street. And A-1 husband material, too."

"Are you going to get married again?" Casey
asked.

"Oh, dear me, no, although Mr. Lancaster is a
delightful fellow, so delightful that I invited him
over for dinner tonight."

Kate turned her head upward, rapidly counting
puffy clouds in an effort to avoid what she sensed
was Evie's latest matchmaking scheme, but all to
no avail.

Evalena waddled up the stairs and sidled up
close to her.

"I've made my prize-winning shrimp casserole
and a double-chocolate brownie torte for dinner.
You and Casey *will* join me and my guest, won't
you?"

"She can't go anyplace," Casey chimed in. "Mr.
Farrell came back."

Kate gave up counting and lowered her eyes

long enough to see Evalena's plump, rosy cheeks light up with joy.

"Ah, Mr. Farrell," Evie cooed. "Now, *there's* a handsome man for you. Husband quality if ever I saw it, even though he has that nasty-looking scar."

"It's not nasty looking, Evie," Kate informed her aunt. "Once you get to know him, you hardly notice it."

"You've been looking, have you? That's a good sign, Katharine. Proves you're interested."

"I'm not interested—"

"He's going to be my daddy," Casey interrupted. "I made a wish on a star. That's almost like praying, I guess."

Kate leaned her head against the newel post and sighed, wondering how she could possibly be surrounded by a woman and child interested in nothing but marriage, when that was the furthest thing from her own mind.

"Well, standing around here chitchatting isn't going to get my basket filled with flowers," Evalena said, maneuvering carefully down the steps and out across the lawn. "Thought I'd steal some of your jasmine and gardenias to sprinkle around the parlor before my guest arrives."

"I'll help you," Casey said, beating her aunt to the raised borders surrounding the porch. Kate could almost hear the jasmine rejoicing as her daughter snapped off one bud after another, tossing them into Evie's basket.

"Can I spend the night with you?" Casey asked,

looking up at Evalena. "I like shrimp casserole, and I really like double-chocolate brownie torte."

"And how do you feel about Perry Como?" Evalena asked with a wink.

"Oh, I really, *really* love Perry Como. What about your new friend? Does he like him, too?"

"Well, we'll just have to find out, won't we?" Evalena twisted around to look at Kate, her basket now overflowing with purple and white blossoms. "You don't mind if Casey stays with me, do you?" she asked, but it seemed more a statement the way Evalena shuffled off across the street, basket swinging in one hand, Casey's little fingers tucked tightly in the other.

"You'll have the house all to yourself," Evalena bubbled. "Well, you'll have Mr. Farrell, too, and . . . and. . . ." Evalena's words trailed off, but her laughter filled the air even after she and Casey disappeared behind Evalena's door.

Kate didn't need to hear any more. She knew full well what was on Evalena's mind. It was the last thing that was on hers. Spending another evening alone with Morgan disturbed her. She didn't know why he'd run away when the doorbell rang, why he'd needed to hide. But that wasn't what bothered her the most. It was more the fact that his soft voice continually hypnotized her, his story entranced her, and the gentle touch of his fingers at her neck soothed away the stiffness in her muscles while enflaming most everything else.

She didn't want to fall in love again—not with him, not with anyone. But she wanted to be held, kissed. She wanted to wake up in the middle of the night to find her head resting atop a strong, masculine chest, or a broad hand lightly draped over her hip.

She didn't want a husband. She didn't even need a commitment. She just wanted someone to help her get through the long, lonely hours of the night.

Looking up at the wishing star, she thought about asking for one night of heaven, but let the thought flit away. She'd already been blessed more times than she could count, so it didn't seem fair to ask for anything more.

The warmth of the evening and the sudden sound of Perry's mellow voice made her forget the need to go inside to pick up toys, to sweep up grass and dirt tracked in by little feet. She didn't want to make preparations for the next day or think about fixing a dinner that she wasn't hungry enough to eat. Instead, she sat on the front porch swing, drew her knees up to her chest, and delighted in the feel of the tufted chintz cushion beneath her feet.

She closed her eyes, resting her forehead on her knees, wishing that warm fingers would once again ease away the returning stiffness in her neck.

And then she felt them—the callused thumbs and strong fingers working miracles along her spine and shoulders.

" 'Tis too lovely a night to be alone," Morgan said, his mesmerizing voice drawing her further into the fantasy that had become impossibly real. "From my room I watched the children departing with their parents. I watched Casey and her aunt roam the yard, then disappear into the house across the street. But I did not see you, Kate, and it was only you I longed to see."

His words sent a shiver from her throat to her stomach, and goosebumps rose on her arms in spite of the warm evening air. *Why?*, she wanted to ask, but it was another question that came to mind.

"What made you run away? It was only Sara's father at the door."

"I am a pirate. A wanted man."

"Three hundred years ago, but not today."

He laughed and sat behind her on the swing, his body close, hot. His hands wrapped around her shoulders and pulled her back against his chest. She could feel his hair against her skin, could feel the warmth of his breath close to her ear. "I was seen on *Satan's Revenge,*" he whispered. "And there's a strong possibility that the authorities think I'm a thief and possibly a—"

"You *are* a thief."

"Ah, but that was three hundred years ago." His fingers spread over her shoulders, along her collarbone, and made soft circles over her throat. "Do not worry, madam. I did not take anything that wasn't rightfully mine."

Her head drifted back as his voice, his touch, worked their hypnotic powers on her much too tired mind and body. Her cheek brushed lightly against a cheek that felt freshly shaved. She could feel him tilting his head, felt soft lips moving ever so slowly along her jaw.

Was he hypnotizing her, drawing her into a spell she might never escape from? His fingers were magic. His kiss was pure enchantment. But the marvels of his touch were going to end all too soon.

Kate threw herself forward, out of his arms, out of the swing, out of the trance. She backed to the far end of the porch, until the railing stopped her movement. She watched him stand, his passionately dark eyes penetrating her soul. He moved to a place where the waning sunlight shone down on deep brown hair that swept over his shoulders like a cloak, making him appear more a mythical creature than a flesh-and-blood man.

She touched her jaw, shivering at the remembrance of his lips whispering over her sensitive skin. "Why did you do that?" she asked, like a foolish schoolgirl.

"Because I am a thief, madam. I saw something I wanted, and I took it."

Willing herself to get out from under his spell, she forced her eyes away from his steady gaze, to his powerful chest, covered quite differently with a white oxford shirt, to his muscular legs clad in tight blue denim. He was no ordinary man, but the charm of the pirate lifted long enough for Kate to once again gain control of her senses.

"Were those clothes something you wanted? Did you take them, too?"

He deliberately rolled the cuffs up on the long-sleeved shirt, baring darkly bronzed forearms sprinkled with nearly black hair. Folding his arms across his chest, he hooked the heel of one black cowboy boot over the lower railing surrounding the porch, his gaze never wavering from her face.

"How easily you turn the conversation from you to me."

"I'm an open book. You, however, are a mystery. You sing, you tell stories, you appear out of nowhere and disappear just as easily. Do you want to know the truth? You scare the hell out of me."

The grin she'd grown used to crossed his face, and the much too passionate eyes twinkled with unheard laughter. "Ah, Katie. I will miss you greatly when I go."

She turned away, looking at the shadows lengthening across the yard. "Then don't go."

"I must—eventually. You know that."

"You said you were leaving last night, too, but you came back. Now you have the nerve to rub my shoulders and make me feel better than I've felt in years. You look at me as if you plan to devour me whole. You kiss my neck like . . . like. . . ." She spun around to face him again. "Oh, hell! If you think I'm going to let you do anything more to me when you plan to walk away at any moment, you're out of your mind."

"I do not make plans to seduce you, madam. It happens of its own accord, as if all control leaves me when you are near."

"Oh." His declaration left her nearly speechless, and heat rose to her face. She turned away so he couldn't see the frustration rushing through her, the emotions she didn't know how to handle.

Taking a deep breath, she tried to speak rationally. "So, how much longer do you think you'll be here?"

"A day. Two perhaps. *Satan's Revenge* is being repaired. Once that is complete, I will find a way to avoid the guards and sail away. 'Twill not be easy without a crew."

"Maybe you could shanghai a sailor or two." She laughed lightly in spite of the anguish tearing through her.

She could hear him walk toward her, felt the soft brush of his chest against her back. "There is only one shipmate I would want at my side," he said softly. "But I cannot ask her to give up her life in this century to go with me."

She ignored his words, fighting to keep her emotions under control. Ignoring the gentle touch of his fingers as he smoothed hair away from the back of her neck was harder to do, especially when he leaned close and whispered into her ear. "Will you miss me when I go?"

Of course she would, but what difference would that make to him? He was going to leave whether she had feelings for him or not.

She pulled away. "Casey's going to miss you. I imagine my aunt will, too."

"That doesn't answer my question, Kate. Will *you* miss me?"

She shook her head, working up the courage to tell him a bald-faced lie—that she wouldn't miss him at all. "You've caused nothing but trouble since you walked into my life," she declared. "You're a pirate, and I'm the widow of a police officer who used to arrest men like you, men who take what they want, when they want it, and to hell with what's right or wrong."

He gripped her arms, pulling her against his chest. *"Will you miss me?"*

"No. I can't afford an extra mouth to feed, and I can't stand having my life disrupted."

His hands fell away from her arms. She heard him take a step back. Heard his frustrated and angry sigh.

Wrapping her fingers tightly around the railing, she stared absently at the jasmine and gardenias.

He didn't move. He didn't touch her. Silence hung around her as heavy and stifling as the humidity in the air.

Without a word he marched from the porch, his heavy footsteps beating like sledgehammers on the planks, on the stairs. She heard the crunch of his boots on the gravel-and–crushed shell walk, then absolute quiet. Suddenly she heard his tread again, as if he'd changed his mind about leaving. She heard him crossing the mushy, rain-soaked lawn, heard the rustle of shrubbery just before his powerful body materialized before her.

Grabbing her hand from the railing, he shoved something small and gold into her palm, then squeezed her fingers into a fist around it.

"That, madam, is a gold doubloon. It is worth a small fortune, or so I have been told by a very curious St. Augustine shopkeeper. I have many of them. I have jewels, too. Emeralds, rubies, sapphires, and diamonds—and any one of them, my dearest Kate, will more than pay for the room and board you have given me."

He took hold of her other hand and placed another doubloon inside, also tightening that hand into a fist. "That is for the generosity you will continue to show me, because I have nowhere else to go and am of no mind to look for other lodging. When I am ready to leave, I will give you even more."

"I don't want anything from you, especially ill-gotten goods."

She started to throw the doubloons in his face, but he trapped her fists in his hands. She could almost hear the grind of his teeth. "You have a closed mind, madam. One that concocts its own beliefs in people, without seeking to know the truth."

"That's not true."

"What do you know of my life before or after I became a pirate? You know nothing, Kate, only what you read in those spurious books in your dead husband's office. I am a thief, a murderer. And I have a black heart that is as cold as the icy Atlantic. Believe the worst, if you want. I will not attempt to tell you anything different. But I will tell you one thing, where you are concerned: I do not always take what I want when I want it. If I did, you would have been in my bed days ago."

With that he was gone, his long legs, his furious pace, carrying him down the street and out of sight.

And tears rushed from Kate's eyes, tears she didn't bother to wipe away, tears that were shed because she wanted him in her life but didn't have the courage to make room for him in her heart.

No one stared at him when he walked into the public house. The men did not seem to care that his hair was longer than most other men's, that he wore rings in his ears, or that he had a menacing scar on his face. They seemed to be interested only in the darts they were tossing, the billiard balls they were hitting, and the comely redhead leaning against the bar watching them with a seductive smile and teasing eyes.

Morgan skirted past them, ordered a rum from the innkeeper, and made his way to a table in a darkened corner of the tavern, not too far from a door with an exit sign above it. Years of hiding, of being cautious, had taught him to look for a ready means of escape, should the need arise.

He leaned back in the hard wooden chair and sipped his rum. It tasted watered down, an inferior quality, to be sure. Still, it warmed his throat, and if he drank enough, it might dull the ache that ripped at his heart.

Damn fool woman! She fought him with every ounce of breath, but beneath her resolve, he sensed passion burning to be shared. She had loved her husband, perhaps she still did, but he'd been dead many a year and 'twas long past time she stopped denying her needs.

He tossed down a swig of rum and thought about the heat of Kate's skin against his, the radiance of her emerald eyes, the silkiness of her hair when it smoothed over his cheek. He longed to hold her in his arms, to sweep his hands along the curves of her body, over her soft, lush breasts. He wanted to taste the sweetness of her mouth, wanted to slide his fingers up the insides of her thighs, and stroke the warm, moist center of her being.

He wanted to love her—at least once before he made his way back to his own time. He wanted to drag memories of her back to the past with him, because, God forbid, he'd never find anyone like her again.

"Would you like another rum?"

The voice startled him, and Morgan looked into the eyes of the tempting redhead he'd seen leaning against the bar. She could readily ease the need raging in his loins, but it wasn't a quick tumble that he wanted.

He wanted Kate. Rum might quench his thirst, but it could never numb his desire.

"One more," he stated, swallowing the last drop in his glass. He pulled a wad of green bills from his pocket and placed one marked with a 50 in the woman's hand. "Bring me a better quality this time. Something stronger."

She stared at the money, then looked at him and

smiled. "Maybe you'd like some company, too?"

He shook his head. "Just the rum."

"You're sure?"

"Aye."

The woman laughed. "Suit yourself."

He wanted Kate, but the rum would have to suffice.

Again he leaned back in the chair and studied the intricate drawings on the paper money. The coin dealer had given him far more than he'd ever expected for a gold doubloon and a silver piece of eight. The man had wanted to purchase even more, but Morgan had seen the gleam in his eye as he'd studied the coins. No doubt they were worth far more than the cunning devil had offered.

Still Morgan had taken the money. Using gold and silver for his purchases the day before had drawn too much attention. The paper money he'd used to pay for his drinks had raised not even one brow. 'Twas best to stay inconspicuous.

The redhead slid another glass of rum in front of him, then sauntered off, her slender hips swaying before his eyes. Disinterested in her too obvious moves, Morgan took a sip of the rum, favoring the way this darker and more potent drink burned his throat. At last he'd found something that suited his needs.

Across the dimly lit room, the door opened, letting in a stream of streetlight and a woman who looked vaguely familiar. Blond. Of average height.

Pretty, even though she had a hardened expression on her face.

She was the woman he'd seen on *Satan's Revenge*.

Morgan leaned back, letting the shadows cover his face, and listened intently to the woman's exchange with the innkeeper and redhead.

"There's a strong possibility he's dressed as a pirate," the woman said. Her back was to Morgan as she addressed the fellow behind the bar. "A big guy. Long dark hair. I'm sure you'd remember him if you saw him."

The redhead turned her head, looking at Morgan over her shoulder. A generous smile curved her painted lips, and she moved over a step or two, so Morgan wouldn't be seen by the woman from the ship.

Morgan winked, pulled another one of the bills from his pocket, and tucked it under his glass, then quietly, stealthily, opened the exit door and slipped out of the tavern.

The night was warm, humid. Dark, threatening clouds littered the sky, but thankfully the streets were still buzzing with people, and he wove between men, women, children, and hand-holding couples until he was far from the inn.

When he neared the shop where he'd sold his coins, he slowed. A crowd swarmed in front of the building, and that same yellow and black ribbon that had surrounded *Satan's Revenge* had been strung up to keep the spectators from getting too close. Red lights flashed on top of nearly half a dozen vehicles, and people in various uniforms scurried about.

Two men bearing a stretcher emerged from the shop. A black bag rested on top, its silhouette taking the form of a man—a man with the same exceedingly large girth as the coin dealer Morgan had spent time with earlier.

He moved closer, peering over the shoulder of an elderly gentleman whose height came close to matching his own. Morgan watched the blond woman from the ship walk up the street and stop beside the vehicle where the stretcher had been placed. She gripped the edge of the door, stared at the black bag for a moment, then shook her head. She twisted around, exchanged a few words with a man in uniform, then looked out at the crowd, searching, Morgan imagined, for him.

"Hey, Sergeant!" someone called out from the door of the building, and the woman turned and walked toward the shop, disappearing into the well-lit interior.

Morgan expelled the breath he'd been holding. He was guilty of nothing, but still he had to hide. Going back to *Satan's Revenge* was his only option. He could stay out of sight there, and when the ship was repaired, he could sail away.

And never see Kate again.

'Twould be for the best, he told himself, although his heart ached at the thought.

Working his way through the mass of bodies, Morgan came to a sudden stop when he saw a pair of cold brown eyes staring at him through the crowd. An instant later, they were gone.

Morgan's pace quickened as he shouldered through the gathering. The eyes had looked familiar. They'd looked evil, vile, like the eyes of Thomas Low. But Low had survived the storm three hundred years ago. He'd died at his estate in Dover—he hadn't traveled through time.

Still, Morgan searched the crowd, looked up and down the street, but he saw no one with eyes like Thomas Low's.

'Twas the murders that had made him see those evil eyes. The coin dealer's death brought back too strong a reminder of what Low had done to Morgan's family. No wonder he'd seen those eyes in the crowd. The sooner he got back to his own time, the sooner he wreaked his revenge on Thomas Low, the sooner his mind would ease, and he'd cease seeing Low in his nightmares—and in the faces of strangers in a crowd.

Chapter 13

'Twas but an instant past—and here he stood!
And now—without the portal's porch she rush'd,
And then at length her tears in freedom rush'd;
Big—bright—and fast, unknown to her they fell;
But still her lips refused to send—"Farewell!"

LORD BYRON, *The Corsair*

It was well past midnight when Kate uncurled her body from the front porch swing and stood at the railing. For long hours she'd waited for Morgan's return. Now, she hoped that if she waited just another minute or two, she'd hear his boots crunch on the walkway, see the moonlight shining on his hair.

But he did not come.

Off in the distance she heard the mournful cry of a siren, the barks and howls of dogs disturbed by the noise. Deep inside her chest, she thought her heart had ceased to beat, that the only thing

keeping her alive right now was the worry that
pulsed in her brain.

Was he hurt?

Dead?

Mad?

Ready to strangle her for being so cruel?

She wondered if she would ever see him again.

His smile.

His scar.

The dimples at the corners of his mouth.

When she shut out all the noises and sights
around her, he came to her in an instant, his azure
eyes sparkling brighter than all the wishing stars
in the nighttime sky, his hair swirling in the wind,
wrapping around her like millions of silky ropes,
pulling her close, so very, very close.

Once again she could feel the whispery touch
of his lips on her jaw, the feathery caress of his
fingers over her cheeks. And his words. My God,
his words. "Ah, Katie. I will miss you greatly
when I go."

"Don't go," she whispered into the air, and
prayed that the breeze would carry it to his ear.

Another siren screamed, its sound reverberating
through the thick, humid night, through her fear-
ful thoughts.

She had to find him. She had to.

If only to see him one last time, if only to kiss
him good-bye.

Running into the house and up to her bedroom,
she slipped out of her shorts and into jeans and
tennis shoes, wrapped a light sweater about her

shoulders, and shoved her house key and wallet into her pocket.

The grandfather clock downstairs struck one time as she rushed through the door and out to the street. The bars in the old part of town would still be open and she hoped he'd stopped off in one for a drink. Of course, there was always the possibility that he was sitting on a park bench, staring at all the new and different things in this century, or that he'd gone to the *castillo*, or to his ship.

He could have left this century entirely.

That thought ate away at her. She had to find him.

No cars passed her as she strolled up St. George toward the center of the city. It was quiet. Much too quiet. Even though she knew it was senseless, she peeked behind bushes, around trees, and in between houses lining the street. She peeked into the dark recesses of one bar, and when she saw no one familiar, she admitted to herself that Morgan would have gone to his ship—and he would be trying to go back home.

She headed for the bridge that would take her to the island where the ship was moored. Just before she reached the Episcopal church, the sound of footsteps joined hers on the street. Her heart slammed in her chest, and she jerked around, but no one was there.

No one.

She walked faster, and the steps caught up with hers again.

Her strides lengthened. Her pace quickened, faster, faster, as a lump formed deep in her throat.

Another block. Another. Still the heavy, evenly spaced footfalls followed her. Could it be Morgan, watching her every move? No, he wouldn't frighten her that way.

She came to a dead stop at Cathedral Place, and spun around, ready to confront whoever was stalking her trail. But there was no one in sight.

Not a man.

Not a woman.

Not a child, or even a dog.

She was all alone.

In the dark.

And she was frightened.

She jogged the next block, wanting to get away from the confinement of buildings, desperately needing to get to the bridge and out into the open where she could have a better view of what—or who—was around her.

When she saw the marina, she took a deep breath and slowed her pace. She hadn't heard the footsteps for nearly a block. She hadn't seen another person at all, and she laughed, sure that her imagination had been playing tricks on her.

"Good evening."

The sudden, unexpected voice surprised her. Her shoe stubbed on a raised section of sidewalk, and she tripped, but an elegant hand reached out and caught her before she fell.

"I did not mean to startle you," the man said

in a slow, deep, vaguely accented voice. "Forgive me. Please."

She pulled away, instantly putting her hand over her chest, trying to calm her rapidly beating heart, but the effort was useless.

The man looked harmless, but still she was alarmed by the way he'd appeared out of nowhere.

"Lovely night for a walk."

"I'm meeting someone. A friend." The words rushed out of her mouth as she backed away, tripping again, and once more she nearly lost her balance.

The tall, slender man with jet black hair and a well-trimmed beard and mustache cupped her elbow. He looked as if he could have stepped out of the pages of *GQ*, but that didn't make Kate want to stop for a chat.

"I really have to be going."

"Perhaps I should escort you. I'm sure your friend wouldn't mind, not at this time of night."

"No, thank you. I'll be fine."

He smiled, and she couldn't miss his pearly white teeth, his icy brown eyes. "Be careful, then."

She rushed off, not looking back, her jog turning into a run as she reached the Bridge of Lions, a run that consumed nearly all her breath, all her strength. At the far end she stopped long enough to look back across the deserted bridge, but the man who'd helped her was nowhere in sight.

She closed her eyes, saying a short, simple prayer of thanks, and adding one for protection, then heard the sound of a car's engine slowing down beside her.

Her eyelids flashed open, but it was only a patrol car, and her sister-in-law sitting behind the wheel shaking her head. "What on earth are you doing out here?" Nikki asked.

Kate let out her pent-up breath and slowly smiled at the most welcome face she'd seen since Morgan had gone away. "Taking a walk," she stated. "What does it look like?"

"It looks foolish. Get inside. I'll take you home."

Kate shook her head. "It's been a long day. It's been an even longer night, and I just want to get some fresh air."

Nikki rested her arms on the open window, her face frowning with skepticism. "What's wrong, Kate?"

"Nothing. Honest. I couldn't sleep."

"Is Casey okay?"

Kate nodded. "She's been at Evalena's the last few nights—plotting, I'm sure. Evie found a man for you, and now they're both trying to find someone for me."

"Might not be such a bad idea. A good man might keep you off the streets at night."

"I'm not looking for a good man, or any man, for that matter. You know that."

"Yeah, I said the same thing until Jack came along. I always thought I'd end up single, or married to a cop. Never in my wildest dreams did I think I'd end up with a museum curator."

Nikki stuck her head back into the car and answered a call on her radio. "I've got to go," she said, turning again to Kate. "Why don't you join Jack and me for dinner tomorrow night?"

"I don't know."

"No arguments, Kate. You need to get out more, and I don't mean walking at night by yourself."

"I like to walk."

"Well, it's not such a good idea. There was another murder a few hours ago."

Panic ripped through Kate, worse than the dread she'd felt when she'd heard the sirens earlier, worse than the fear she'd felt when she'd seen the stranger on the street. "Not anyone we know?" she asked, trying to sound calm.

"A coin dealer. Someone fairly new in town."

Kate let out a rapid sigh of relief.

"You're awfully edgy tonight," Nikki said. "Let me take you home."

"I'm fine. All I want to do is walk. Be a friend, please. Don't nag."

"If I didn't have to go, I wouldn't give up so easily," Nikki said, shoving the car into gear. "Tell you what: I'll come by for coffee in the morning, and then I'll nag you until you tell me what's troubling you."

Another call came over the radio. Nikki smiled and brought their conversation to an abrupt end. "Gotta go."

Kate watched Nikki's car speed across the bridge, and when it was out of sight, she picked up her jogging pace, making her way down old familiar streets as she headed toward the ship.

The disquiet of the night prickled her nerves, made her jump at every abrupt noise. Down a dark alley she heard the clank of a metal trash can tipping over, heard the sounds of two dogs yipping, as if they were fighting over the garbage.

A black-and-white cat darted out from the shrubs and raced across her path, and a scream froze in her throat.

Don't be afraid, she told herself. *You're almost there. Just a little further. A little further . . .*

Just as she thought those words, *Satan's Revenge* came into view, the ancient warship rising above the water like a phantom from another world.

Someone had set up searchlights at her bow and her stern, and they waved now, back and forth through the night. Yellow crime scene tape had been strung from one end of the ship to the other, and a makeshift gangplank ran from the pier up to the deck.

Kate worked her way to the police car parked at the edge of the dock, waiting, watching for the guard to disappear, or at least move to the far end of the ship so she could run up the plank and sneak on board.

Her wait wasn't long, but the gangplank wasn't going to work. It was too visible, too lit up. There was only one other thing she could think of. She'd have to climb the anchor chain hanging from the bow of the ship into the water below.

Never in her life had she done something so crazy. She told herself she should go back home, but she'd come this far, and she wasn't running away now. This was her last chance to find Morgan.

Crouching low, trying to stay out of the searchlight beams, she raced toward the bow and didn't stop to think before she leapt the short distance from the pier and grabbed onto the heavy chain.

Her hands slipped on the cold, damp iron, but she managed to dig her fingers between the links and hold on tight, climb quickly to the top, and then swing her feet over the railing and onto the deck.

Bending over, hands on knees, she took a few seconds to catch her breath, then slowly stood, realizing suddenly that she was on a vessel that had traveled across centuries—in the blink of an eye.

Her entire body trembled at the thought, and she reached out a steadying hand and gripped one of the cables securing the mast. She closed her eyes for a moment, then opened them, having the oddest feeling that she'd stepped back in time, but the searchlights waved through the sky, and the familiar black-and-white lighthouse stood watch in the distance.

Still, she could almost hear the shouts of sailors as if the ship clipped across the waves, the clash of steel against steel, and booming cannon fire as if pirate fought pirate and galleon fought warship.

And she could easily picture Morgan Farrell standing at the helm, legs spread wide for balance, arms folded powerfully over his chest as he shouted out orders.

Above her she could hear the creak of the mast, the snap of rope, the whistle of wind blowing in from the sea, and behind her the soft, almost silent step of a booted foot.

Her body tensed.

Oh, God. What had she gotten herself into?

Another step in the dark.

She opened her mouth to scream, but a hand clapped hard over her lips, and a powerful arm wrapped around her chest and dragged her kicking and struggling away from the moonlit deck, into the deep, dark shadows of the night.

Chapter 14

There be none of Beauty's daughters
With a magic like thee;
And like music on the waters
Is thy sweet voice to me . . .

LORD BYRON, *STANZAS FOR MUSIC*

K ate punched, clawed, and jabbed, trying to free herself of her captor's arms, but her battle was useless. If only she could open her mouth and scream, the guard would come running and she'd be safe, but the hand clamped down too tightly. Somehow, she had to work her way out of its grasp.

Again she struck backward with her foot, hitting something hard, and heard a short, teeth-clenched gasp. The blasted hand loosened on her mouth, not a lot, but enough that she could work her lips and teeth apart, and then she attacked, chomping down on the vile appendage that threatened to cut off her air.

There was no gasp this time, just a hiss, and a threatening whisper. *"Damnation, woman! Stop your struggling before you bring the bloody guards down on us."*

"Morgan?" she mumbled through the warm hand clapped over her lips.

"Who the bloody hell do you think it is?"

"I bloody well thought you were a murderer. Now, let me go!"

She stomped down hard on his booted foot, and took advantage of having the upper hand, even for just one moment. Spinning around, she punched him hard in the stomach, which didn't seem to faze him a bit. Fighting back the urge to scream out loud, she stretched up on tiptoe and got within inches of his face, letting her words seethe out, very low and very dangerous. "You touch me like that ever again, and so help me, Morgan Farrell, I'll get that damned cutlass of yours and run it through your scurvy hide. *Do you hear me?"*

His lips slanted into a grin. "I hear you, Katie," he whispered, caressing a strand of hair away from her mouth. " 'Tis an angel you are, to fill my ears with such sweet affirmations of your devotion."

She gritted her teeth in anger-filled frustration and jerked her head away, but Morgan's finger touched her chin and tilted her face so she could see nothing but his hot blue eyes lowering ever so slowly toward her.

"She had emerald eyes," he said softly, as if he were telling a story, and his voice once more captured her in his spell. *"Her hair was the color of honey, her voice sang with the sound of a fine golden harp, and he knew she'd been sent to him from heaven."*

And then he kissed her, sweetly, tenderly, his fingers at the nape of her neck, inching their way through her hair. She could feel his hand at the small of her back, dragging her against his strong, hard body. She could feel his heart beating in time with hers, and oh, God, it felt so good.

Hesitantly she opened her lips, wanting the kiss to deepen, wanting his mouth to linger, their tongues to mingle in a dance she'd almost forgotten.

He drew back just long enough to smile, just long enough to sigh, to whisper, "Ah, Katie. For many a day and many a night I have longed to know the taste of you."

Her heart boomed hard, heavy, as he captured her lips again, and breathed a bit of his life into her. With one powerful arm he lifted her feet from the deck till only her toes touched the wood, then even they left their connection to earth. She was suspended in his arms, held tightly, and all she could feel, all she knew, was this man from another world who had blown into her life in the midst of a hurricane and had wreaked havoc on her soul.

Her fingers, which until now had done nothing

but dig into the muscles of his arms, slowly slid across his shoulders and into his magnificent hair. Like threads of the finest silk, she drew the long waving strands about her shoulders, making herself a part of him. And then she found herself whispering words she'd never thought she'd utter, words that sounded foreign to her ear. "Make love to me."

He pulled away, and suddenly she felt herself sliding down his body until her feet once again touched the deck. Fear raced through her. Had she asked too soon? Did he think she was far too forward? Was making love the last thing on his mind?

She didn't want to open her eyes, but she couldn't prolong the agony of seeing the disgust on his face.

But he kissed her eyelids, and when she opened them she saw a sparkle in his eyes, a gentle smile on his lips.

He put a silencing finger to his mouth and whispered, "Follow me."

Holding her hand tightly, his long, strong fingers woven with her smaller ones, he drew her through the shadows, down a darkened hatch, and along a narrow, even darker corridor. Pushing open a door, he led her into a magnificent room lined with rich wooden bookshelves and cabinets, all subtly lit by a hint of moonlight and nothing more.

Beneath her feet she felt the gentle rocking of the ship, a lulling motion that eased the built-up tension in her body. Slipping away from Morgan's hand, she wandered about the room, wanting to explore the place that seemed so much a part of him. The shelves were lined with leatherbound books, with tankards of hammered gold, with ornate pistols and daggers. Vivid red velvet drapes hung at the corners of the massive bed, which was piled high with pillows of silk, velvet, and satin.

Kate ran her fingers over a blanket of thick, plush fur, and a shiver of fear mixed with desire trickled from her throat, to her stomach, to the intimate depths of her very lonely body.

Behind her, she heard Morgan closing the door, heard the click of a lock, and then the sound of his footsteps moving toward her.

Gentle hands slipped over her arms, dragging her easily against his chest. "Is this what you want, Katie—when you know I must leave?"

She swallowed her nagging apprehension. "I don't want to think about tomorrow, I just want to think about tonight, about being with you."

There was no turning back when his fingers combed through her hair, exposing her neck to the warmth of his breath, to the heat of his lips. Tender. So very, very tender. His strong hands swept away her sweater and rested on her upper arms, while his mouth, his tongue explored her shoulder, the sensitive hollow below her ear, her temple.

Dear Lord, this was what she'd been dreaming of for days. This was how she wanted to spend the long hours of night, every night.

Or just this night, if that was all she could have.

But all too suddenly he pulled away, and she could hear his heavy sigh, his quick pace across the floor.

She spun around. "What's wrong?" she asked, when she saw only his back.

"We have much to talk of, Kate Cameron. You do not trust me. You believe I am more corrupt than I really am. I believe, madam, that it is far too soon for us to consider making love."

"Too soon?" she asked incredulously. "Wasn't making love what you had in mind when you tried to hypnotize me on my front porch?"

"I had seduction in mind, I will not deny it. But you brought that to a very sudden halt."

"Oh, so turnabout's fair play?"

He lifted a decanter of liquor from the table in the center of the room, removed two cut crystal goblets from inside a glass-fronted cabinet, and poured a healthy—or near deadly—amount of liquor in each. He took a short swig, then walked nonchalantly toward the window.

" 'Tis not often—no, that is not true. I have never, madam, told a woman that I would miss her. I have never before suggested that I would have a woman, let alone a beautiful firebrand, sail at my side. Yet I opened myself up to you, thinking there might be one ounce of tenderness in your heart toward me. And, madam, you chose to take my heartfelt words and toss them to the wind."

"I did no such thing."

"You called me a thief. A murderer—"

"You said that word. Not me."

"But you were thinking it, Kate, at the same time you were yelling at me like an old sea hag."

"That's not the way I yelled."

He grinned. "Very well. Perhaps I exaggerate your berating tone. Perhaps you did not yell, but you did not tell the truth, either. You said I was trouble."

"You *are* trouble."

He tilted the glass once more to his mouth, his eyes never leaving hers. "Was I trouble when you shaved my face? When you ran a finger over the scar on my cheek, thinking I was asleep? And what of the time when you stripped away my undergarments? Was I trouble then, Katie?"

"I didn't look."

"Ah, but you did. I could feel the heat in my loins, I could feel your cool fingers trailing over the scar on my hip, I could—"

"Okay," Kate stammered. "I looked . . . but not for long." She grabbed one of the glasses he'd filled and took a quick swallow. The liquor set fire to her tongue, burned all the way down her throat, and flamed in the empty pit of her stomach.

She tilted her head toward him and smiled. "I looked," she said, her eyes fluttering down to the zipper of his jeans, then back again to meet his steady gaze. "I liked what I saw. After all, I'm only human." She swallowed another big gulp of liquor and waited for the burning to stop before she crossed her arms over her chest and glared at him. "That," she said, pointedly looking once more at his zipper, "is the only reason I'm here now. You got me all fired up, had the nerve to run off, and now I fully aim to finish what you started."

His laughter filled the cabin.

" 'Tis an angel you are, Katie. And I am the devil himself." He tossed down the rest of his rum, then went back to the table and filled his glass again. "Before you give me the pleasure of making love to you, I suggest you know who it is you are allowing to touch you."

"Well, since I foolishly begged you to make love to me in the heat of some totally impulsive and quite unexpected passion, and since you've managed to douse the flames of whatever it was that overcame me, I guess . . . I guess I'll let you tell me about yourself."

She held out her glass and suffered the rise of his questioning eyebrow as he filled it again. Then, quite dramatically, she flounced to the bed and made herself comfortable, sitting cross-legged in the very center. "Make it fast, will you?" she said, taking a tiny sip. "It's late and I have to work in the morning."

Morgan sat down in the heavy leather-and-mahogany armchair, stretching out his legs and crossing them at the ankles. He took another sip of his drink, watched her mimic his action, and wondered just how long it would be before she keeled over from the potent rum.

He should take the liquor away from her. Bloody hell! He should have tossed her on the bed, stripped her clothes away, and tasted every inch of her body. But beneath the guise of a pirate there lurked a gentleman who longed to tell her of his life, who had a need for her to know the truth of what he was, and why. He laughed to himself. He longed to tell her one truth while he lied about another. *Satan's Revenge* had been repaired. He would be gone tomorrow, but he could not tell her now, for if she knew, she might run away.

And he needed her to stay. God, how he needed her.

He swirled the rum, watching Kate over the top of his glass.

"Where would you have me begin? Before I became a pirate, or after?"

"I want to know it all, but give me the condensed version—please."

"I wasn't always a pirate."

"You mean, you didn't pop out of your mother's womb with a scar and an eye patch?"

"No, madam. I popped out with the proverbial silver spoon in my mouth, in a glorious room, in a great house, on one of the finest estates in Kent."

He watched the slant of her doubting brow, but didn't give her time to dash off a flippant comment. He had to hurry, lest she drink too much of the rum. A moment ago he believed he should tell her his story, thought she should know him better before they made love, but as he looked at her beauty, as he saw the fire radiating from her, he realized he needed her now, and wished that he'd waited until later to tell her so many things that needed to be shared.

Being a gentleman was a bloody nuisance!

He tossed down a swallow of rum and then another to control his desire.

"My grandfather was a wealthy man, a merchant who was a favorite of the king. There is no need for me to give you a history lesson now. Suffice it to say, I had money, stature. I traveled throughout Europe as a young man, studying the arts, and spending many nights and many days amongst scholars who talked of what life could be in the future, if only man had the knowledge and the power to dream."

"You were a scholar?" she asked, stretching out on her side on the bed, looking lovelier by the moment, with the rum tingeing her cheeks a delightfully rosy pink.

"I had a desire to write great books."

"Like Shakespeare?" she asked, kicking off her shoes and sending them flying across the room.

"I did not wish to be a playwright, but a novelist, like Cervantes. My father, God rest his soul, was the second son, and as he did not inherit my grandfather's estate, and only a portion of his wealth, desired a home of his own. So my mother, my sister Melody, my father, and I sailed for the West Indies. There would be no time for books and writing there, not at first, but I shared my father's ideals, and had great visions of a powerful sugar plantation."

"Then why did you become a pirate?"

That was always the hardest part of the story, the part he'd never told a soul, the part he'd relived again and again in his dreams.

"The voyage to Jamaica was not a successful one. Our ship's captain, Thomas Low, was much more than he appeared. He was a rich man—a pirate, some would call him. A privateer, others would say, awarded with commissions that gave him the right to steal from the enemy, as long as his profits were shared with the Crown. Sometimes he used his power against those who were not enemies of the king—like my father. Sometimes he used his power to steal from wealthy men—like my father. And most of the time . . . he killed."

"Your family?" she asked.

"Aye. Like fools, we believed Captain Low to be a gentleman of the highest order. Again like fools, we loaded great riches onto his ship. I remember full well the servants packing my mother's cherished wedding presents, her plates and cups of gold, her sparkling crystal, her linens and lace. I remember the chests of priceless jewelry, and those of gold, the fortune that would turn the bare land we had purchased into the finest estate in Jamaica."

Again he swallowed a gulp of rum, remembering far too much. "Thomas Low took it all," he told her, "and ever so much more."

Morgan rested his head against the back of the chair and closed his eyes, reliving the horror, the pain. He clutched his shirt, the ring and the cross hanging behind the fabric, and thought of the last time he'd seen the ones he loved, remembered the way Low had stripped his mother and father, and bound them together, back to back, so they could not see each other as they died. He remembered the way Low had laughed as he'd wrenched the wedding ring off his mother's finger, examining the emerald, the diamonds, the gold, saying, "I have admired your ring throughout our voyage. 'Tis beautiful, madam. Quite beautiful. And now it is mine." Morgan remembered struggling against his chains as Low's men had tied lead weights to his mother's and father's feet, remembered the way four men had hoisted them high in the air, remembered his mother's screams and his father's prayers as they were tossed into the sea.

And he remembered begging his sister to jump overboard rather than suffer the ravages of Thomas Low. He remembered being thrown over the side of the boat himself, long after he'd been flogged mercilessly and was presumed dead. He remembered the pain of the salt water on his wounds, remembered swimming for what seemed like hours, until he reached the island where he'd found his little sister, her life nearly gone.

She'd smiled at him as he clutched her body in his arms. "I love you, Morgan," she whispered, and then she'd closed her eyes—and died. He'd held her lifeless body against his chest for more than a day, as he cried, and swore, and vowed to get revenge. . . .

He had to go back. . . .

But first he wanted to know Kate's comfort, wanted her to hold him through the long, lonely night.

It was wrong not to tell her he was leaving tomorrow, wrong not to tell her that she'd burrowed so deeply into his heart that he'd thought about staying.

But he had to go. He had to.

He heard the light sound of footsteps on the floor, felt the soft touch of fingers stroking his cheek, and a hand sliding gently over his chest until it rested against his heart. "Make love to me, Morgan," Kate whispered, crawling into his arms, bringing him the solace he desperately needed, as if she could feel his pain and knew just how to soothe it.

Slowly she released the top button on his shirt, and moved down to the next, while one slender arm wove around his neck and fingers combed through his hair. "I know you're going to leave me," she said. "And I think I can understand why you have to go back."

"Can you?"

"All too well, I'm afraid. My husband was shot, and I stood beside him for hours, watching him die, knowing there was nothing I could do. And then he was gone."

Kate rested her cheek against Morgan's, remembering the thoughts that went through her mind

that night in the hospital and for many weeks after Joe's death. "I wanted to kill the man who'd
murdered him. I wanted to put a shotgun to his
chest and blow him away, but someone else had
done it for me. I was mad for the longest time,
and then I went through every other emotion
imaginable, including blaming myself for what
had happened." She kissed the scar on Morgan's
face, wishing she'd been able to give him comfort
all those years ago. He'd been alone, yet she'd
been surrounded by loved ones and those who
cared. Still, she'd hated the man who had killed
her husband, just as Morgan hated the man who
had killed his family.

"I know what you're feeling, Morgan. You want
to go back. You want to take the life of the man
who took the lives of those you loved."

"Aye. 'Tis the only reason I have for going."

He kissed her, then cupped her cheeks in his
hands and looked deep into her eyes. "You are a
blessing, Kate Cameron. And I would stay with
you if I could."

"I don't need any promises. No commitments.
I know you're going to go, and I want something
more than words and smiles to remember you
by."

"With no regrets."

She shook her head. "No regrets."

"Ah, Katie . . . you are more intoxicating than
the finest of rum," he said, setting aside his glass.
"You are far more beautiful, more valuable, than
a treasure chest full of jewels."

"You're full of pretty words, Morgan Farrell. But right now I just want you to carry me to that bed and . . . and . . . I'm sure you can figure out what to do once we're there."

He laughed, swept her up in his arms, and in two long strides, lay her down in a bed of velvet, silk, and fur, a soft, warm place that seemed to be made of clouds.

His wonderfully strong body balanced above hers. His hips lightly brushed over her thighs, and his powerful chest pressed ever so softly against her breasts. His lips, oh God, his lips, opened over hers, teasing them as if for the first time, loving them as if it were the last.

Wrapping his arms tightly about her, he rolled in the magnificent bed until she was above him, looking down at a face she needed to memorize before the night was through.

" 'Tis a shame the sun is not shining," he said, tugging at the hem of her blouse and drawing it upward.

The touch of his hands on her sides sent shivers through her, made breathing nearly impossible. Somehow, she muttered, "Why?"

"So I could easily see every movement you make." He slipped the blouse over her head. "So I could see you smile and laugh, and know that I am pleasing you."

She closed her eyes as his hands swept over her lace-covered breasts. "Don't worry, Morgan. You're pleasing me very much."

His fingers circled her nipples, tracing the edge

of the lace, and a soft moan escaped her lips.

Sliding his palms over her shoulders, he brushed away the thin straps of her bra. She leaned close and he rose up to meet her. She loved the feel of his tongue and lips on her skin, wanted to remember the thrill of that exquisite heat.

She felt his fingers flowing over her shoulder blades, felt them fumbling with the hooks at the back of her bra. Heard his frustrated sigh.

"Bloody hell! I could remove a corset in less than a minute, but—"

Kate silenced his words with a kiss. She reached behind her, touching his fingers, guiding them toward the hooks, and in mere seconds showed him what to do.

"It's not so difficult once you get the hang of it," she said. Suddenly her bra was gone, and when his mouth swept over her breast, warm, wet, and . . . and she'd never felt anything so wonderful.

He curled his arms about her. One second he was beneath her, the next he was above, straddling her, breathing raggedly, and in the dim light of the room she could see his smile. "You are beautiful, Kate," he said, teasing each taut nipple with the rough tips of his thumbs. "So beautiful."

And then he leaned over and kissed her.

Slowly.

Oh, so slowly.

One night with this man would never be enough.

But she would not ask for more.

Soft kisses whispered against her chin, down the curve of her neck, and over and around each breast, bringing forth soft moans from her throat as he worked his way down her belly. Warm fingers found the snap of her jeans, the catch on her zipper, and she let him draw them away from her legs, toss them somewhere across the room, then slide his fingers under the last remaining bit of lace.

He drew her panties away, then swung his legs from the bed, pushed off his boots, jeans, and shorts, and joined her once more, stretching his long, strong body above her.

He kissed her lips and her eyelids, and his glorious hair flowed about her, caressing her tender and oh so sensitive breasts.

"I have dreamed of you this way, Katie, long before I knew you. 'Twas an angel who came to me as I slept all alone, an angel with emerald eyes and hair of honey." He drew a finger lightly over her lips. "She whispered softly of heaven-filled nights and sun-kissed days, when she would hold my head against her breast and smooth away my nightmares."

"I'm no angel, Morgan."

"Ah, but you are." His hands slid over her legs, then lifted them about his waist. He moved close, closer, until she felt him hot and hard against her. "I need you, Kate, more than I've ever needed anything." In one swift thrust he was inside her, and he sighed as if he'd found his home.

As gentle as the sway of a ship on the water, they moved together, their eyes open to watch each smile, their hearts and ears tuned to each gasp, each cry of pleasure, each moan for more.

And then the storm came, fast, wild, all consuming. It raged on and on. He held her tight, tighter.

Suddenly he rose above her, a tall, powerful wave building up momentum. He grasped her hips and drove deep, holding on with all his might, his body shivering and beading with sweat. With one last gasp for breath, he wrapped his arms around her, and the wave crashed powerfully on her shore.

For long minutes they lay bound in each other's arms, his heart beating fast and heavy against hers. It calmed ever so slowly.

But she felt that hers would never slow down again.

Cupping her face within the palms of his hands, he looked deeply into her eyes and whispered, "What the bloody hell am I going to do without you, Katie?"

She forced a smile. "You'll get by, just as you did before."

"Nay. I will have sweet memories, but my heart will long for you."

"Then don't go."

He rolled to his side, keeping her close, cradling her head in the crook of his arm. Tugging the fur over them, he absently traced circles around and around on her shoulder.

He was silent for far too long. Was he thinking about staying? Was there any chance that she could be more important to him than the vengeance in his heart?

All too soon she knew the answer.

"I must go, Katie," he said, his lips lingering after he kissed her brow. "I have no choice. No choice at all."

Chapter 15

She was his life,
The ocean to the river of his thoughts.

LORD BYRON, *THE DREAM*

Somehow Kate slept, waking once with her head nestled against the warmth of Morgan's chest, once more with his hand draped possessively over her hip, and now, with the last hours of darkness pouring through the cabin window, she stirred from sleep to see him standing, looking out to sea.

She crept from bed, pulling the soft fur blanket with her, wrapping it about both of them as she rested her cheek against the scars on his back, scars that seemed miniscule in comparison with the scars she knew must be on his heart.

"Did Thomas Low do this to you, too?" she asked softly.

He did not turn toward her, just continued to stare out the window. "Aye."

"Why?"

" 'Tis not a story to burden yourself with."

"Don't keep anything from me. Please. I need to know everything about you, things to remember after you go."

"Then remember what we shared during the night."

She smiled and slid around him, wanting to see the man who sounded so pensive when throughout the night he'd laughed and teased as he'd loved her thoroughly. Curling her hands around his neck, she stretched up on her toes to meet his lips. "I'll always remember what we shared. But I need to know more."

He gazed down at her with brooding eyes. "Even those things that are painful?"

She nodded. "Pain is a part of life. It's what makes us who we are."

"It has made me a vengeful man."

Warmth filled her as she thought of what he truly was. "I've seen you cuddle a child. I've listened to you sing and tell stories. And I've been held in your arms. You're the most gentle man I've ever known."

One dark brow slanted, and the devilish grin she'd grown so fond of tilted his lips. "You, dearest Katie, are a most *persistent* wench."

"Aye, that I am."

He swept her up in his arms, carrying her to the comfort of a big leather chair, where he cradled her close, kissing her softly before he began his tale.

"We were but a few days from our destination. 'Twas the twenty-third anniversary of my parents' marriage, and my father wanted to celebrate his fortunes. We'd brought cases of wine to stock the shelves in our new home, but Father wanted to share his bounty with everyone. He was a good man—but much too foolish, especially that day.

"Low watched the gaiety from his place at the helm. He had a crew of eighty men, and they drank my father's wine, danced, and sang for a good part of the afternoon. And then, when my father had had too much to drink, Low approached him."

Morgan drew in a deep breath, closing his eyes for one moment, his fingers clenching her arm, and she knew his pain. She should tell him to stop, tell him she'd heard enough, but he was opening his heart and his life to her. She imagined the story he was telling her was one he'd never before shared, and that made her feel a part of him, as if they were one—if only for the moment. She had to accept whatever he could give her now. For soon enough he'd be gone.

"There was something evil about Thomas Low. I'd watched him every day on that ship. He spoke little. He was elegant, refined, yet there was something vile in his heart. I remember him watching me, remember the hate in his eyes whenever I came into his view. But I never knew why. Of course, I hated him myself when next he spoke.

"He looked at my father as if he were his equal, which he could never be, and he said, 'I would have your daughter.' I remember my father's laughter, and then his face sobering when Low pulled out his dagger. I remember my mother's shock, and I remember Melody, my sweet little sister, cowering behind my mother's skirts."

Morgan's body tensed. Kate could see his jaw tighten, and she understood his hatred. She would feel the same if somebody dared hurt Casey or anyone she loved.

"What did your father do?" she asked.

His gaze flickered down to her face, then toward the window. "My father was too numb, too drunk to do much of anything. But I hadn't touched the wine. Low was standing close to my father with his dagger drawn, but that didn't stop me. I pulled my own and went after him.

"I was inches away from his throat when his men grabbed my arms and legs and dragged me away. I struggled, but I could do nothing as they clapped chains about my wrists and ankles. Low gave my father a choice. 'Your daughter,' he said, 'or watch as your beloved son is flogged to death.' "

"What kind of choice is that?"

"It wasn't a choice my father could make. He refused to give over his daughter, and he begged Low to spare his son. But Low only laughed. I remember him walking toward me. I remember how white his teeth were when he smiled. And I remember him putting the tip of his dagger next to my eye and dragging it slowly down my cheek."

Kate touched the scar, drawing a finger lightly over its length, and a tear spilled from her eye.

"Low wanted to show my father that he gave no mercy. He wanted everyone to know that he was the master."

Morgan rested his head against the back of the chair. "He flogged me once, twice, while his men held on to my mother and father. I remember Melody screaming. I remember Low running a hand over her hair. Then he . . ."

Morgan clutched the ring at his neck, and held it tight. "My parents drowned," he told her, his breath ragged as he said the words. "I begged Melody to run away from Low, to jump overboard. I knew she'd drown, but I saw no other choice."

Kate could feel the rapid beat of his heart, the anguish pulsing through him. "I'm sorry," she said. "If I'd known, I never would have asked you to tell me."

His hands tightened around her arms. His eyes were full of fire and pain, and his lips came down hard and heavy over hers, pouring out his grief. "Don't be sorry. Please," he begged between kisses. "I have kept the horror bottled up inside me for seven long years."

He drew in a breath, and smiled from deep within his heart. " 'Tis time it came out. 'Tis time to heal."

He carried her to the bed, laying her down on

sheets of the finest silk, and he loved her, filling her with his need, his want, soaking up her softness, her caring, her passion. She took his breath away, smiling down at him with her wavy hair tousled and flying about her shoulders and face as she straddled his hips and made sweet blessed love to him.

He gasped for air, trying to hold on to the feeling of her wrapped tightly around him. And when he thought he'd explode, he pulled her beneath him. He captured her lips and buried himself deep, deeper, until he filled her with his love—an emotion he had thought he no longer possessed, an emotion he'd never given a woman.

He kissed her eyelids, her nose, her lovely pink lips, memorizing everything about her, this woman he longed to live his life with, this woman he'd searched for and finally found—this woman who could never be his.

What the bloody hell was he going to do without her?

If only she had come to him sooner, in another time, another place. . . .

If only he wasn't going to leave when the darkness came again. . . .

If only the first shot of pink wasn't rising on the horizon. . . .

Tasting her lips again, he whispered against her mouth, " 'Tis time to leave."

She sighed, the warmth of her breath spreading about him like the sweet mist of morning. "Does reality have to creep back in so soon?"

"Aye. I'm afraid so."

With one more kiss, he forced himself from the bed, pulling her with him. He gathered up her clothes and handed them to her piece by piece, watching her slide slowly into the trousers he wished he could once more remove.

"You must hurry if you're to be off the ship before daylight."

"What about you?" she asked, her beautiful smile turning suddenly to a frown as she slipped on her shoes. "Aren't you going with me?"

He shook his head. "I can hide here . . . until I leave."

"But you don't know how long you'll be here. Wouldn't you be more comfortable at my house?"

"Aye. But I must stay here."

"You don't have any food. The place is being watched all the time."

Frustration rushed from her, and he watched her fighting for something to say.

He wished there were something he could tell her to ease her mind.

"What about Casey?" she asked. "You've got to tell her good-bye."

He shook his head. " 'Tis best if I stay here. This is my home, Kate. I know my way around. I know secret places I can go if someone comes on board. And—" He shoved his hands through his hair as he turned away, walking toward the window, "I learned shortly before you appeared last night that the ship had been repaired. My plan is to sail tonight. Not tomorrow. Not next week, and I can't risk leaving the ship now."

Silence.

Deafening silence.

He looked back at her, at the tear flowing slowly down her cheek. "Why didn't you tell me earlier?"

"I needed you, Kate. I was afraid you'd go if you knew we'd have only one night together."

She drew in a shaky breath. Her lip quivered, and then she turned away. "I wouldn't have left. I told you when I got here what I wanted—and you gave it to me. I said I'd have no regrets. I said I didn't need a commitment, and I meant it."

"I would give you a commitment if I could."

"Yeah, well, you can't." He heard her sniff back a tear, then watched her search the room as if she'd lost something. Finally she grabbed her sweater from the top of the table and wrapped it around her shoulders. "It's late," she said, looking over his shoulder at the sun just beginning to appear through the window. "I shouldn't have stayed all night. I shouldn't . . . Oh, hell! I've got to get home before Bubba gets there."

"Stay a while longer," he pleaded, but she shook her head.

"I hope . . ." A trembling smile touched her lips. "I hope you'll be happy back in your own time."

"There is no happiness for me there."

"Then . . . then I hope you find Thomas Low."

He reached across the widening void between them and caressed the softness of her cheek. "I'll always remember you."

She backed away from his touch, and gripped

the edge of the door. "The first day we met, when I said I didn't want anything to do with you, you told me you weren't an easy man to forget. I thought you were crazy. I couldn't imagine anyone wanting to remember someone like you ... but I was wrong."

He smiled, hoping she would step into his arms and tell him she'd sail back with him to 1702.

"I love you," he whispered, but she didn't move toward him or acknowledge his words. Instead, she rushed from the cabin and disappeared from his life.

Chapter 16

⚔

I only know we loved in vain;
I only feel—farewell! farewell!

LORD BYRON, *FAREWELL!*
IF EVER FONDEST PRAYER

Kate climbed through the hatch, and stood in a daze on the rain-soaked deck. It had stormed sometime during the night, and she hadn't even known. A hurricane could have swept across northeast Florida and she would have been oblivious. She'd been too caught up in her own hurricane, something wild and wonderful, something she'd dreamed of, something she'd wanted desperately.

The reality of it all suddenly crashed down on her.

Morgan was going to leave, and she'd never see him again.

Never . . .

She'd just walked away from him, left him standing in the middle of the cabin where they'd made love for hours.

He'd whispered, "I love you."

And she'd ignored his words, ignored the fact that he'd given her his heart. But she couldn't ignore how her own heart had broken, the moment he'd said he was leaving, the moment she'd realized that going back was more important to him than staying here with her, the moment she'd known that one night with Morgan would never be enough.

Kate sniffed back her tears and slipped through the shadows until she reached the bow of the ship. For the first time that morning, she actually noticed the sun rising on the horizon, saw cars with their lights on driving along the road that paralleled the beach. They were filled with men and woman on their way to work, men and women with normal lives, who didn't know that an eighteenth-century pirate had traveled through time, who didn't know or care that she was running away from the man she loved.

Turning, she looked toward the hatch, hoping she'd catch one last glimpse of her pirate, hoping he'd call out for her to stay, but the place where she looked was as empty as her heart.

Cautiously she swung her legs over the side of the ship, dug her feet into the anchor chain and climbed down, swinging at last to the wooden dock.

The guard stood near the stern, far enough

away that she was able to sneak across the wharf without being seen. She crept past a patrol car, around the back of crates, and into an alley that morning light had yet to touch. She breathed rapidly, her chest rising and falling with each quick beat of her heart. It was late, she had to get home before the children arrived, and she needed to forget about Morgan and return to her calm, ordinary life.

If that were at all possible.

"Well, well, well. We meet again."

Kate's arms and shoulders tensed at the sudden sound of the deep, refined voice, and when the man appeared like a specter out of the dark, she moved backward until her retreat was halted by a cold, damp brick wall.

"I have frightened you yet again. I am truly sorry."

She recognized him as the man she'd seen last night. Had he followed her here? Had he been on the ship? Did he know who she was? Kate inched away from the wall and stumbled over a trash can tipped on its side. Her heart thudded. "Who are you?" she asked shakily.

"A man who's interested in the same thing as you."

"And what's that?"

"*Satan's Revenge*, of course. If I'd known last night you were coming here, I would have joined you." He smiled, his white teeth and brown eyes shining in the first rays of light. He looked toward the ship. "She's a beauty. I imagine a man would do just about anything to possess something so exquisite."

"I suppose."

"I like beautiful things. Ships. Women . . ." He faced her again. "Like you."

"You don't even know me."

"That could be changed quite easily."

"I don't think so."

She backed away, but he took a step closer.

"I've got to go," she said nervously.

The man touched her, his long, slender fingers wrapping around her upper arm. "Must you leave?"

Kate nodded.

He smiled again. "Your lips are quivering. I'm not surprised. It's rather wet out this morning, and there's a slight chill in the air. One would think one was in England rather than Florida."

Behind her Kate heard the rumble of an engine and the unmistakable sound of a police radio. She took a deep breath, pulling away from the stranger as headlights flashed down the alley and illuminated him from head to toe. Impeccably dressed, stunningly handsome, but there was something in his deep brown eyes that made her shiver.

The door of the car opened, light footsteps moved into the alley. "Good morning."

Kate spun around, relieved to see Nikki's frowning face. Her sister-in-law was shaking her head, one brow raised, and then she turned to the stranger. "Good morning, Mr. . . . . I'm sorry. We met yesterday on the ship, but I've forgotten your name."

"Lancaster. Gordon Lancaster."

"That's right. The historian from England."

"You have a good memory, Miss Cameron."

"Nikki," she corrected, then laughed in her usual style, looking from Kate to Mr. Lancaster, then back again. "I take it the two of you have met already."

"We ran into each other last night," he said, holding out his hand to Kate, "but we haven't been formally introduced."

Kate reached out hesitantly. Gordon Lancaster slid his fingers around her hand. His touch was cool, and he held on far too long. A foreboding tremble raced up her spine.

"I'm Gordon Lancaster," he repeated. The name sounded familiar, something she'd heard before this morning, but she couldn't remember where.

He squeezed her fingers. "And you are?"

"Kate Cameron."

"You and Nikki must be sisters."

"Sisters-in-law," Kate stated.

Nodding, he smiled as he looked at Nikki. "It would be easy to mistake you for sisters, considering the resemblance, not to mention the fact that you're both quite beautiful."

Kate frowned when she saw the blush rise in Nikki's cheeks. The man had all the airs of a gentleman, but he gave Kate the creeps, and she didn't like the way always-in-control Nikki was falling for his slippery smooth words.

Kate linked her arm through Nikki's and took a step toward the car. "It was nice to meet you, Mr. Lancaster—"

"Gordon. Please."

Kate smiled. "I hope you'll enjoy your visit, but I have to get to work, and Nikki's here to take me home."

"I quite understand. Perhaps I'll see you both before I leave?"

"Actually," Nikki said, "Kate's having dinner with my fiancé and me tonight. We'd love to have you join us."

"I'd be honored."

Arguing would have been useless, so Kate stood quietly while Nikki gave Gordon the time and place. Kate had no intention of going out to dinner, and she didn't like the way Nikki was adopting Evalena's matchmaking ways. There was only one man who interested Kate—and by nightfall, he'd probably be back in 1702.

"We'll see you at eight," Nikki said, and Kate reluctantly gave Mr. Lancaster a half smile before dragging Nikki toward the car and climbing in-side.

"Why did you tell him I was going out with you?"

"Because you are," Nikki answered. "You need some other interests besides your day care center and walking around town in the middle of the night. Which reminds me, the officer guarding the ship said he saw a woman fitting your description sneaking off the ship."

Kate shrugged, wanting to ignore Nikki's implied question, but Nikki had the gift of reading peoples' minds.

"What were you doing there?"

"Looking around."

"All night?"

"I was tired after my walk. I fell asleep."

Nikki shook her head. "Well, you won't be out walking tonight, and you won't be alone. Gordon Lancaster seems like a nice guy."

"Too refined for my tastes."

"He could grow on you."

"You find him more interesting than Jack?"

"Of course not. But he seems perfect for you."

Gordon Lancaster seemed perfect, and that was the problem. Kate didn't want perfect. She wanted a man with scars inside and out, a man who could hate as passionately as he could love.

A man who was gone from her life.

She stared out the window as Nikki drove away. Looking back at *Satan's Revenge,* she watched the sheets slapping against the masts, the sunlight striking the black-and-white skull and crossbones flapping in the wind, and, high up in the crow's nest, she saw a man with long dark hair billowing about his head and shoulders. He was nothing more than a phantom from another world, but Kate could see him touching his fingers to his lips, then blowing a last parting kiss toward her.

A tear slipped easily from Kate's eye, and she whispered, "Good-bye."

*   *   *

Kate walked through the living room, pulling a comb through her tangled mass of just-washed hair. Sara and the triplets were playing in the middle of the floor, and she patted heads and caressed cheeks on her way to the kitchen. Bubba held his little arms out to her and she scooped him from the high chair, as if that was the most natural thing in the world to do.

Pressing a kiss to his plump pink cheek, she sat across from Nikki and took a sip of her first cup of morning coffee. "Thanks for watching everyone while I showered."

"No problem."

She lifted a knife from the plate in the center of the table, cut a wedge of coffee cake, slipped it onto a napkin, and broke off a piece with her fingers, avoiding the questioning look on Nikki's face. She'd told her on the drive home that she'd talk about what was troubling her, but only after she'd showered, only after she'd had a little while to collect her thoughts.

And now she didn't want to talk.

"What's going on, Kate?" Nikki asked over her cup of coffee. "And don't tell me nothing, because I won't believe you. I want to know what you were doing on that ship, why you were out walking, why you're acting so strange."

Offering a bite of cake to Bubba, she popped the rest in her mouth, and picked at the crumbs on the napkin. "I met a man."

"Well, that's a good sign."

"I spent last night with him. On the ship."

"On the ship? What is he, a thrill-seeker or something?"

"Or something." She couldn't tell Nikki that the man she'd spent the night with was a pirate, and she definitely couldn't tell her that she'd forgotten to use the condoms she'd carried around the last few weeks—just in case.

"Do I know this guy?"

"No." Kate wiped crumbs from Bubba's mouth, then looked back at Nikki. "Could we change the subject? I'd rather talk about your wedding than—"

"Yoo-hoo!"

Evalena burst through the living room door with Casey trailing rapidly behind.

"Hi, Aunt Nikki. Hi, Mommy." Casey threw her arms around her mother's neck and slid a kiss quickly across her cheek before climbing into the chair beside her. "Guess what? Evie and I made lovebirds out of frosting last night. We're going to put them all over Nikki's wedding cake."

"They're just the cutest little things," Evalena bubbled, lowering her body into a kitchen chair. "You'll absolutely love them, Nikki."

"I thought we'd decided on something simple," Nikki said. "You know, a few white roses, a few leaves."

"That was before I thought of the lovebirds." Evalena said, patting Nikki's hand. "Don't you worry your pretty little head. You'll love the cake, no matter what I put on it."

"I hope so."

Evalena moved in close to Nikki. "I'm sure glad I ran into you this morning. You just *have* to tell me all about this latest murder." She leaned over and whispered into Nikki's ear, but still Kate could hear her meddling aunt's every word. "Is it true the guy was naked?"

Kate watched the smile curve on Nikki's closed mouth, watched her shake her head.

"You know I can't give you any details."

"Well," Evalena murmured, "I thought, just this once you might tell me at least one little thing that no one else knows. You know I'll keep it a secret."

"Can't do it, Evie."

"Well!" Evie pushed out of the chair, brushed a kiss across Kate's cheek, rolled her eyes at Nikki, and headed for the door. "Guess I'll go see what the TV reporters have to say. They usually have the best scoop, anyway."

"Talk to you later," Kate called out, as Evie scurried through the living room, patting little heads on her way out the door.

Bubba squirmed in Kate's arms, and she looked to her daughter for help. "Do me a favor, Case— would you take Bubba in with the other kids? Tell them a story or something, so Nikki and I can have a few minutes to talk."

"You're not going to talk about my pirate, are you?"

"Pirate?" Nikki asked. "What pirate, Casey?"

"Mr. Farrell. He lives with us now."

Kate quickly thrust Bubba into Casey's arms. "Scoot," she said. "Nikki and I won't be long, then maybe we'll finger paint or something."

"That's not fair," Casey mumbled, yet she took Bubba's hand as they walked from the room. The little boy toddled for a moment, then dropped to his knees and crawled after Casey.

"What's this about a pirate?" Nikki asked.

"It's Casey's imagination. Joe filled her head so full of that pirate stuff that she imagines everyone's a pirate."

"But this one has a name," Nikki said pointedly. "*Mr. Farrell.* I heard it quite distinctly." Nikki took a sip of coffee while keeping her eyes fixed on Kate. "Is he the one you spent the night with?"

Kate nodded.

"And he's living here now?"

"Not anymore." Kate pushed up from the table and walked to the kitchen window, staring out at the bright blue morning. "I'm never going to see him again."

"Why?"

"He's gone. Far away."

Kate could hear the kitchen chair scraping on the floor. A moment later, Nikki stood at her side. "You really liked him?"

"Yeah."

"Did he dress like a pirate?"

"Does that matter?"

"It matters a lot. I've been looking for a pirate."

"Does Jack know you're in the market for another man?" she asked, laughing lightly, hoping Nikki would veer away from talk about Morgan.

"This isn't funny, Kate. Two men have been murdered since that pirate ship showed up. We've had strange reports coming in day and night about a pirate hanging around town. And just the other day I saw a guy dressed as a pirate sneaking away from the ship." Silence. A frown marred Nikki's face. "He was big. He had long dark hair—and a scar." Nikki shook her head and laughed. "I should have put two and two together when you called me yesterday morning asking about the first victim. You wanted to know if he had a scar, if he had long dark hair."

Kate paced across the room. "Morgan's not a murderer."

"You're sure?"

She nodded, but knew that he'd killed people in his own time. Could he have killed here, too? She didn't want to believe it, but. . . .

"What kind of evidence do you have against him?"

"Not much." Crossing to the table, Nikki picked up her cup and sipped her coffee. "I shouldn't tell you any of this, but I think you should know everything, just in case he comes back."

"He's not coming back."

"I hope not. He's a suspect, Kate. Two men are dead, and whoever did it sliced their throats, stole their wedding rings and wallets, and stripped them of all their clothes."

"Why would someone take their clothes?"

"I don't know. We found the coin dealer's things in a dumpster, but the cowboy's clothes haven't shown up yet. His wife said he was wearing a brand new pair of boots. Maybe our suspect wanted something to wear besides a pirate costume."

Kate's heart sank. She remembered so well the black cowboy boots Morgan had been wearing the day of the first murder. But that wasn't enough evidence to prove he was guilty. She couldn't believe it. She couldn't.

"It doesn't sound like you have any evidence at all. It sounds like you're guessing."

"There was a gold doubloon in the second guy's fist."

"He was a coin dealer, for heaven's sake!"

"He's dead, Kate! He had a gold doubloon in his hand that looked like it was nearly in mint condition. A pirate has been wandering the streets. A pirate ship mysteriously appeared on shore, I saw a pirate sneaking off the ship, and I found a gold doubloon just like the one the coin dealer had lying on the cabin floor. Now Casey says a pirate was living here. Is that all coincidence?"

A tear slid down Kate's cheek. "Morgan's innocent."

"What do you really know about him?

"Enough to know he wouldn't *murder* anyone. Please don't interrogate me, Nikki."

"That's not my intention, and you know it. We're friends. You take care of me, I take care of you, and right now I'd like to prove this friend of yours is pure as the driven snow, but I can't do that without your help."

Kate opened a cupboard door and absently put dishes from the drainer away on the shelf. She refused to believe Morgan was guilty, but Nikki would continue to pry until she learned every last detail about her relationship with the pirate.

Slowly she turned around and leaned against the cabinet. "What do you want to know?"

"How'd you meet him?"

Should she tell the truth, a lie, or something in between? She decided to skip the parts about Morgan traveling through time and about him being on the island, and figured the part about the gash on his head was better left unmentioned. Finally she asked, "Does it matter?"

Nikki raised a brow. "Guess not. So, where's he from?"

"England."

"Does he have a job?"

"He's independently wealthy."

"Or so he says."

"It's true."

"Then why was he staying here, instead of some expensive hotel?"

"Look, Nikki, these questions aren't helping you, and they're definitely not making *me* feel any better."

"Since when are interrogations supposed to be fun?"

"You're going to hound me until I tell you everything, aren't you?"

Nikki nodded.

"Okay, here's the condensed version. I met him by accident. He's sort of eccentric—well, more than eccentric—but he intrigued me. I let him stay here a few days because he asked, and because . . . well . . . because he was good with the kids, because Casey liked him."

"Surely there were more reasons than that."

"I was lonely, okay? And he was so damn irresistible, not to mention drop-dead gorgeous, that I slept with him." She took a deep breath. "Now he's gone and I hurt like hell. End of story."

Nikki shook her head. "No, it's not. Endings are never that cut-and-dried. You want him back, I can tell. But why you want a man who dresses like a pirate is beyond me."

"He's eccentric. I told you that."

"I suppose he carries around a cutlass?"

"Sometimes, but if you'll remember correctly, Joe had a penchant for the blasted things, too."

Nikki sipped at her coffee. Slowly, her no-nonsense expression softened with a smile. "Casey likes him, huh?"

"She wants him to be her daddy."

"And you?"

"I told you. He's not coming back."

"Did you have dinner with him before meeting him on the ship?"

"No. He left the house about six o'clock."

"You didn't meet him for drinks or something

between then and the time I saw you on the bridge?''

Kate shook her head. ''I wish I had. There's so much we could have talked about, so much more I'd like to know about him. There just wasn't enough time.''

''Sometimes you can learn all you need to know in an hour or two.''

''We didn't have much more time than that.''

''But I thought he was here a few days.''

''He was sick the first two.'' How easily she could see him lying in bed, his face freshly shaved, a patch covering his eye. She felt herself smiling as she looked at Nikki. ''I took care of him morning, noon, and night. And then he left.''

''Sounds ungrateful to me.''

Kate shook her head. ''Not Morgan.''

''But he left you.''

Shrugging, as if it didn't matter, Kate went to the table, clearing away empty cups and crumb-coated plates which she took to the sink.

''Did he hurt you, Kate?''

''No. Not really.'' Kate turned around and smiled at her sister-in-law. ''I don't want to talk about it anymore.''

''Just one more question?''

Somehow Kate managed to laugh. ''God, Nikki. I've been pouring out my soul, and you've been treating it as just another interrogation.''

''I'm a cop, what do you expect? I've got two murders to solve, and a friend who's out of her

ever-loving mind. Just a few more questions—
then I'll stop."

Bubba cried in the next room, and that was
more than enough excuse to escape. "Sorry," Kate
said. "Inquisition's over."

But Nikki was insistent. "When was he here,
Kate? I need to know the days and times."

Kate stood with one hand on the swinging door,
wishing none of this were happening.

"Sunday night," she answered. "All day and
night Monday and Tuesday. He was here on
Wednesday, too."

"What about Wednesday night?"

Kate shook her head. "You already told me you
saw him on the ship. I'd be lying if I told you
anything else."

"What time did he leave on Wednesday?"

"I don't know. Nine, ten . . . it was dark."

"Did he come back after that?"

"Yesterday afternoon. I had a headache. The
kids were awful, but he came back and made
everything perfect." A tear slipped from Kate's
eye. "He's not a murderer, Nikki. I know it."

"For your sake, I hope that's true." Nikki put a
comforting hand on Kate's arm. "For your sake, I
hope he has another alibi, because you just told
me he wasn't with you when the murders occurred."

Chapter 17

In him inexplicably
mix'd appear'd
much to be loved and hated,
sought and feared.

LORD BYRON, LARA

Kate opened her bedroom window, letting in the sounds of children playing in the street, the fresh scent of rainwashed gardenia and jasmine, along with the warm breeze that had driven away the afternoon storm clouds. Drawing in a deep breath, she wished the wind could also drive away the anguish that had dampened her day.

With not more than an hour's sleep, she had no idea how she'd made it through temper tantrums, tears, games of chase, a broken vase, and Casey's incessant questions about Mr. Farrell. "He'll be here later," she told her, not wanting to face the truth. Later, when she herself could accept his reasons for leaving, she'd tell Casey that he was gone. And then they could cry together.

Right now, she had time only to wonder and worry about her conversation with Nikki.

Could Morgan be the murderer Nikki was looking for? Impossible. Yet many impossible things had happened in the past week, like a man traveling through time, like her losing her heart to a pirate, like her sleeping with a man without a commitment—and without a condom. Disease didn't seem possible—not with Morgan. Yet . . . she sighed at her foolishness, swearing she'd never again get so caught up in the moment that she forgot to protect herself, then let another consequence capture her thoughts.

Again she turned her attention outside to the children at play. There was a game going on in the center of the street—two boys and a girl, batting and catching softballs, the same thing she and Nikki used to do with Joe. Further up the street she heard what sounded like a squeaky wheel, and she turned to see a little girl pushing a baby doll carriage along the edge of the road.

She smiled softly. Another child was something she'd always wanted. Not using a condom hadn't been smart, but. . . .

A distant rumble made her look off in the distance, where she saw a blanket of black clouds rolling in from the sea. A storm was coming—the kind Morgan would need to take him home, to take him far, far away.

She swallowed the ache in her heart, and closed

the window and French doors to keep out the coming rain. She wished she could close her thoughts as easily.

Once more she looked at the little girl with the baby buggy and let thoughts of another child capture her mind as she wandered down the stairs, trailing her fingers along the banister. In the living room, she picked up blocks and cars and dolls from the floor and tossed them into the toy-filled laundry baskets sitting in the corner. Sweeping up the worn and stained Raggedy Andy, she held it close to her chest. One of the hands was wet, and she remembered Bubba chewing on it most of the day in an attempt to soothe the ache of an incoming tooth. Casey had done the same thing when she was a baby, and so many fond memories of those early days came rushing at her.

Joe's parents giving Kate and Joe the house he'd grown up in, the one Kate had always loved.

Joe holding her hand in the labor room, scared half out of his mind that something would happen to her or the baby.

Joe sitting in the middle of the living room floor, fumbling with his very first diaper change.

But no matter how hard she tried, she couldn't remember the touch of Joe's hand, the feel of his kiss.

When she thought of being held, the only man who came to mind was one with dark brown hair flowing over his shoulders and chest. A man with big gold hoops in his ears. A man with scars much deeper than her own.

Carrying Raggedy Andy with her to the story-teller's chair, she curled up in its big, overstuffed comfort and thought about holding another baby. Her baby—and Morgan's. A little boy or girl with pink cheeks and ten tiny fingers and toes. A little boy or girl with curly dark brown hair and azure eyes.

A child who'd always remind her of the few brief days she'd enjoyed with a pirate from an-other century, a pirate who'd pulled her easily into a fantasy and reminded her just how won-derful life could be if she'd once again believe in dreams.

A pirate who'd pillaged and plundered, who'd slashed other men with the sharp blade of his cutlass, and, heaven forbid, bedded wenches in far too many ports.

Wenches just like herself, she imagined, who'd fallen for a devilishly handsome face, a mesmer-izing voice, and a touch both soothing and pas-sionate.

Had they known what was inside him, though? Had they shared his anguish? His grief? Had they watched the way he'd held a baby, or listened to a child's chatter? Had he told any of them that he wished they'd sail at his side on *Satan's Revenge?*

Or had those special things been reserved just for her? A woman who had fallen in love with a man who'd killed in his own time, and was sus-pected of being a murderer in hers.

Morgan, a murderer? It seemed impossible, yet it nagged at the back of her mind.

Pulling from her pocket one of the gold doubloons Morgan had given her, she held the shining coin in her palm. It looked newly minted, just as Nikki had said when she'd talked about the one they'd found on the dead man. Perhaps Morgan had sold a few to the coin dealer right before the man had been murdered. That seemed the only possible explanation.

But what of the shirt, the jeans, the shoes? Only tourists walked around St. Augustine in cowboy boots, yet that's what Morgan had chosen to wear. Could they possibly have belonged to the dead cowboy from Texas?

She'd asked him where he'd gotten the clothes, but he'd avoided her question. Was that a sign of guilt?

Kate rested her head against the back of the chair and tried not to think such horrid thoughts.

Morgan was not a murderer. He'd had good reason for what he'd done in the past, and no reason to do it in the present.

She wouldn't believe it.

She wouldn't. Not of the man who'd held her so tenderly, who'd kissed away all her loneliness, who'd sung her to sleep, and loved her when she woke.

Kate's eyes opened when she felt a child bounce onto her lap and pull the Raggedy Andy from her arms.

"Were you asleep?" Casey asked.

"Just dozing," she answered. "What about you?

You've been quiet as a church mouse since the other kids left."

"I've been sitting on the front porch, waiting for Mr. Farrell to come back."

Kate couldn't lie any longer. She had to tell Casey the truth. Morgan was gone and he wasn't coming back. She'd console Casey, hold her and love her and make her understand. Then she'd tuck her in bed and wander off to a place where she could be alone with her own broken heart, a place where no one could hear her cry.

Kate wrapped a finger around one of Casey's curls and kissed her daughter's forehead. "Did Mr. Farrell tell you where he came from?"

"He said he came from really, really far away."

"That's right. And he had to go home, to a place you can't sail to, or fly to, or even get in the car and drive to."

"Like heaven?" Casey's lips trembled. "He didn't die like my daddy, did he?"

"No, Case." Kate pulled her close, tucking her curly head against her neck. "He didn't die, honey. It's hard to explain, though."

"Why?"

How could she possibly tell her that Morgan had traveled through time, that he was from another world and had wanted to go home? And then she remembered an old and favorite story, and a movie she and Casey had watched many times together.

"Remember in the *Wizard of Oz*, when Dorothy and Toto got swept up in the tornado and ended up in a place far, far from Kansas?"

Casey nodded.

"Well, that's pretty much the same thing that happened with Mr. Farrell. You said a prayer, remember?"

"Uh-huh."

"You asked God to send you a pirate, and He did. He swept Mr. Farrell up in a hurricane and tossed him down on our island. Just like Dorothy, Mr. Farrell liked the new land he'd come to, but it was strange to him. He liked the people he met—especially you and me—but he still wanted to go home."

"He doesn't have ruby slippers, does he?"

"No, honey. He has a ship—and that's what's taking him home."

"Is it magic?"

Kate nodded.

"Will he ever come back?"

"I don't think so."

"But I wanted him to be my daddy and live with us all the time."

"I know, Case. I know."

A tear spilled from Kate's eye, and Casey reached out and wiped it away. "Don't cry, Mommy."

Kate smiled, and buried her face in her daughter's hair. "We're going to miss him, Case, but we'll always have memories of our time together."

"We can dream about him, too."

"That's right. Pleasant dreams. Ones that make

you happy all through the night. Ones you remember the next day and the next."

Casey snuggled close, and Kate rocked her gently. When she heard her daughter's soft, gentle
breathing, she carried her up the stairs and tucked
her into bed. Smoothing a curl away from her
brow, she kissed her.

"I love you," Kate whispered, then wanted
nothing more than to go to her own bedroom—
and dream.

But her room felt big, and far too empty. Wind
and the smell of rain blew in through the open
French doors. She thought she'd closed them earlier, but maybe she hadn't. She shut and latched
them now, then sat on the edge of the queen-sized
bed she'd shared with Joe, and touched the white
ceramic frame that held a picture she'd taken of
him on their sailboat. He'd been her dearest
friend. Her lover. He'd been her life for so many
years that it had seemed nearly impossible to go
on without him. But she *had* gone on, and she'd
found Morgan.

Morgan. She could still see his beloved face,
hear the sound of his hypnotic voice, feel the beating of his heart. Memories of him were strong and
powerful. Her fingertips could almost feel the
sleek line of the scar on his face and the growth
of whiskers breaking through on his cheeks. Her
lips could almost feel the thick welts on his back,
the curving scar on his hip. She knew the feel of
the hair on his chest, brushing ever so lightly over
her sensitive breasts, the taut stomach muscles

she'd kissed when she'd begun her first intimate exploration of his body, the softness of his lips on her mouth.

She felt the comfort of his arms encircling her, the happiness that he poured into her with his kiss, his voice.

"I love you," he'd whispered, and she'd been too foolish to whisper the same words back, even though she'd felt them in her heart.

He was gone, but she'd never forget him or stop loving him. He'd given her much more than he'd ever know—he'd given her hope, he'd given her a reason to stop dwelling on the past and start looking forward to the future.

He'd shown her that a heart could break—but a heart could also heal, and move on.

She lifted the picture of Joe that she still held in her lap, and looked at the old familiar face. She touched a finger to her lips and then to Joe's smiling face, holding it there until she was able to smile. She took a deep breath, opened the dresser drawer, and put the picture inside.

"I'll always love you," she whispered, then closed the drawer.

Wiping a tear from her cheek, she left her bedroom and walked down the hall to the room where Morgan had slept. She leaned against the doorjamb and looked inside, just as she'd done that day Casey had read to him in bed. His big, worn leather boots sat beside the nightstand, desperately in need of leather wax. His gray trousers with too many brass buttons in front hung over the back of a stiff wooden chair. The room seemed empty, but felt so full. This is where she'd shaved away his beard, where she'd kissed his wounds, where he'd asked her, in the midst of his fever, to climb into bed and keep him warm.

Someday she might be able to close Morgan's memory away in a drawer, but not now.

She curled up in the bed where he'd slept, and drew his battle-and sea-weary velvet coat into her arms.

"I love you," she whispered, and hoped he could hear her.

She closed her eyes, but sleep refused to come. Hunger gnawed at her belly, her heart ached, and she wanted nothing more than to be inside a ship's cabin that smelled of cedar and salt water, where the floor swayed, and a strong, loving man stood looking out to sea.

Climbing from the bed, she slipped into Morgan's coat, fastening the fifteen brass buttons in front. It hung past her knees, beyond her fingertips. It felt warm, and it carried Morgan's scent, the natural muskiness of his body that reminded her once more that he'd been born more than three hundred years ago, that he was very different from a twentieth-century man.

He'd tried to be modern. He'd changed his clothes, but underneath the oxford shirt beat the heart of a pirate.

Smiling at all the memories she had, she went to the tall dresser to tuck in a bit of white cotton sticking out of a nearly closed drawer. She pulled it fully open, and looked at a stack of neatly folded undershirts inside, with an assortment of colored boxers beside them, and at least half a dozen pair of white cotton socks.

Her mind quickly conjured a picture of Morgan going into a department store, feeling completely out of place in his pirate clothes. She saw a sales clerk coming up to him. "May I help you?" she'd ask, and his eyes would quickly scan her body before he'd accept her offer.

How odd it must have seemed to him to purchase clothes in 1998 instead of 1702. She wondered if he'd been baffled by the prices, by the plastic wrapping, and if he'd attempted to pay for his purchases with a gold doubloon, or a ruby or emerald or diamond.

She wished she'd been with him to ease him through the newness of everything. If he came back, she'd have another chance. There was so much about this time that she could teach him. And there was so much about life that he could teach her.

The black-and-white bag Morgan had asked Casey to take upstairs rested underneath the shirts, folded just as carefully as the underwear, and Kate took it out.

A cash register receipt rested at the bottom, face up, and she saw the price for each of the things in the drawer, but saw nothing noted for the Levi's, the boots, or anything else.

The fear that had nagged at her earlier came back again with full force. She pulled out the re-

ceipt, hoping another one lay beneath it, but there
was nothing more in the bag.

*Where had he gotten the boots and clothes he'd been
wearing?* she wondered.

She rifled through the shorts and the socks, and
in the toe of one she felt something thick and
heavy, and also something round. Sticking her
hand deep inside, she pulled out—

A wallet.

A man's wedding ring.

Tears fell unbidden from her eyes as she looked
at the plain golden band, at the inscription inside:
AMF loves EDT—1963. When she opened the wallet, the Texas driver's license stared up at her, and
the face of a dead man.

Her fingers trembled, not so much with fear, but
with the fact that she'd just found evidence that
suggested Morgan was a murderer.

Damn you, Morgan! Damn you!

As if they were hot coals, she dropped both the
ring and the wallet back onto the underwear and
slammed the drawer shut. She didn't want to look
at them or touch them. She wanted to forget they
were there, wanted to forget she'd ever seen them,
but the part of her that had been a cop's wife told
her she had to call Nikki, told her that no matter
how much she loved Morgan, he'd done something vile, something unforgivable.

And she'd slept with him.

What a fool she'd been.

Behind her she heard the sound of heavy boots.
Cowboy boots.

Morgan's distinctive walk.

Her heart hammered. Why couldn't he have walked in five minutes before she'd found those horrid things in the drawer?

His fingers softly brushed over her hair. The heat of his body radiated through her clothes, warming her skin, wrapping around her cold, frightened heart.

"I have come to ask you to go home with me."

One hand settled on her shoulder, the other caressed hair away from her neck, sending shocks of electricity skittering through her insides. Warm breath, like the whisper of an island breeze, swirled about her ear.

She jerked away, moving across the room, cowering beside the bed. Love had nothing to do with the feelings racing through her now.

He'd murdered in his past. She had evidence pointing to him as a murderer in the present. Yet he stood before her now, asking her to go far, far away with him, to be part of his life.

"Do not run away from me, Kate. I apologize for last night," he said. " 'Twas wrong not to tell you I would be leaving tonight."

Anger, love, and fear shot through her heart, her soul, more painful than anything she'd ever known. "Do you think I care about that anymore? Do you think I care for you at all, now that I know what you are?"

"I have told you nothing but the truth about myself. I have held back little of my past."

"I don't care about your past. Not now. I don't

care about your future, either. Just get out of my house."

He came toward her, his head shaking, a smile on his face. She wanted to rush into his arms, she wanted him to hold her and tell her he wasn't a murderer, but she wouldn't believe it. Not now.

She couldn't let him touch her, couldn't look into his eyes and fall back under his spell. She had to get away.

She rushed past him, out of her bedroom, down the stairs, and stopped when she reached the kitchen. She stood at the counter, staring down at the cold, white, empty kitchen sink.

Behind her she heard the swing of the kitchen door, the slow, heavy step of his boots on the hardwood floor.

Suddenly, strong, powerful hands pulled her back against a chest as hard as granite. Fingers clutched at her arms, refusing to let her go.

"Have I hurt you so greatly that you cannot look at me? Have I wronged you so much that you would send me away without a smile, a kiss?" His chest rose and fell heavily against her back. "Not even a farewell?"

Warm lips kissed her jaw, the hollow beneath her ear, and her head fell back against his powerful body.

"Do you not love me, Katie?"

The damnable knot that he could so easily cause to form in her throat settled there again. *Of course* she loved him. If she didn't, she wouldn't be hurting so badly right now.

Still, she shook her head. "I don't love you," she said, turning slowly in his arms, daring to look into his eyes before she pushed away from his chest and moved a safe distance across the room.

She took a deep breath. "How could I love you when you've killed two people since you've been here?"

His eyes narrowed, and then he laughed. "I have killed no one . . . recently."

"There's evidence that says you have."

"And what, pray tell, is this evidence?"

"Cowboy clothes."

"I do not know the word 'cowboy.' "

Kate hated hearing the sound of mock innocence in his voice. "*Cowboy*," she said emphatically. "A man dressed in boots like you're wearing. A man in jeans."

A grin teased his lips. Damn it, she didn't want him making light of the moment. Every time he did that he pulled her deeper into his hypnotic spell.

He looked down at his boots, at his jeans, then shrugged. "The haberdasher explained to me that this clothing is not customary in St. Augustine. I did not, however, choose to purchase the short pants and the odd-looking white shoes he thought would be the better choice. The fact that I'm wearing cowboy clothes seems to be flimsy evidence. Is there something else that makes you think I've murdered two men here in your city?"

"Gold doubloons."

"I have many."

"There was one in the dead coin dealer's hand."

His devilish laughter rang out again. "He was a coin dealer, madam, or have you forgotten?"

"Of course I haven't forgotten. But it's that gold doubloon that's making the police look for a pirate. For you."

"I've been branded before with even less evidence. But my dearest Kate, I would have thought you'd give me the benefit of the doubt, especially after last night."

"Don't make light of last night."

" 'Tis not me who has forgotten what we shared. 'Tis you who calls me a murderer, even though you have no proof."

"I do have proof."

His eyebrow raised. "What? Another gold doubloon? These articles of clothing I wear? I beg you to tell me, Kate. What other proof do you have?"

"The things you left here."

"I left many things behind. A jewel-hilted cutlass that saw me through many battles. A pistol. The dagger you once used to hold me at bay. I also left behind the coat you're wearing . . . and my heart. I will not need that if I leave alone."

She turned away, unable to look into the dark fathoms of his eyes. "What about the other things? The things you hid? Weren't you afraid I'd find them?"

"My treasures?" He laughed. "I have riches hidden on my ship, on my island, and in ports too numerous to mention. I'm not the least concerned that you found a few dispensable trinkets. What do jewels or other riches mean to me if I can't have you?"

She spun around. "How can you be so cold?"

"I might ask you the same question."

"You're a murderer."

"Ah, that again. You have evidence, weak as it is, but you have not asked me where I was at the time of the murders."

"You weren't with me. I know that much."

"I read in your books that a person in this country is innocent until proven guilty. That does not seem to apply to me, though, does it?"

"I *want* you to be innocent. With all my heart I want to believe you."

"Perhaps you should, but I have no alibi that can effectively ease the ache in your heart. I cannot tell you where I was when the first person was murdered, I'm not even sure where I was when the second murder occurred, but I did spend some time last night in one of your public houses, trying to get drunk."

"Why?"

"So I could forget about you. Alas, I was not successful. No amount of rum will ever make me forget you. That is all that matters, Kate. Evidence be damned! My love for you should be enough to erase anything that attempts to come between us. Now, lest you have forgotten why I came here tonight, I will tell you again: I wish to take you back with me."

"I'm not going anywhere with you," she said, forcing out each word. "Not now. Not ever. I've made

myself accept the fact that you had to kill people in your own time, but you have no excuse for it now."

"I offer no excuses, madam. Perhaps if you would stop haranguing me like a sea witch—"

Tears came. She couldn't help it, not with the tone of his voice, that wouldn't allow her to keep her anger at full force. "I'm not a sea hag," she said amidst the flow of tears.

" 'Tis not a sea hag I have called you, Katie," he said too tenderly. " 'Tis a sea *witch* you are. You have *bewitched* me, and not even your accusations will dampen my feelings for you."

He tilted her chin and wiped away her tears with the rough pad of his thumb. He leaned over and kissed her lightly, his lips soft, tasting rich and wonderful.

"Go with me, Kate. I cannot bear to go back to my time without you."

"I can't."

She took a deep, ragged breath, trying to collect her wavering emotions, and walked out of the kitchen, going to the living room and curling up in the storyteller's chair with Raggedy Andy.

"I will ask you just once more: Go with me?" He stood in front of her with his feet spread wide, as if he were already standing on his ship, sailing back to the eighteenth century. Looking up through damp lashes, she could see his arms crossed over his chest, his glorious hair hanging over his shoulders so it brushed his folded arms.

Gold rings gleamed in his ears, and a scar slashed across his face.

He was the most handsome man she'd ever seen.

He was the most tender man ever to touch her.

He was a pirate.

She loved him.

And he'd offered no excuses to prove his innocence.

He remained steadfast, never once changing his stance, looking all powerful as he stood above her.

Swallowing the anguish she felt inside, she looked down at the floor and whispered, "I can't go with you."

Kate watched one boot move, then the other, and finally heard him pace across the living room. She looked up just long enough to see him standing with his back to the screen door. His eyes burned deep into hers, and she quickly looked back down at the floor.

"Have you forgotten what we shared last night?" he asked.

That was something she'd never forget. "No," she whispered.

" 'Tis impossible for me to believe you. 'Tis easier for me to believe that what we shared was love on my part, and a sham on yours."

"That's not true."

"Nay? Let me refresh your memory, madam. You came to the ship and begged me to make love to you. When I asked, like a gentleman, if that's what you truly wanted, you told me, quite frankly, I might add—that *that* was the only reason you'd come."

"I didn't know what else to say."

"That's obvious, madam. You know quite well when to use your tongue and when to hold it. Too many times I have professed my feelings for you only to be met with silence or indifference. Now you accuse me of murder!"

He laughed, not devilishly this time, but with anger and scorn.

The screen door opened with a creak. "Do not feel that you have accused me wrongly, Kate. As I have told you before, I *am* a murderer. I have killed many, and when I return to my own time, I will, no doubt, resume that activity and continue it until I find Thomas Low. I am also a thief. Unfortunately, I have not been able to steal the only thing in this century that I have wanted. That, madam, is your heart. I'm afraid you keep it locked up far too tight."

A tear spilled down Kate's cheek when the screen door screeched shut. She didn't bother to wipe it away, not when it was being joined by even more tears. Instead, she pulled Raggedy Andy into her arms and looked toward the door and the darkness outside.

"I love you, Morgan," she whispered. "I love you."

Chapter 18

*And after all, what is a lie? 'Tis but
The truth in masquerade.*

LORD BYRON, DON JUAN

The knock came unexpectedly, waking Kate from storm-tossed dreams of a sailing vessel fighting high waves, thunder, and lightning, while two men battled on her deck, fury etched deeply in their faces as swords slashed with deadly intent.

Again she heard the knock, and she stumbled from the storyteller's chair, with a whispered prayer flowing from her lips: "Please let it be Morgan." They needed to talk—or maybe she just needed to listen. In spite of the evidence, she found it impossible that the man she loved could have killed so brutally.

She wanted to show him the wallet and ring. She wanted him to stare at them and look puzzled. She wanted him to say he didn't know where they'd come from.

But they'd been in his room, hidden away in one of his socks. He'd said they were nothing more than dispensable trinkets—things he could replace quite easily with just another slash of his blade.

She put her fingers to her lips to stop their trembling, then opened the door.

"Good evening."

Gordon Lancaster stood on the other side of the screen door with his hands tucked into the pockets of khakis. He wore a dark blue summer-weight blazer, a pale blue shirt, and a smile that conjured visions of Count Dracula—charm and sophistication masking an evil mind.

She shivered. "What are you doing here?"

"We were invited to dinner with your friends. Had you forgotten?"

"No, I hadn't forgotten, but I never accepted."

He continued to smile. "I hope you will. We could talk about our common interest in sailing ships, maybe old clothing," he said, his laughing eyes trailing up and down the velvet coat she wore. "Or we could merely talk about each other."

"We could also talk about how you found my house. I didn't tell you where I lived, and I doubt Nikki did, either."

His smile turned to a much wider grin. "I met your aunt a few days ago. In fact, we had dinner together just the other night—even your daughter joined us."

Now she remembered why his name had sounded so familiar when they'd met in the alley. Mr. Lancaster—Gordon—was Evalena's A-1 husband material.

"Your aunt told me a lot about you, and I was quite pleased to learn that Evalena's cherished niece was the same beautiful woman I'd bumped into on the street."

"My aunt talks too much sometimes." The grandfather clock struck and Kate turned to look at the time. Eight o'clock. "It's late," she said, facing Gordon again. "My daughter's asleep, and I honestly don't feel like going out."

"I understand completely. However, I am in town for only a few brief days. Perhaps I could keep you company here this evening? There's no need to entertain me. We could simply sit out here on your porch and talk."

"Not this evening."

He put his hand on the door. "Just an hour or two. That's all."

The phone rang, its piercing chime skittering through Kate's nerves. "Excuse me a moment."

She rushed to the phone. "Hello."

Nikki was on the other end, her voice scolding as she asked what Kate was doing at home when they had plans for an evening out.

"I couldn't shuttle Case off to Evalena's tonight. She needed me, and besides, I told you I didn't want to go out."

While Kate listened to Nikki's lecture, she caught sight of Gordon leaning against the newel post, his penetrating eyes studying her through the screen. "Gordon Lancaster is here," she told Nikki. And it didn't look like he planned to leave. "Why don't you and Jack pick up some Chinese and come over?" she asked, quickly coming up with a way not to be alone with the man.

There was happiness in Nikki's voice as she gave Kate a definite yes.

"Okay. I'll see you soon."

Kate put down the phone and ran her fingers through her hair as she walked toward the door. Pushing open the screen, she stepped onto the porch. "Nikki and Jack are coming here, instead of us joining them."

His eyes narrowed slightly, but a smile quickly replaced his frown. "It will be delightful to see your sister-in-law again."

"I hope you like Chinese."

He nodded.

"I need to change," she said, remembering that she was still bundled up in Morgan's coat. "Why don't you make yourself comfortable out here on the porch? I'll be just a few minutes."

She didn't wait for an answer. Instead, she attempted to walk casually back into the house, feeling the glare of his eyes on her back with each step she took.

Rushing up the stairs, she peeked in on Casey and tucked the sheet and blanket that had drifted down to her waist back around her shoulders. She brushed a curl away from Casey's lips and planted a kiss on her cheek.

She wanted to crawl in bed with Casey and sleep just as soundlessly, anything to block the memories of the days she'd spent with Morgan, to interrupt the persistent need she had to see him again, in spite of everything.

Put him out of your mind, she told herself. *Forget him.*

Wandering to her room, she removed Morgan's coat and draped it over the back of a chair. Suddenly she saw him sitting there, the velvet stretched across his muscular arms and chest, his hair cascading over his shoulders, his devilish smile watching her as she removed her shorts and blouse, then went to the closet and pulled a flowered sundress from a hanger and slipped it over her head.

His make-believe smile turned to a look of need, of desire, and her body ached, wanting so much to be held by him again.

But he was only a dream this time. A dream that would fade eventually—if she could find the nerve to push him from her heart.

She went downstairs again. She was almost to the front door when she heard the familiar squeak of a floorboard. Gordon Lancaster was standing near the back door when she entered the kitchen, his hand braced against the wall next to her key rack, staring out into the yard.

"I heard a noise," he said, turning slowly. "I had the oddest feeling that someone had sneaked into your home, but I saw no one inside or out. I hope I haven't frightened you."

She shook her head, but he had frightened her. His very presence made her uncomfortable, but she didn't know why, and she wished he were still outside on the porch, wished Nikki and Jack would arrive shortly.

She peered out the door, hoping the noise Gordon had heard had been Morgan stalking around outside, but all she saw was darkness. She latched the door and turned to Gordon. "Would you like a drink?"

"Brandy, if you have it."

"I have wine."

"That will do, thank you."

He wandered about the kitchen, just as Morgan had done that first time, touching the refrigerator, the stove.

"You have a lovely home," he said, when she handed him the glass of wine.

"Thank you." She leaned against the kitchen counter and sipped her Chablis. When she heard footsteps on the front porch, she sighed with relief.

"Nikki and Jack are here."

"Good. The more, the merrier."

She hadn't seen Jack in several weeks, and he hugged her when they entered the door. His sandy-colored hair was windblown—but it looked that way even when the weather was calm. He wore wire-rimmed glasses and looked far better than she ever imagined a museum curator should look. He reminded her of Indiana Jones, and he was the perfect man for Nikki: rugged, intelligent, and definitely in love.

Introductions were made, white containers of Chinese food were heaped in the middle of the kitchen table, and Kate set out plates, silverware, and wineglasses while Jack popped the cork on a better bottle of wine than the one she'd already opened.

Nikki laughed at one of Jack's jokes, Gordon sipped at his wine, and Kate tried to relax. It had been far too long since she'd sat at the kitchen table and enjoyed the company of other adults— without any children present.

"I've been to England many times," Jack said, leaning casually in his chair as he talked to Gordon. "Where exactly are you from?"

"Dover. Ever been there?"

"Once," Jack said. "I took part in an archaeological dig in the area. I wouldn't mind going back."

"It's a beautiful place," Gordon stated. "No matter where I travel, I'm always eager to return home."

Kate dipped a battered shrimp into tangy sauce and nibbled at the end while Gordon talked of his home, a magnificent estate not far from the white cliffs.

"Has it been in your family a long time?" she asked.

"Several centuries. It was a gift, for services rendered to the Crown."

"Pretty nice gift." Nikki laughed.

Gordon nodded slowly, swirling his wine before taking a sip.

"Nikki tells me you're a historian," Jack said. "Any particular era?"

"Late-seventeenth, early-eighteenth centuries. I consider myself an expert on the pirates of that period. That's why I find the ship that appeared here so interesting."

"Jack thinks it's authentic," Nikki said to Gordon. "What about you?"

"I'm not the expert that Jack is, but from the little I've seen of it, I'd venture a guess that it's close to three hundred years old, and that it's a ship called *Satan's Revenge* that disappeared in seventeen-oh-two."

"I agree," Jack said. "It's aged better than any other ship I've seen, which is a mystery. Of course, there's also the mystery of where it's been for the past few centuries."

"I wish it hadn't shown up here," Nikki said. "But unfortunately it was in the harbor a few minutes ago."

"It's still there?" Kate asked, her heart slamming hard against her chest.

"Where else would it be?" Gordon asked, a well-defined black brow raising slightly.

"Oh, I don't know." Kate laughed nervously. "I thought someone might have sneaked on board and tried sailing it away."

Nikki frowned at Kate, and she was afraid she'd said too much.

"It would be impossible for one person to sail

a warship like that all on his own," Gordon said. "It would take an entire crew, or at least two very skillful sailors."

"Kate's one of the best sailors I know," Jack said. "Think you could handle something that size without any help?"

"Of course not. I wouldn't even want to try."

Gordon refilled his glass of wine and took a sip, staring over the top of the glass at Kate. "I've heard stories that the pirate Black Heart once tried to sail *Satan's Revenge* by himself—and failed."

"Did he drown?" Nikki asked.

"No," Gordon said, "he disappeared, just like his ship. No one knows what happened."

"It shimmered," Kate said, then noticed all eyes had turned to her for an explanation. "I read an account about it. There was a prisoner on board. Thomas Low. He was thrown overboard in the storm, but he saw *Satan's Revenge* vanish in a flash of light."

"Lightning, more than likely," Nikki stated. "Things don't just disappear into thin air."

"It seems highly plausible to me," Gordon said. "I've heard many such stories of ships disappearing in the waters not far from here."

"The Bermuda Triangle?" Jack asked.

"Yes, exactly." Gordon poured himself more wine. "This story of Low's has me puzzled, though. I was under the impression he disappeared at the same time as the ship."

"No. He died at home. In Dover," Kate said.

Gordon laughed. "I assure you, he did not die

in Dover. He was an ancestor of mine. A great-uncle many times over on my mother's side. A remarkable man, by most accounts." He sipped his wine. "I can only assume the man who told that story about the ship disappearing in a flash of light must have been an impostor. I know Low's true history inside and out—and Kate, he disappeared the same time as Black Heart and *Satan's Revenge.*"

Kate's hands shook. She put her glass on the table and stuck her hands between her knees so no one could see them trembling.

Nikki reached across the table for the wine and refilled her glass. She was laughing. So was Jack. So was Gordon Lancaster. But Kate didn't find anything humorous in the ongoing discussion.

"You know," Nikki said with a grin, "a pirate's been roaming the streets lately. I even saw a pirate on that ship. Maybe it's Thomas Low. Maybe *he's* the one responsible for the murders in town."

"Highly unlikely," Gordon said. "Thomas Low was an honorable man. I would imagine if you wanted to place the blame for these killings on an eighteenth-century pirate, you should look toward Black Heart. You may not be aware of this little known fact, but Black Heart was such a vile and despicable man that he murdered his own family."

"That's impossible," Kate blurted out, just as a streak of lightning bolted across the sky and thunder shook the pictures on the walls. "He wouldn't have done something like that."

"You act as if you knew him personally," Nikki said.

"No, of course I didn't. But Joe knew everything about him."

"History books are not always full of accuracy," Gordon stated. "The truth is often stretched or misrepresented. Would you like to hear the actual facts about Black Heart?"

"No," Kate said firmly.

"I would," Nikki said. "Come on, Kate. There's a storm coming. This will be just like telling ghost stories when we were kids."

Jack refilled everyone's glasses. "Go ahead, Gordon. I'm always ready for an interesting tale."

"The story isn't pleasant, but it is the truth."

Kate drank her wine, trying to steady her jittery hands while Gordon told a tale similar to Morgan's. He painted a clear picture of the voyage to the West Indies, of hot days and balmy nights, and a party to celebrate an anniversary. And then he told of a mutiny attempt, when the sailors were drunk and didn't know what they were doing. He told a tale that Kate found impossible to believe, of Morgan despising his father, of wanting him dead so he could inherit his wealth.

"The man who would someday be known as Black Heart had captured Thomas Low and part of the crew. The rest of the men he'd pulled under his spell. From all accounts, Morgan Farrell had a certain charm about him."

"Morgan Farrell?" Nikki frowned, looking at Kate. "Isn't that the name of your friend?"

"I'm sure it's just a coincidence," Kate stammered, and even though she didn't want to hear any more of the story, she insisted that Gordon continue.

"Farrell was mad with his sudden power," he said. "He had control of the ship, he had control of Thomas Low, and he had control of his own father. 'I have taken orders from you long enough,' he said, standing before his sire, brandishing the cutlass he'd taken from Thomas Low. " 'Tis my turn to give the orders, and what I want most of all is for you to leave this ship.' "

"How was he going to do that?" Nikki asked.

Gordon grinned. "There was only one way. Overboard. Morgan Farrell was beyond reason. His mother was frightened and angry, and she slapped him, but Morgan laughed. 'Bind them together,' he shouted to the drunken sailors. 'Toss them over the side.' Thomas Low struggled in the arms of his captors. He wanted to save his passengers, but he could do nothing. He heard the Farrells begging for mercy. Suddenly . . . their cries stopped.

"That's when the child—Melody was her name—grabbed a dagger from one of the sailors and ran at her brother. She slashed at him with the knife, cutting his face. He was enraged that his own sister would do such a thing. He told her to jump. Again and again he yelled at her. She was crying, but he didn't care. 'Jump,' he said. 'Say your prayers, and jump.' And Black Heart laughed as the child disappeared over the side.

"It was at that moment that the sailors who'd turned against Low realized what had happened. Farrell had murdered his own family. They knew they couldn't trust a madman, so they turned on him. Low was freed. He was back in command, and Farrell was taken prisoner. Twenty-four lashes with the cat-'o-nine tails was the order. Eight was usually the maximum, but Low tripled it—eight lashes for each victim."

Kate pushed away from the table, refusing to hear any more. Her glass tipped, but Gordon caught it before the remnants of her drink spilled across the oak tabletop.

"Are you okay, Kate?" Nikki asked.

"It's just the heat," she said, going to the kitchen sink where the breeze blowing through the window hit her face.

Behind her she heard Nikki, Jack, and Gordon discussing the story. How could they believe such a thing? Morgan would never have killed his family. He'd loved them.

She'd seen the tears in his eyes when he'd talked of his sister. Seen them even in his sleep.

No man could cry that way if the deaths of his family had meant so little.

She looked out the window, into the dark, wondering if Morgan had gone, wondering if he was still waiting for his chance to sail away on *Satan's Revenge*.

Damn it! He couldn't go. Not until she knew the truth.

Outside she heard a noise, the rustle of bushes,

the crack of what sounded like a fallen tree limb. Next door a dog barked. Further away another dog howled.

Suddenly, Gordon stood next to her, holding out another glass of wine. "I apologize if the story upset you."

"I've just been a little on edge lately."

"Drink this. Maybe it will help."

She took the glass of wine from him. He was smiling. Out of the corner of her eye she saw Jack lean over and kiss Nikki.

Thunder rumbled again.

Lightning flashed through the sky.

And outside she saw a face.

Morgan's face.

The wineglass slipped from her hand and shattered on the floor.

Another bolt brightened the night—and the face was gone.

Nikki was beside her, an arm around her, offering her comfort.

Jack was cleaning wine and glass from the floor.

One picture after another flashed before her eyes, like an old-fashioned movie, but the scene she wanted to see—Morgan's face—didn't return.

Gordon Lancaster was staring out the window. Frowning. "It's getting late," he said. "I hope you'll forgive me if I leave."

"So soon?" Nikki asked.

"I like taking a walk at night." He looked out the window again. "I should go before the rain comes."

"Would you like a ride somewhere?" Jack asked.

Gordon shook his head. "No. No, thank you. You've been delightful company this evening, the food and wine were delicious, but now I must go."

They went to the living room door. Thunder rang out again as they were saying their good-byes.

"Mommy."

The sound of Casey's sleep-filled voice drew Kate's attention. "What is it, honey?" she asked, walking halfway up the stairs and pulling Casey into her arms.

"I couldn't sleep. The thunder's too loud."

"Don't worry about the thunder or the light-ning. I'll take care of you."

Kate joined her guests again at the door.

"Hello, Casey," Gordon said, smoothing his hand over her curls. "Remember me?"

Casey rubbed her eyes and nodded.

Gordon smiled at Casey, then stepped onto the porch. "Good night, everyone. Thank you again for the evening."

"Good night," Kate said, glad to finally see him go, glad to see him disappear when he passed the hedges and a stand of palms.

"Nice guy," Nikki said, linking her arm through Jack's. "Do you think you'll see him again?" she asked Kate.

"No. He's not my type."

Nikki shrugged, thankfully not nagging her

about the man, then leaned against the doorjamb.

From across the street, Kate could hear Perry Como playing on the hi-fi, his melodious voice filling in the quiet moments when thunder wasn't booming through the night.

"What do you say we all go across the street and see Evalena?" Nikki suggested. She grabbed hold of Jack and danced around the room. "I think we could use a little light entertainment to polish off the night."

"Why don't the two of you go?" Kate said. "I'm going to tuck Casey back into bed and try to go to sleep myself."

"I want to go to Evie's," Casey said. "Please, Mommy."

Kate smiled. How could she refuse her daughter's plea, when she herself wanted and needed a distraction? Perry Como had eased Evalena's heart and soul for over fifty years; maybe he could ease hers tonight.

Chapter 19

St. Charles Street was quiet, except for the sounds of Thomas Low's footsteps and the incessant thunder and lightning. It *was* Low's evil eyes Morgan had seen in the crowd in front of the coin dealer's shop. He hadn't imagined it, after all.

Thomas Low . . . their paths were destined to cross—but Morgan promised himself that this would be the very last time.

He crept along the edge of buildings, staying deep in the shadows as he followed his enemy. He could spring on him now and snap his neck, but killing Low out in the open was foolish. Already he was accused of murder. When Low died, Morgan would cover his tracks so no evidence would point his way.

Low stopped in front of a window, smoothed his hand over his hair, then turned. His pearly white grin shone in the light of a street lamp. His dark, depraved eyes stared directly at Morgan's hiding place.

"She's a beautiful woman," Low said, his smile widening. "But it's the child who interests me most. So much like Melody."

Low laughed, and Morgan's anger erupted. He ran across the street and down a narrow alleyway, chasing after Low. He wanted to put his hands around the murderer's throat. He wanted to squeeze the life out of him, then clap him in chains and let his body rot in a public place.

But Low was fast. Too fast. He pushed on a stack of crates and sent them careening down into the narrow road. Morgan hurdled over one and dodged another. Low turned to the left at the end of the alley and continued to run, zigzagging between buildings, up dark passageways, through small backyard gardens, with Morgan not far behind.

He couldn't lose sight of him. He couldn't.

Low jumped a fence, ran across a street, and still Morgan followed. Up one street, down another, right into the path of an oncoming car.

The driver slammed on his brakes and Low made it to safety, but the wheels screeched, and the car slid out of control on the damp pavement.

Morgan stumbled and fell.

The back end of the car spun around, heading straight toward him.

He lurched forward, getting out of the vehicle's way just as it hit a lamppost.

And then Morgan ran again.

But it was no use. Thomas Low had disappeared.

Standing in the middle of a grassy park, with thunder and lightning shattering the night, he cursed his foolishness. He should have killed Low when he'd had the chance. Damn the evidence against him!

He looked up and down the street one more time, wanting to find Low, but it wasn't vengeance that screamed through his thoughts, it was Kate, and Casey, and protecting the two people he loved more than anything on earth.

Again he ran, this time toward Kate. He'd hold her, shake her, and make her listen. He had not murdered the cowboy or the coin dealer, but he had a good idea who had. Thomas Low—the man who'd laughed with Kate this evening, but probably had more than merrymaking on his mind.

He had to protect her from that bastard. But he didn't want to frighten her, didn't want her to think that her life and Casey's were at risk.

He had to keep Thomas Low's presence a secret—for now.

Kate's house was empty when he arrived. Too damn empty.

The back door was latched, but the front door was open. He searched every room, every hiding place, but Kate and Casey were gone.

Lights shone brightly through the windows at

Evalena's. A man's soothing voice oozed through
the screens, and silhouettes danced about the
room—a child, an older woman, and the beautiful
lady he loved.

He smiled, and took a deep, thankful breath.
They were safe.

Morgan kept a watchful eye on the house across
the street as he checked doors and windows, making sure Kate's home was locked and secure.
When everything was just as he wanted it, he
splashed cold water on his face, dragged a razor
across his cheeks, and tried to look like the gentleman he longed to be again. Kate deserved a
gentleman, not a pirate.

He snapped a white gardenia from one of the
bushes before walking across the street and up the
steps to Evalena's house. He listened to the giggling inside, to the sweet strains of music, and
then he knocked.

He'd expected Evalena to answer the door, but
it was Kate, sweet, beautiful Kate, who stood before him, looking more delicate, more perfect than
the flower he held.

"Good evening."

"What are you doing here?"

"Ah, Katie." He tucked the flower into her hair
before she could protest. " 'Tis good to hear your
voice again."

"Go away."

"I cannot. I will not."

Behind Kate, Morgan saw Evalena shuffling toward the door. "Mr. Farrell! How wonderful it is to see you. Come in. Come in."

Winking at Kate's frown, he stepped past her and into a room as colorful and welcoming as Evalena herself.

"Morgan!"

Casey ran toward him and he swept her into his arms, swallowing back the emotion that was filling him now. How could he ever have thought he could leave?

"You came back," Casey said.

"And I plan to stay."

"Forever?"

Morgan looked at Kate, at the way she was biting her lower lip, at the redness in her cheeks. "Forever, Casey. 'Twould take more than a hurricane to pull me away from any of you."

"Well," Evalena bubbled, "this calls for a celebration."

Kate didn't believe him. *Forever?* How could he say that to Casey when he knew it wasn't true? It had to be a ploy, some way of charming all of them. He was going to leave. She knew it, and she was going to hurt like hell when he left again.

"Do you like Perry Como?" Evalena asked.

He nodded at Evalena, as if he knew who Perry Como was, then he turned back to Kate. He didn't move toward her, he didn't smile, he just stared at her with those mesmerizing blue eyes of his that she wished would look somewhere else.

"Do you dance, Mr. Farrell?"

"It has been many years. I fear someone would have to teach me."

"Me! Me!" Casey chirped.

Kate tore her gaze from Morgan and looked at Evalena. "You know, Evie, I'm awfully tired. I think I'll go home and let you entertain Mr. Farrell."

"No, Mommy." Casey grabbed her arm and pulled her to the center of the room. "You can't leave. We've got to teach him to dance."

"That's right, Katharine. You can't leave."

She felt trapped.

Evalena bustled over to the old hi-fi, lifted the needle, and set it on the shiny black album spinning around and around. The opening strains of "It's Impossible" filled the room.

"Why don't you do the honors, Katharine?" Evalena suggested. "You're such a good dancer. I just know you can teach Mr. Farrell in no time flat."

"Oh, no. I think I'll sit this one out. Probably the next ones, too."

Kate sat in the S-shaped loveseat and watched Evalena put Morgan's right hand around her more than ample waist, then take his left hand lightly in hers.

"Casey, sweetie, would you start the song again?"

Casey ran to the hi-fi, very carefully lifted the needle, and set it perfectly on the record.

"All right, Mr. Farrell," Evalena said. "Follow me."

Kate watched the sparkle in Morgan's eyes as his big feet followed the path of Evalena's scruffy slippers. A few times he came within inches of stepping on her toes, but when he did, he merely laughed and tried again.

" 'Tis not at all like the minuet," Morgan said.

"Oh, Mr. Farrell, you do say the funniest things," Evalena quipped. "Of course it's not like the minuet. Men and women are allowed to touch in this dance. In fact, it's the number one ingredient. Why, dancing without touching would be like a wedding cake without the frosting—sweet, but not nearly sweet enough."

"I want a turn. I want a turn," Casey cried out, jumping up and down.

"Just you hold on a moment, sweetie. It might take one or two whole songs before Mr. Farrell has the hang of this."

It looked to Kate like he'd gotten the hang of it and mastered it, too. And Evalena was soaking up his charm. She laughed with more enthusiasm than normal, her eyes positively beamed, and her cheeks continually blushed as Morgan plied her ears with one gentlemanly comment after another.

And then it was Casey's turn. Too small to be held the way he'd held Evalena, Morgan swept the little girl up in his arms and danced her about the room like a delicate porcelain doll.

Casey's pink cheeks brightened with a glow Kate hadn't seen since Joe was alive. She giggled, clutching her hands behind Morgan's neck.

Morgan beamed, too. His eyes never left Casey's. His smile never dimmed.

If she'd believed even one word of Gordon Lancaster's story, she would have plucked Casey from Morgan's arms and forced him out of the house. If she'd honestly believed he was a murderer in the present, she would be on the phone to Nikki right now—even if it meant interrupting her night with Jack.

But at least an hour ago, sometime during Gordon Lancaster's story, she'd come to the conclusion that she didn't believe any of it. Her heart told her to believe in Morgan, and she'd decided to listen. Still, she sure as hell wished she had something to refute all the evidence against him.

"Dance with my mommy, now," Casey said, and coming out of half a daze, Kate saw two tiny bare feet, two big black boots, and small fingers tucked into a large, powerful hand.

"May I have the honor of the next dance?" Morgan asked.

Kate shook her head. She felt like a temperamental child, but she was afraid to touch him, afraid to want him. Most of all, she was afraid to lose him.

"Come on, Mommy. It's fun."

All she saw when she looked from Casey to Morgan were a pair of intense hypnotic blue eyes. "One dance, Katie. 'Tis all I ask."

She shoved up from the loveseat, avoiding his touch, and stood in the very center of the room. She looked at Evalena standing by the hi-fi. "Why don't you play 'Hot Diggity, Dog Ziggity'?" Kate asked. "You know, something fast. I can teach Mr. Farrell a totally different way to dance."

Evalena frowned. "Nonsense, Katharine. 'Temptation' is what the two of you need to hear right now."

Morgan smiled, his eyes glinting as he took hold of Kate's right hand and placed his left around her waist.

She slapped it away. "The music hasn't begun yet."

"You are wrong, madam," he said, his fingers inching around her side. " 'Tis a beautiful melody I hear whenever you are near."

"Like hell!"

He pulled her closer. "I believe, madam, the customary thing is for you to put one hand on my shoulder as we dance. I believe it's also traditional for you to smile at the man who holds you."

"I don't go along with the traditional anything, Mr. Farrell."

Evalena bustled across the room, bumping Kate's bottom with her own, knocking her easily off balance and into Morgan's chest.

"I taught you to be polite, Katharine. As long as Mr. Farrell's in my home, you'll show him the utmost courtesy. And, as you know full well, dancing is something we do in this house, and when we're fortunate enough to have a man to dance with, we move in close and rub bellies. Am I making myself clear, Katharine?"

Kate glared at her aunt.

"Good. Now, I'm going to start the music. I'll make it good and loud, too, so it will drown out all that nastiness you keep spouting."

Evalena bustled over to the hi-fi and put it on the outermost edge of the record. Amid the scratches, Kate heard Evalena scuffle away, taking Casey's hand in hers. "Come on, sweetie. Why don't the two of us go into the kitchen and test the sweetness of my latest batch of lovebirds?"

"But we already tried them," Casey moaned.

"The second time's usually the best. Trust me on this."

Evalena and Casey disappeared much too quickly.

The music clashed against the walls, so loud Kate feared the neighbors might call the police. Then, Perry's low tones echoed around her as Morgan inclined his head and hummed along with the words he'd heard only once before, but seemed to know already. He nibbled softly on her ear.

"You are temptation," he sang in that lilting tenor that made her stomach quiver. Her heart started to dance with the music, and her legs felt as if they'd been made of frosting, and were melting from Morgan's warmth.

Oh, God! What was he doing to her? She had to back away from his seductive touch before she lost all control.

His power was much too strong, though. She couldn't break away. Still he continued to sing, his words not exactly following Perry's, but Kate couldn't care less at the moment. The words were aimed at her soul, words meant to mesmerize her thoroughly.

"I give you my heart," he sang, his breath warm against her ear. "Take it, Katie. Take it, and tell me we'll never part."

Tell him we'll never part? Ha!

She pushed out of his arms and backed away.

Into a wall.

Morgan approached, slowly, methodically, and his mouth slanted over hers.

She was lost.

Thomas Low stood at the window, anger building inside as he watched the dance and the kiss. He crushed a gardenia in his tightening fist, wishing it was the woman's throat.

The bitch simpers at his feet. Did she not believe the evidence I placed so carefully? Did she not hear my words about his treachery?

Look at the way he fondles her hair, strokes her cheek, so easily pulling her into his power.

Damn him for taking what should be mine!

Damn him for loving and being loved in return!

His fingers relaxed around the gardenia. He opened his fist and gazed at what had once been a thing of beauty and now lay lifeless in his palm.

He saw the woman's face. The child's. Beautiful flowers, who could die just as easily as the gardenia.

A smile crossed his face.

Turning her against you, Black Heart, could never be as pleasant as taking her from you.

I will enjoy watching you suffer when the woman and child are gone—for good.

Kate stomped on the toe of Morgan's boot as if that one small action could tear him away from her lips. Kissing her was all he'd thought of since she'd left him on the ship. 'Twould not be easy for her to push him away.

She struggled, but still he feasted on the sweetness of her mouth. Her tongue danced with his in spite of the fight the rest of her body was waging.

And then he felt her hand skimming over his chest, across his belt, inching ever closer to the part of him that had ached with need since she'd left him yesterday morn.

Softly she cupped him, her fingers slipping about his balls as the rest of him stretched and strained from her caress.

She tightened her hold.

Tighter.

Tighter.

"Let go of me," she cursed against his lips, "or I will twist the living daylights out of those jewels you carry so proudly between your legs."

"Damn it, Kate!" he groaned, backing an arm's length away. Still her clenched fingers remained steadfast.

"Don't 'damn it' me, Morgan Farrell. What the hell are you doing here, and what were you doing hiding in my backyard earlier tonight?"

Across the parlor, Morgan could hear the swing of the kitchen door, heard the shuffle of Evalena's slippers, heard a gasp and then a giggle.

"It appears you two are doing just fine without me. Why don't you pretend I never popped my head out of the kitchen?"

The door closed again, and all was silent except for the singer Evalena had spoken of so fondly, and the heavy, angered breathing of the woman still clutching what she thought of as his jewels.

He attempted to grin, but her fingers tightened again. Not enough to do any permanent damage, but enough to let him know that she considered herself in charge at the moment.

"I'm waiting for an answer."

"In my agony, dearest Kate, I believe I forgot the question."

"What the hell are you doing here?"

" 'Twas an urgent need to see you, to talk to you, to make you see that I am not the murderer you think I am, although now I'm beginning to wonder at the sanity of my action."

"I already changed my mind about you being a murderer—in this century, that is. Call me crazy, because I've got all this evidence against you, but I just can't believe it."

" 'Tis good to hear, madam, but could we continue this discussion without you holding that part of my anatomy I value so richly?"

He received his answer with another light squeeze that made his shaft grow ever harder against the fabric of his pants. Damn her!

"You were saying, madam?"

"I'm going to say this very plainly, Mr. Farrell. I may not believe you're a murderer, but I think you're mean and awful. I don't like being hurt, and you've had a field day plucking up my emotions, tossing them high in the clouds, and then letting them smash down to the ground."

"Could you speak plain English, madam?"

"All right. This is as plain as it gets. I will not let you kiss me again and then walk away from me."

"Why?"

"It hurts, damn it!"

"Why?"

"Because . . . because . . . because it does!"

She jerked her hand away, and for the first time he could see the tears in her eyes.

She ran to the kitchen. "Come on, Case, we're going home."

"Is Morgan going, too?"

"No. Maybe. I don't know."

Morgan stood in silence as he watched Kate and Casey rush across the street. He saw Kate try the door which he'd locked when he'd left the house, then reach under the doormat, pull out a key, and let herself and Casey inside.

What a fool he was to let her leave him yet again.

"My goodness. Did something go wrong? A lover's quarrel, perhaps?" Evalena asked, peeking through the kitchen door.

"Nay. It has been a long week—a very long day, and Kate felt the need to sleep." He feigned a yawn. "I myself am tired, so if you'll pardon me, madam, I will take my leave."

Morgan backed away, offering Evalena a short, gentlemanly bow, then walked from the house.

He stood on the porch for the longest time, watching the light go on in Casey's room, then go off again. Moments later he saw Kate step out on her balcony and gaze off toward the ocean. He could almost hear her heart beating, the softness of her sigh. He imagined a tear sliding down her cheek, and he wanted to kiss it away. He wanted to hold her and comfort her—for the rest of his life.

He followed Kate's gaze toward the sea. Thunder and lightning were moving in, inching ever closer, sounding much like the storm that had come out of nowhere a week ago—shortly before he was swept into Kate's loving arms.

Wind beat against him while he looked at the clouds overhead, rolling and pitching like breaking waves. If he wanted to go home, this would be the night to do it.

Looking across the rooftops toward *Satan's Revenge*, he thought of the century he'd left behind, thought of what waited for him there.

Nothing.

He looked at Kate again, at her honey-colored hair that glowed with each flash of lightning. The warmth he'd known since meeting her burned deep within his chest, and brought peace and contentment to his soul.

He smiled as he looked at the woman he loved, and he knew where he wanted to go.

To Kate—for she was his home.

Chapter 20

And to his eye
There was but one beloved face on earth,
And that was shining on him.

LORD BYRON, THE DREAM

Kate sat on the darkened balcony outside her bedroom, the perfect vantage point for looking at Morgan, who stood tall and majestic on Evalena's porch. She watched him gaze off in the direction of his ship, toward her house, then back to the ship again, and part of her wished he'd just go away. She didn't believe in forever. He might have said he would never leave again, but she found that too hard to believe. There were too many reasons for him to run away.

Two of those reasons rested in her hands—a dead man's wallet, and a dead man's wedding ring. They saddened her, made her want to cry for the men who had died, for the doubt that still ripped away at her mind.

Had he murdered those men?

She couldn't trust her heart to answer that question. Her heart had told him earlier that she believed his innocence; her mind continually thought of the evidence that proved his guilt.

He looked again toward the east. The wind was strong, and it beat against his back, pushing him toward the sea, toward his ship. But he didn't go. Instead, he turned slowly, walked across the street, halfway up her walk, across her lawn, and leaned casually against a palm tree.

His long hair whipped about his face. His eyes almost sizzled as he looked at her.

" 'Tis not a good night for a man to stand outside."

Kate's gaze nonchalantly followed the movement of a palm frond as it flew down the street, and the rapid spinning of the weathervane on top of Evalena's roof, then finally settled on Morgan's mesmerizing eyes.

It was obvious that all he wanted was one more night of passion, one more night of lust that Kate could easily give him, because she had absolutely no control of her emotions when he was around. She only wished she could forget all her doubts and just enjoy the night—for surely it would be the last they'd ever share.

Tomorrow she could worry about all the rights and wrongs of her actions. Tomorrow she could suffer over losing him and nurse her broken heart.

She put the wallet and ring into her pocket and leaned close to the edge of the balcony. "No, I suppose it isn't a good night to be outside." She looked across the street at the lights still on in her aunt's house. "I'm sure Evalena would lend you a couch."

" 'Tis your bed I prefer."

Heat rushed to her cheeks.

"Casey's home."

"She'll be asleep soon. I promise to be quiet."

"I'm not interested in another one-night stand."

"Neither am I." He pushed away from the tree, his devilish grin serious now. "We must talk."

"I'm listening."

"Let me in, Kate. Either we speak in private, or I shout out for Evalena, Casey, and all your neighbors to hear."

He left her no choice. "The door's unlocked."

"You should keep them locked, Kate. 'Tis not safe in this town."

"The only person I have to fear is you. You can either come up or go away—it doesn't matter."

A bolt of lightning lit up the sky as well as the grin on Morgan's face when he moved toward the house.

She heard the heavy sound of his boots on the porch, on the stairs, in the hallway outside her room. He moved slowly across the hardwood floor, as if he needed time to think—or to plot his seduction.

Meeting him downstairs would have been the smart thing to do, but her intelligence was losing a battle with her raging desire. On top of that, her legs refused to move.

A high-backed wicker chair angled toward her rocker. Morgan sat, stretching his long legs across the deck until they nearly touched her toes.

He belonged there, sitting at her side every morning drinking orange juice and coffee, reading the paper dressed in only his boxers.

He didn't belong to the past anymore. Didn't he realize that?

"What do you want to talk about?" she asked.

"You. Your husband. Your future."

"Can you be a little more specific?"

"I need to know how deeply you loved your husband. If you love him still."

She was silent a moment, remembering that day nearly twenty years ago when Joe had invited her outside to play ball. She remembered all the good times. She smiled softly when she looked at Morgan.

"I'll always love him," she said. "I fell in love with Joe the moment we met. I was only eight, but right then and there I made up my mind to marry him. I never wanted anyone else."

" 'Tis a long time to love one man."

"It wasn't nearly long enough."

"Is it your wish never to love again?"

She looked away from his eyes, turning to see the lights going out at Evalena's.

"For the longest time I tried to live on memories—not just the good times, but the bad times, too. I thought I could keep him with me that way, that memories of what we'd shared would be enough. I was afraid if I allowed someone else into my life, they'd make me forget all about Joe." She stole a glance at Morgan. "I can't live on memories any longer."

"Then you would consider marrying again?"

"I don't know. Maybe if I was madly in love."

"Are you in love with anyone now?"

She shook her head. "No."

He stood, and walked across the balcony until he disappeared behind her chair. He touched her hair, sweeping it away from her neck, and a shock as powerful as the lightning streaking across the sky skittered through her insides. His fingers curled around her shoulders. His breath was warm against her ear.

"You lie, madam," he whispered. "Your body betrays you."

"What makes you think you know so much about me?"

"Because you are as much a part of me as I am of you. Because even when we are separated, I feel your heart beating with mine."

Kate laughed nervously. "Well, good. When you're back in seventeen-oh-two maybe you'll know how light my heart beats because it's not burdened by so much worry."

"What do you worry about?"

She pulled away from his touch, from the warmth of his voice, the heat of his body. "What does it matter? You'll be leaving soon."

He followed her through the bedroom, trapping

her in his arms before she reached the door. In spite of the control she heard in his voice, she felt the heavy beat of his heart against her back.

"I cannot go," he whispered in the dark. " 'Tis impossible for me to leave when my heart is here with you."

"You say that now, but how long will it be before you change your mind? Have you forgotten Thomas Low? What about that damned vengeance that's so important to you?"

He hesitated a moment, as if there were something he had to tell her, and then he smiled. "You are more important than Thomas Low or vengeance."

If only she could believe that.

Her heart told her he was a good man, an honest man. Unfortunately, her brain continued to remind her that he'd been a pirate, a thief, a cutthroat, and heaven only knows what else in his own time.

If only the doubts she had about him could fly away on the wind raging outside.

She tried to pull out of his arms, but he held her far too tightly.

Turning in his embrace, she took a deep breath and said, "Tell me the truth, Morgan, and please don't make light of this any longer. Did you kill the coin dealer and the man by the ship?"

She could see the tension in his jaw. "Must we go through this yet again?"

"I have to know."

"Do you trust me so little?"

She could neither nod nor shake her head because she had no answer.

The warmth in his eyes turned cold. Suddenly he let her go, brushing past her as he stomped heavily from the bedroom and down the stairs. She waited for the slam of the door, the sound of his boots on the porch and walk.

Instead, she heard only thunder.

Her fingers trailed lightly over the banister as she walked down the stairs. Morgan was sitting in the storyteller's chair, his angry gaze focused on her every move.

"Ask your questions, Kate," he said much too coldly. "I will answer truthfully. 'Tis up to you, of course, to decide whether or not you wish to believe me. When we are through, I will ask you one question. I will expect the same honesty."

She paced the dimly lit room, sweeping a tiny toy truck up from the floor. She spun the wheels and watched them turn around and around. Right now, she couldn't look into his eyes.

"The other night, when you saw *Satan's Revenge* on television, where did you go?"

"To the ship, madam," he answered brusquely. "Going home 'twas the only thing on my mind."

"Oh," she said softly, then stole a glance at his eyes. She smiled weakly. "Casey and I weren't on your mind at all?"

"That question is irrelevant at the moment, Kate."

"You're right," she said. "Sorry." She took a deep breath and continued her interrogation, realizing she sounded more like Nikki than herself. "Okay, you went to your ship but something kept you from sailing away. Since you had nowhere else to go, you came back here. But you didn't do that until late the next afternoon. You weren't on the ship the whole time. What *did* you do?"

"I roamed your fair city. There was much I wanted to see, much I wanted to learn. Unfortunately, I did not find many people interested in conversing with a man attired as a pirate."

"No one?"

"Only the haberdasher who sold me the clothes I wear now. He gladly took one gold doubloon in payment—an exorbitant price, I assure you—then suggested I see a coin dealer before I attempt any further purchases."

She dropped the tiny truck she'd been playing with into a toy basket and continued her steady back-and-forth march across the room.

"So you went to see the coin dealer next?"

"No, madam, I returned to you."

"Why?"

One dark eyebrow rose, and she half expected him to tell her that wasn't a relevant question. But it was, damn it!

"As much as the city intrigued me," he said, "it was you I longed to see."

She stopped her pacing, remembering the stories he'd told the children, the way he'd sung so beautifully, the way he'd made her headache go away. She looked up from the floor and smiled at Morgan.

"Did I ever tell you I was glad to see you?"

"No, madam. You did not. If you will recall, that is why I left again. I was angry, and quite tired of having to prove myself to you. I needed to get away and had nowhere else to go. That is why I went to see the coin dealer, and that is why you now think I'm a bloody murderer."

"I have more reason than that."

"As you said earlier tonight. My clothes. The gold doubloon."

Kate put her hand in her pocket and pulled out the wallet and wedding ring. "I found these in your room. They belong to the cowboy."

Morgan stared at her hands as she opened the wallet to show him the face of a man not yet sixty, a man with a wife, three grown children, and five grandchildren. "Did you kill him?"

"No."

He rose from the chair and went to the window, looking out at the rain that had finally started to fall. "I would imagine that trusting me is difficult, considering what I have done in the past. But I would have you know that until my family was killed, I never entertained the notion of taking another life."

"I believe you."

"Then believe this too, Kate. I did not murder the cowboy or the coin dealer, but 'tis my belief you know the man who did."

"Who?"

"The man who was here earlier tonight."

Kate thought of Jack, and that was impossible.

Then she thought of the stranger in town, the man whose every word made her shiver. "Gordon Lancaster?"

"Is that what he's calling himself now? When last I saw him, he went by the name Thomas Low."

Kate sank down in a chair. She should have known, should have suspected.

"He has come through time, Kate."

She looked at Morgan and saw something close to fear in his eyes. "Is that why you decided to stay here?"

"I did not know Low was here until I saw him through your window. But he is not the one who makes me want to stay. You are the reason I am here. You are the only reason."

She smiled, letting his words work their way to her heart. But thoughts of Thomas Low would not leave her. "What are you going to do about Low?"

"Kill him."

"You can't. We should call Nikki and tell her. She can arrest him, put him on trial. He'll go to jail."

"Jail?" Morgan's cynical laugh filled the room. "Once before I sought the help of the authorities, but 'twas a mistake to believe they would arrest the bastard. Little did I know that Low had long been filling their pockets with gold and jewels he'd plundered. I learned I could not trust the law. I learned that the only way I could get revenge was to go after Low myself."

"But things are different now."

"And I am a different man than the one who wanted Low to stand trial for what he'd done. Trust me, Kate, if I don't rid our world of Thomas Low, he will find a way to evade the law, and. . . ."

"And what?"

"He will try to kill me, but he will take his time. He enjoys watching people suffer." Morgan looked at the wallet and ring Kate had dropped on the coffee table. "I imagine he put those in my room."

"How?"

" 'Tis easy, Kate. You do not lock doors or windows. I imagine he sneaked in."

Kate sighed at her foolishness, and started to rise, but Morgan put a hand on her arm.

"Where are you going?"

"To lock everything up. To make sure Low doesn't get inside . . . to hurt you."

"I was here earlier. Everything is closed, locked. Low cannot get in without us hearing."

"Then you're safe?"

"I am safe, Kate. But. . . ."

"But what?"

"I do not worry for me."

"Then who?"

"You. Casey."

"Why?"

"He wants you. Both of you, and he will let nothing stand in his way."

Casey? Oh, God.

Kate rushed up the stairs and down the hall. She could hear Morgan behind her, could feel his hands touching her shoulders as she opened Casey's door.

She walked to the bed and looked down at her daughter's precious face. Asleep.

Morgan wrapped his arms about her, and pulled her against his chest. "I will let no harm come to either of you," he whispered. "Believe me, Kate."

She turned in his arms, and he looked down at her with heated intensity. Taking her fingers, he led her out of the room and quietly closed Casey's door behind them. He started for the stairs, but she pulled back, then reached up, lightly caressing the scar on his face.

"I believe you," she said, and before she could smile, before she could tell him that she'd never doubt him again, his lips pressed against hers, hard and passionate. She forgot how to breathe, but that didn't matter. He was breathing life into her.

Opening her mouth to his kiss, she felt his tongue mate with hers, felt his hands sweeping over her body, felt her sundress rising to her waist and being pulled over her head and tossed somewhere across the hall.

His fingers were in her hair, holding her mouth close, so very, very close, as he kissed her deep and hard.

Gradually, the kiss softened, the beat of his

heart slowed, and he cupped her face in his palms and looked lovingly into her eyes.

"I have never loved a woman before," he said. "I have never wanted a woman so much that all other thoughts but her cease to exist. You have taken away my pain. You have made me happy, Kate, an emotion as bewildering and foreign to me as this century. Much has been written about me. I would imagine that stories about my exploits also abound. Some are true, I am sure, for I do not claim to be a man of many virtues. But many more are probably false. I cannot change any of that. I only hope I can make you believe the truth of my love for you."

She would have told him she believed him. She would have told him in a hundred different ways that she loved him, but he kissed her instead.

Then he lifted her in his arms and carried her to her room. It was cloaked in darkness. She could see nothing, but that didn't matter. She could feel, and she remembered so very well every wonderful thing that she'd felt last night when she and Morgan had made love.

He set her down in the massive Spanish chair made of dark walnut and wide straps of leather that Joe swore had once belonged to a pirate. It was a place for hanging dirty clothes, a jacket or sweater. It wasn't a place for making love.

"What's wrong with the bed?" she asked, scraping her fingernails across his shirt as he pulled away.

" 'Tis not yet time for bed."

"But—"

"*Shhh*," he said, touching an index finger to her lips. "Have you forgotten, Kate? 'Tis my turn to ask a question of you."

Her fear had washed away and now passion consumed her. He would care for Casey, for her; there was no need to worry. And now she wanted him desperately.

"Couldn't you ask your question later?"

"I could. But I won't."

"Then ask your bloody question."

He laughed. "You must answer truthfully. Either yes or no."

"Okay. I'm waiting."

His smile did little to ease her frustration. "Do you love me?"

"Of course I do."

"You don't often show it."

"What do you want me to do? Beg you to make love to me every ten minutes or so?"

" 'Tis not a bad idea. Perhaps we will practice your begging in a moment or two, but there is something else on my mind at the present."

"What?"

He reached into his pocket and withdrew the emerald and diamond wedding ring that had belonged to his mother.

" 'Twas my intention to give this to you earlier," he said. " 'Twas my intention to ask you once more to go with me. But it is a future I want with you, Kate. I do not want to drag you with me back to my past."

He knelt before her, lifted her left hand gently in his. She wondered if he could feel the trembling that raced from her fingers all the way down to her toes, wondered if he could hear her heart beating double time.

He slipped the ring onto her finger, then turned his hypnotizing blue eyes on her.

"Marry me, Katie."

A tear slid down her cheek, and he captured it with his thumb.

"The proposal was not meant to bring tears to your eyes."

"Do you really want to stay here?" she blubbered. He'd said those words over and over, but she hadn't believed them until now. "Do you really want to marry me?"

He nodded. " 'Tis *all* that I want."

"Oh, Morgan." She threw her arms around his neck. "I love you so much."

" 'Tis about time you said those words, madam. 'Tis my hope I will not have to give you jewels every time I need to hear them."

"I've never needed jewels or money or anything like that. I just want to be loved."

"Then I will give you much. Every day. Every night."

"I love you," she repeated, laughing as she kissed every part of his face. "Could we please make love now?" she pleaded in between kisses. "Just like last night?"

" 'Tis not a night like that that you need. Last night was much too hurried, for I feared I would be leaving soon."

"We can do it slow and easy some other time. Just take me to bed, please."

"Nay, I will not. 'Tis a pirate I am. A thief. You, my dear, sweet Katie, are the treasure I intend to plunder, one jewel at a time. Starting here."

He kissed her ear, the warmth of his lips and tongue whispering over the curve of her neck while his fingers lightly traced the sensitive skin just below the lacy edge of her bra.

Skyrockets shot off inside her, ricocheting around and around, as his hands inched their way about her back, deliciously tormenting her skin with the roughness of his fingers.

One by one he loosened the catches on her bra, then drew it away from her body, as if he'd done it a million times before. He teased her breasts with the wet tip of his tongue, with his mouth.

"Oh, Morgan," she moaned. "Please. Make love to me."

" 'Tis what I am doing. Slowly, Kate. Very slowly."

He pulled her panties down her legs, one torturous inch at a time.

"Do not move," he said, rising before her.

"Why?"

"You shall see."

"You can't leave me sitting here stark naked."

"I will be gone only a moment. I realize patience is not one of your virtues, but trust me,

Kate. I will make the wait worth your while."

The room was impossibly dark, lit occasionally by streaks of lightning, and when they flashed, she could see the glint of light on his belt buckle. She heard a sizzle. She saw a flaming match, and Morgan's godlike body moving from one part of the room to another, setting fire to candle after candle until the room flickered with fiery glow.

"Where did all those candles come from?" Kate asked.

"I put them here earlier. Before I went to Evalena's."

"You had this planned?"

"A good pirate always has a plan." He knelt before her. "You, my sweet Katie, are too beautiful to hide in the dark. As I said last night, I want to see the pleasure on your face as I make love to you."

He smoothed his hands over her breasts, kneading them gently, and a soft sigh escaped her lips.

"I assume that means you like this?" he asked.

"I like a whole lot of things, so try them all. If you do something I don't like, I'll let you know."

She saw the devilish grin on his face before his mouth brushed over one breast, then settled on the other. His tongue swirled over one very taut, very needy nipple.

Every ounce of her body quivered at his touch. Her hands shook, but somehow she managed to get them into his hair, wrapping long silky strands about her fingers in an attempt to keep him near.

And he stayed close, very close, lifting her

breasts in the palms of his hands, kissing them, nipping them tenderly until a low moan of pleasure rose from deep inside her.

He looked up and smiled. "Tell me you love me again," he whispered, half order, half plea.

It was the easiest thing she'd ever been asked to say. "I love you."

Slowly he stood, his jeans-clad legs nudging her knees apart. Heat rushed to her face. Flames erupted between her thighs. He unbuttoned his shirt while his eyes caressed the secret parts of her body as erotically as the hands of a master seducer.

He threw his shirt to the floor, then lightly stroked her cheeks, her lips. She opened her mouth and sucked one of his fingers between her teeth, tasting the saltiness on her tongue as she swirled it about his knuckles, his fingernails, the very tip.

It was Morgan's turn to moan, Morgan's turn to gasp for breath.

"Do you like that?" she asked.

"Aye."

Suddenly she was enjoying every moment of her agonizing wait.

He lifted one of her hands to his buckle, but she let it slide over the hardness beneath his jeans. She teased him lightly, watching the dance of candlelight in his eyes, listening to the raspy sound of his breathing as her fingers waltzed up and down the length of his straining zipper.

When she leaned forward and kissed the spot

where her hand had been, he groaned.

"Bloody hell, Kate. I will not last through the night if you do that again."

She smiled and teasingly kissed him again, releasing the buckle, the button of his jeans, and slowly slid open the zipper.

She tucked her fingers inside his jeans and boxers and cupped him, relishing the silky smooth feel of him in her hand, wanting to feel him inside her. "I'm ready to make love, Morgan," she said softly. "I think you're ready, too."

"All in good time, madam. All in good time."

She might have hated him if he hadn't laughed, if she hadn't known that each moment he lingered increased her desire in full measure with his.

He stood back, and she watched with fascination and awe as he hastily shoved off his boots, his jeans and underwear.

Oh, God, he looked magnificent, and her body throbbed, every sensitive speck of it.

He knelt before her again and smiled his devilish smile as his fingers meandered up the insides of her thighs, followed by his lips and tongue.

She threw her head back against the hard leather, grabbing onto his hair, twisting it, pulling it, as his hands slid under her bottom and lifted her so his mouth could move closer, closer.

"Oh, God!"

She felt the warmth of his lips, the erotic swirl of his tongue aimed at the very center of her body, and for one moment she thought she'd die from the sheer ecstasy of every stroke.

Her insides pulsed so rapidly she was afraid she'd explode, and then she did, again and again and again.

"Make love to me," she begged one more time.

There was nothing he wanted more.

The time had come and he could wait no longer.

He swept her from the chair and carried her to the bed. Flinging back the covers, he lay her soft, sweet body on the cool white sheets and covered her completely, kissing her as he entered her warm inviting haven.

Thunder rolled through the night, through his head, through his body, and wicked streaks of lightning shot across the sky. The windows and doors rattled, the floor seemed to shake, but it was no more tumultuous than the feelings shuddering through him.

He moved within her, slowly, deliberately, savoring each moment, learning as he loved her what stroke brought forth a gasp, which one a sigh.

Suddenly he didn't want to learn anything more; he wanted to take and give and forget everything else.

He buried himself deep within her, rocking back and forth, driving both of them to frenzy.

He forced himself to hold on, wanting her to know the same exquisite joy that he found just looking at her.

Her fingernails dug into his shoulders, scraped over the scars on his back, and he prayed that she would add one more scar to his body, one that would always remind him of her love.

Her breath was coming out now in short, moan-filled gasps, and he caught them between his lips, kissing her hard and feverishly, until he could hold on no longer.

The thunder came again, and he rolled beneath her, letting her ride out the last moments of the storm above him. Her face lit up as the lightning struck. Her emerald eyes blazed down upon him, warm and full of love.

Weaving his fingers into her honey-colored hair, he rose up to meet her smiling lips. He kissed their blessed softness, whispered, "I love you," and spilled his heart and soul and life deep, deep within her.

Chapter 21

Hark! To the hurried question of despair:
"Where is my child?"—an echo answers, "Where?"

LORD BYRON
THE BRIDE OF ABYDOS, CANTO II

It wasn't much of a noise, but he'd heard it distinctly in between the thunder and lightning and the scratch of a tree branch against the side of the house. Maybe it was just a soft step on a floorboard. But he'd lain awake most of the night listening for even the slightest of sounds, and this one was enough to pull Morgan from the tangle of Kate's hair. Quietly he slipped from the bed, stepped into his trousers, and went to the door.

He listened, but heard nothing.

Kate stirred, rolled over in bed. Still asleep.

He went into the hallway and immediately turned to Casey's room. A sliver of light shone under the door. He started to move toward it when he heard the footstep again.

The door opened slowly, and a little girl walked out of the room rubbing her eyes.

Morgan sighed with relief, and whispered, " 'Tis much too early for you to be up."

Casey smiled. "I couldn't sleep."

He scooped her up in his arms and she put her soft cheek against his whiskered face. He started to hum, softly, an old tune of his mother's. Carrying Casey down the stairs, he checked the front door, the windows in every room, and the door to the backyard. All were safely locked.

He carried Casey up the stairs, and went through the same ritual of checking windows in every room, before returning her to bed.

"Will you tell me a story?" Casey asked.

"One short one," he answered, "and then you must go back to sleep."

Casey turned on her side, tucked her hands beneath her cheek. She closed her eyes and smiled when Morgan began his tale about a man who'd found an angel and fallen in love. He whispered the words, smoothing a fallen curl away from Casey's cheek, and when he knew she was once again asleep, he kissed her brow, and returned to Kate.

"Is everything okay?" she asked, waking only when he crawled back into bed.

"Casey was awake. I told her a story—and checked all the locks again."

Morgan leaned against the headboard and

pulled Kate against him. Her head rested against his shoulder and she traced small circles over his chest.

"Would you tell me a story, too?"

"I would rather talk of our future." He kissed the top of her head and let his lips linger. "I love Casey as if she were my own, but I would like more children. Many of them."

"Joe and I wanted more, too, but. . . ." She raised her head and looked at him. "What if we can't have any more?"

He squeezed her tightly. " 'Tis not something to fret over. If the good Lord chooses to bless us, we will celebrate. If not," he said, caressing the silkiness of Kate's skin, letting his thumb swirl over the roundness of her breast, "I do not believe our efforts will have been in vain."

"What about a job? You'll have to work."

"Are you forgetting, madam, that here in this very house I have a bag of jewels and another of gold and silver doubloons, which, I have been told, are worth many fortunes? Have you forgotten that I have treasures scattered in many other ports?"

"We can't live off your ill-gotten gains."

"I do not consider these things ill gotten. 'Tis but a portion of the riches my family had before Thomas Low took everything. This is something I will not discuss."

She started to protest, but he kissed her instead, rolling her beneath him and pinning her to the bed. "I have thought of one job I might like," he said, in between tasting her lips. "I would like to write books—history books, I imagine, ones that tell the truth of my time, not falsehoods."

"You'd be good at that."

"I am good at many things, madam. Would you like me to show you one of my greatest skills?"

Kate smiled. "Aye."

And he did, making love to her until the wee hours of the morning.

Kate woke with a long roll of thunder rattling the windows and shaking the picture frames and knickknacks on the dresser. Morgan's hair was wrapped around her hands, and he slept soundless beside her. She smiled, and kissed his brow.

She loved him. She had no doubts about anything any longer.

Outside she heard the crunch of footsteps on the gravel and shell path, on the porch, and a knock on the door.

Morgan didn't stir, even when she rushed from the bed and peeked out the window into the storm-darkened morning.

Nikki's patrol car was parked at the curb.

The knock came again, and then Kate heard the door open.

Kate grabbed a pair of cutoffs from the back of a chair and struggled into them, and was pulling a T-shirt over her head when Morgan jerked up in bed. "What's wrong?"

"Nikki's downstairs."

"Good. We can tell her the truth, and she can

begin looking for Low—even though I'll find him first."

"You're not going anywhere," Kate said in a rush. "Give me a chance to tell her everything. If she sees you she'll overreact—she'll probably arrest you and ask questions later."

She thought he was going to argue with her. Instead, he smiled. "Very well, madam. You talk to Nikki, and I'll check on Casey."

"Thank you."

Kate blew him a kiss as she dashed out of the bedroom and down the stairs.

Nikki stood in the center of the living room. In her hands she was holding the wallet and ring, and she looked at Kate as if they were strangers. "Is your pirate here?" Nikki asked.

"No. I told you he left yesterday."

"I don't believe you. Not anymore."

Nikki brushed past Kate, her hand moving to her gun as she put a foot on the first stair.

"Don't go up there. Please," Kate called out, but Nikki ignored her.

Upstairs a door slammed, and Morgan's haunting cry echoed against the walls and through Kate's nerves. "Casey!"

Glass shattered.

Something hit the floor.

Kate ran, but Nikki beat her to the top of the stairs.

Morgan was lying on the floor in the doorway to Casey's room.

Nikki drew her gun and motioned for Kate to

stay back, but all Kate could think of was Casey, and Morgan. She slammed against Nikki's shoulder in her rush to the room, throwing Nikki off balance.

The gun fell to the floor, and Kate saw a booted foot kick it away as Nikki bent to retrieve her weapon.

A hand clamped over Kate's mouth, and she heard the familiar voice.

"Well, well, well. We meet again."

Thomas Low's arm tightened around her waist, and the fingers that covered her mouth worked their way down to her breasts.

"Let her go," Nikki said, sounding calm, in control.

"That is not possible. After all, she is what I came here for."

Kate fought the fear rising inside her. "I was going to tell you about him," Kate stammered. "He's the one you've been looking for, not Morgan."

"You?" Nikki asked. "You're the murderer?"

"Aye, that I am," he said proudly, no hint of remorse in his voice. "Murder is something I do quite well."

"What have you done with my daughter? Please. Tell me," Kate cried, struggling to look toward the empty room, the unmade bed, and the man she loved lying lifeless on the floor.

"She is alive. Have no fear. As for your friend— I imagine he's dead."

Kate tried to control her anguish, to free herself of his hold, but she wasn't successful at either. Tears filled her eyes, blurring everything around her, even Nikki.

But she saw her sister-in-law move in spite of the sword held against her, saw her go for the gun, saw Thomas Low lunge, thrusting the blade into Nikki's stomach.

Kate screamed.

She saw the pain in Nikki's face, saw the dark red stain forming on her shirt as she crumpled to the floor.

Low pulled her away. "Do not struggle, Kate. Be good, and you will see your daughter again."

He dragged her through the house and kitchen, his hand returning to her mouth to keep her from screaming. His strength was too powerful to resist, and the knowledge that he had Casey made her willing to go anywhere he asked. The garage door was already open, and he shoved her through the passenger door of the Chevy. He climbed in behind her, coaxing her toward the driver's seat with the tip of his blade.

"Head toward the ship," he told her.

"I need my keys."

He held them toward her. "You should not keep these where just anyone can find them, Kate. You made it quite easy for me to get into your house, and now you're making it easy to drive away. Go."

Her hands were shaking so hard she was afraid she wouldn't be able to start the car, but the engine turned over immediately and she pulled out of the garage, down the driveway, and headed toward the bridge.

Her heart ached for Morgan, for Nikki. They could be dead or dying, but she could do nothing to help. Right now, she had to think about Casey, and it was her fear that kept her going.

"Where's my daughter?"

"On the ship. If you do as you are told, I might let you see her again."

"What are you going to do to us?"

"I have not decided." The edge of the sword wedged at the base of her neck. "You have seen the scars on Black Heart's face and back. Those, as you no doubt have heard, are the results of my handiwork." He laughed. "Do you think the man you slept with last night will find you as pretty if you are scarred, like he is?"

Morgan thought his head had been split in two, but still he managed to push himself from the floor. There was blood on the carpeting. It coursed over his forehead and into his eye. He was dizzy, and then he stumbled over something behind him.

The blond-headed woman he'd seen on the ship lay on the floor in a pool of blood. Nikki—Kate's sister-in-law. He knelt beside her, turning her gently. He saw the agony in her face as her eyes opened.

"Gordon Lancaster," she whispered, then gasped for breath. "He has Kate . . . and Casey. You have to help them."

"Aye. But I must help you first."

"No. Please."

He didn't listen. He scooped her up in his arms and carried her to Casey's bed, tugged the sheet away from the mattress and ripped away a strip. He folded it into a compress and placed it over the gash he knew full well had come from the tip of Thomas Low's blade.

"Hold this against you."

He lifted her hand and put it on top of the now blood-stained sheet.

"Call nine-one-one," she told him, looking toward the small pink telephone sitting on the table next to Casey's bed. He had never used the telephone before, did not know what "nine-one-one" even meant, but he did as Nikki'd said.

He listened to the voice at the other end, and he asked for help, answering every question he possibly could until he finally shouted, "I don't have time to answer any more of your bloody questions. A woman needs help."

He slammed the phone down, and smiled weakly at the woman looking up at him with a slight grin on her face and tears dripping out of the corners of her eyes.

"Hurry. Please."

A moment later, Morgan was downstairs, recovering his weapons from the top of the cabinet where he'd left them but a few days before. He strapped the leather belt about his waist and shoved his cutlass, dagger, and pistol into their appointed places.

Thomas Low would surely die this day.

He ran outside into the driving rain.

Thunder bellowed.

Lightning crackled and snapped.

And suddenly he was three hundred years in the past, living the horror all over again.

Chapter 22

He left a corsair's name to other times,
Link'd with one virtue and a thousand crimes.

LORD BYRON
THE CORSAIR, CANTO III

Nikki's car sat at the end of the walk. Morgan hadn't driven without Kate's assistance, but that wasn't going to stop him. He ran to the car and climbed behind the wheel, confused by the great number of instruments that stared at him— far more than were in Kate's vehicle.

But the keys were where he expected, and he turned them just as he'd watched Kate do. He released the brake, pulled the lever to drive, and pressed on the right pedal.

The car shot forward, and he eased his foot away. Too slow. Too slow. He touched it again, gradually building up speed, until he was moving down familiar streets.

The wind howled through the doors. It beat against the car. Palm fronds blew across the street, and paper and other trash slashed at the windows. Still he continued to forge ahead.

The city was coming to life, but few people challenged the storm. Darkness prevailed, leaving no room for the early morning light. Only an occasional vehicle passed.

The car roared right along with the storm. He headed over the bridge, swerving almost uncontrollably with each blast of wind. Ahead of him he saw the lighthouse, and the masts of *Satan's Revenge*.

Kate's car was parked not far from the ship, and he stopped next to it. The doors were open, and there was no one inside, but he gave thanks that his ship was still in the harbor, and he prayed that Kate and Casey were safe.

Satan's Revenge rode the roiling waters like a harpooned whale, and he ran toward her as she was breaking free of her moorings, and straining away from the dock. The gangplank was gone. He couldn't make it to the ladder stretching up her hull, so he ran along side her, vaulted across a stretch of sand and sea, and caught one of the mooring ropes as it snapped from the ground. He swung across the foaming water and slammed against the hull.

A wave hit him, threatening to tear loose his hold, but he'd not be stopped.

He climbed, hand over hand, dragging himself to the deck of the ship. He gripped the railing and peered over the side, hoping to see Kate and Casey, but he saw nothing.

He slid over the side and dashed across the rain-slick deck, hiding behind a stack of crates.

Through the pounding rain he heard a well-remembered voice.

"That sweet little daughter of yours will be mine tonight, if you do not do as you are told."

Bile rose in Morgan's throat as he remembered what had happened to Melody and his parents. He refused to think of something similar happening to Kate and Casey.

He peered over the wooden crates. Kate stood at the helm, her hands holding fast to the wheel. Rain pelted her. Wind swept her hair into the swirling gale. But she aimed her fiery green eyes directly at Low.

"*I told you*," she screamed, her voice full of tears and hate. "*I don't know the first thing about sailing a ship this big.*"

"You will before the day is out. It is impossible for me to sail it on my own. That means, my dear, that you must be the crew."

In his hand, Low carried the cat-'o-nine-tails, one of his favorite weapons, and he cracked it against his hand as he paced the deck in front of Kate.

"Where's my daughter?"

"Do not concern yourself with that."

"You told me she's on the ship?"

Low inclined his head, his short dark hair streaming with rain over his brow. He smiled, a look Morgan remembered too well. "She waits for me below."

Kate lunged toward Low, but came to an abrupt stop. Morgan saw the length of rope binding her wrists to the wheel. He had brought this pain upon her. God forbid, he had to save her.

"It is useless to struggle, Kate," Low said. "You are powerless against me."

"Go to hell!" she screamed. Her lips quivered in anger and fright. But Morgan knew damn good and well it wasn't for herself she feared. It was for her child.

He crouched low, stealing across the deck, and slipped down the hatch leading to his cabin.

It was dark inside, but the whimpering of a child led him toward the bed.

"Casey?" he whispered.

He heard naught but a soft, tear-filled cry.

When his eyes adjusted to the dark, he found Casey curled up on the center of the mattress, her hands and feet bound, a gag tied about her mouth.

He lifted her into his arms, cuddling her close as he removed the rag.

"Shhh," he cooed, softly pressing his lips to her forehead. " 'Tis all right, Casey."

"I'm scared."

"I know." Her hands and ankles had been bound with rope that was cutting into her skin. Carefully, hoping to cause her little pain, he loosened a knot around her wrists, and pulled her close when she cried.

He hummed an old lullaby as he untied the

other knots, then rocked her gently, hoping to ease some of her fear. "I will not let him hurt you," Morgan whispered. "Do you trust me, Casey?"

She nodded.

"Then you must do whatever I tell you. You might be frightened, but I promise no harm will come to you."

"Where's my mommy?"

"She's on the deck. We have to save her, too. But you have to be quiet. No matter how scared you are, you can't scream, or cry, or run from my side—unless I tell you to. Do you understand?"

Again she nodded.

Morgan felt her little hands weave around his neck as he carried her from the cabin. He drew his cutlass as they made their way to the deck.

Satan's Revenge had reached open water. She pitched and tossed, and Morgan fought to keep his balance.

Stealing across the deck, he hid behind the crates and held a silencing finger to his lips when he set Casey on the wooden planking.

"Are you frightened?" he asked, pushing wet ringlets from her face.

"Yes," she said, her lips quivering as she spoke.

"So am I." He smiled as he drew his dagger and handed it to Casey, wrapping her little fingers tightly around the hilt.

"Do not play with this, Casey. 'Tis not a toy."

"I know." She lightly touched the remnants of the scab at his neck.

" 'Twas not your fault, but I don't want you accidentally hurting anyone again. What I want you to do is hold the blade down to your side." He drew her fist to her hip, then looked deeply into her eyes.

"I'm going to get the bad man's attention, and draw him away from your mother, hopefully to the far end of the ship. When I call your name, and yell, 'Now,' I want you to walk very slowly, very carefully, toward your mother. Don't run. Promise me?"

She nodded.

"When you get to your mother, give her the dagger. Then tell her to stay with you at the wheel. Do you understand?"

Casey's lower lip jutted out as she nodded.

"Are you going to leave us again?" she asked, tears mixing with the rain beating against her face.

"Not if I can help it. I'd rather stay here and marry your mother."

"And be my daddy?"

"Aye, Casey. There is nothing I want more."

He hugged her, kissing the top of her head. And then he whispered in her ear, "I love you."

Leaving Casey there was one of the hardest things he'd ever had to do. But he had no choice.

He dashed toward the mast where canvas flapped, and climbed a good ten feet from the deck. Lightning flashed through the early morning sky, and all on board was illuminated.

Kate saw him first, and a smile shone on her beautiful face. God, he'd never seen anyone or anything so radiant.

And then he turned his attention to his enemy.

"Thomas Low," he shouted. " 'Tis a word I would have with you."

Low spun around, hate oozing from every pore in his body.

"I was hoping you'd come," Low declared, sauntering toward Kate. He drew his cutlass and aimed it at her neck. " 'Tis a fair wench you've bedded. Of course, she will not be nearly so comely with her head separated from her body."

" 'Tis true," Morgan laughed, attempting to look and sound unconcerned, when deep inside his stomach knotted. But he knew too well how Low worked. He would toy with Morgan before bringing any harm to Kate. He liked the thrill of watching his victims squirm, and Morgan was just as much a victim now as Kate and Casey.

That knowledge was the only thing that kept Morgan sane.

"I have something for you, Low. Something you may find more appealing than taking the woman's life."

"And what is that?"

"Carving another scar on my face. I have an unblemished cheek ripe for the taking."

Low's pearly white smile shone in the next flash of lightning. He slapped the cat against his side as he strolled away from Kate.

Morgan grinned at Low, realizing that his hastily devised plan was working. "I would even bare my back for you should you care to have another go at ripping the flesh from my body."

"You would do all that for a woman?"

"Aye. All that and more."

"You are a fool."

"Nay."

Morgan jumped down from the mast and spread his feet wide on the deck to steady himself on the rocking ship. He resheathed his cutlass and held his arms out to his sides.

"I am yours, Low."

"What assurances do I have that you will not run?"

"I may be a pirate, but first and foremost, I am a gentleman. Have I ever lied to you?"

"Not that I recall."

"Then come and get me."

Low advanced slowly, his cutlass zigzagging methodically in front of him.

Closer and closer he came, the wind and rain pummeling him.

Morgan remained steadfast.

Water dripped from Low's cutlass, from his hand, from the tip of his beard as he neared.

Still, Morgan held his ground, staring at the man he hated.

Low raised the tip of his blade toward Morgan's left eye, then lunged, but Morgan dodged the deadly thrust, drawing his cutlass from its scabbard. Taking advantage of Low's confusion, he danced behind him, then coaxed the bastard further away from Kate with swift swings of his blade.

Low sneered. "You lied to me."

"Perhaps I am not the gentleman I believed myself to be."

Morgan laughed as he jabbed again, dancing right and left to avoid Low's crazed and wild swings.

Thunder crashed. Lightning streaked, hitting a coil of chain lying on the deck. Sparks flew, and Morgan thrust again and again until he had Low far from Kate.

And then he shouted. "Casey! Now!"

Low's eyes widened as he looked past Morgan's shoulder. Morgan didn't dare look, he only prayed that Casey would remember his words. *Walk very slowly. Give the dagger to your mother. Stay by the wheel.*

"You will not take the child from me," Low screamed. "Not again."

"You are wrong."

Morgan had no more time for words, for sport. Low was a vicious dog who deserved nothing less than a blade through his evil heart, and Morgan intended to give him his due.

"Morgan!"

He heard Kate's scream an instant before the block hit him in the head. He stumbled, ramming his shoulder into the mast. He tried to right himself, tried to ride the wave of nausea and dizziness.

Low rushed at him, his cutlass extended. Morgan was unable to move, and he prayed for help.

"Get away from him, you bastard!" Kate yelled. Her small body rushed at Low, knocking him in the side, her hand flailing at Low with the dagger.

That was all Morgan needed to regain his senses, his strength. He pushed up from the deck, staggering just a moment, and went after Low again. He grasped Kate's arm, yanking her away from Low as he swung his sword.

"My thanks, madam," he managed to utter. He smiled at Kate, then shoved her away from the man he meant to kill.

"Be a man, Low," he hollered. "Fight me and not a woman and child."

"I will kill you. And then I will kill them, just as I killed the others." Low grinned, flashing the diamond and emerald ring he wore in front of Morgan. "I have retrieved the treasure I wanted so badly."

Hatred filled Morgan as visions of his mother, his father, and Melody came vividly to his eyes.

He parried and trust, wildly driving his anger against Low.

Lightning crashed against the foremast, and just as before, Morgan heard it snap, heard the rip of wood before it toppled down to the deck, separating him from Kate and Casey.

Thunder roared. A giant wave rolled against the hull. He and Low were thrown from their feet and slid across the deck. Low's cutlass flew through the air. Morgan's slid across the planking, disappearing from sight.

Low struggled with the ropes that he'd collided with. Morgan was trapped beneath a dozen heavy crates. He pushed against them, desperate to see

Kate and Casey for what he feared might be the last time. They huddled together against the base of the mizzenmast, their arms woven through the rigging to keep from going overboard.

Using his back for leverage, Morgan shoved the crates away just as Low lunged toward him. They wrestled, rolling over and over across the deck, and somehow Morgan trapped Low's arms and wrenched the wedding ring from his finger. It belonged to Kate, and no one would ever take it from her.

No one.

He slid it on the end of his little finger as another bolt of lightning skittered across the ship, striking down an oil lamp. Flames shot across the deck, burning steadily beneath the rain-soaked canvas on the fallen mast.

Low kneed Morgan, shoved out of his hold, and stumbled backward as *Satan's Revenge* surged on a wave.

Morgan lunged at Low, hitting him in the belly with his shoulder. Again they rolled across the pitching deck, trying to reach the cutlasses that slid back and forth on the slippery planks.

Flames shot high in the air as the canvas caught fire. It trailed along the mast in spite of the pouring rain.

Another bolt of lightning ripped from the clouds and struck the hull. Like a cannonball, it burst through the wood.

Another bolt hit.

Another.

Morgan could hear *Satan's Revenge* groan as she split nearly in two.

Low screamed when the deck cracked beneath him, and Morgan managed to get his feet up to Low's chest. He pushed hard, sending his enemy crashing against the side of the ship.

Rising quickly, Morgan rushed toward Kate and Casey, but the flames and the ragged opening in the deck kept them apart.

Kate held a crying Casey in her arms. He saw the fear in her eyes as fire leapt between them. And then he cried out, "Jump. Please, Kate."

"I'm afraid."

"Don't be. Please. Say a prayer for all of us, and jump."

"I don't want to leave you."

He smiled, dragging in a deep breath. "I'll always be in your heart, Katie. Always."

"I love you."

"I know."

Tears coursed down his cheeks.

Satan's Revenge pitched. The crack in her deck widened.

"Jump!" he screamed, and watched with an aching heart as Kate and Casey disappeared over the side.

"They will die."

He heard Low behind him, and when he turned, Low held his cutlass mere inches from Morgan's heart.

"As I always predicted, Low, we will die together."

Low grinned, then lost his balance as *Satan's Revenge* broke apart.

Water rushed over the rapidly sinking deck.

Morgan wrapped his arm through the rigging and grasped his own jewel-hilted cutlass as it slid past him on a wave of water.

Low rose, laughing like the devil himself. He raised his cutlass, making a crazed attempt to charge at Morgan.

Thunder rolled.

"Help me, Lord," Morgan prayed—for himself, for Kate, for Casey.

Taking a deep breath, he heaved his cutlass at Low as lightning streaked across the sky. It hit the blade, and sparks skittered along the steel as it buried itself in the center of Low's chest.

Low's eyes widened, and blood dribbled from the corner of his mouth.

Another bolt of lightning struck the blade, and Thomas Low faded before Morgan's eyes, then disappeared completely from sight, as if he'd been nothing but a nightmare.

Satan's Revenge shimmered in the firelight. Lightning struck her figurehead, and just like Low, she started to fade.

Morgan struggled against the rigging that had captured his legs. Fire shot around him, burning everything that floated. He felt the heat at his feet, against his legs.

At last he broke free.

Satan's Revenge made one last valiant attempt to

hold on to life. She groaned as Morgan worked his way to her splintered railing.

He said good-bye to the ship that had been his life for many a year. He said another good-bye to the man he'd been in another time, and dived for the open sea.

Kate fought the wind and waves, treading with all her might to keep her head and Casey's above the treacherous water.

"I'm scared, Mommy."

"Me, too, Case. Me, too."

Salt water rushed into her mouth, stinging her lungs, as she watched the fire leap from the mast on *Satan's Revenge* to the carved figure of a woman at her bow. She heard the crack and groan of wood as the ship ripped apart and made one last pitch toward heaven.

Suddenly *Satan's Revenge* shimmered like a mirage on a hot summer day. She glowed brightly, lighting the darkened sky, and then she disappeared—not under the water, but into thin air.

Tears raced down Kate's cheeks along with the rain and salt water. Her chest felt as if it would collapse—her heart had vanished along with the ship.

Morgan was gone. She'd never see him again.

"I love you," she whispered. "I love you."

Water bubbled about her. Something brushed against her feet, along her legs. It grasped her waist. Fear ripped through her at the thought that she might have gotten caught in some strange undertow, or that Thomas Low had survived—to carry out his threats.

A head suddenly burst through the surging water. Long dark brown hair rose on the waves, and hypnotic blue eyes smiled at her as Morgan pulled her and Casey into his embrace.

He kissed her, breathing a new resolve to live into her heart.

The thunder ceased.

The lightning was swallowed up by the dark.

The clouds broke apart and flew away, leaving behind only the mid-morning sun.

And a rainbow arched over the suddenly calm waters of the Atlantic.

" 'Tis going to be a lovely day, madam," Morgan said, kissing her trembling lips and Casey's forehead.

"Beautiful, I think. But what about Low?" she asked.

"Gone. He won't be hurting anyone in this century, or in any other."

Kate kissed him softly, and he winced when she brushed her fingers over a gash on the side of his head.

"You're hurt. Oh, God. I forgot."

" 'Tis nothing a good nurse—or preferably, a loving woman—cannot heal. I quite look forward to a few more days in bed, and your lovely face looking down at me as you shave my whiskers and soothe my burning brow."

"Can I tell you more stories?" Casey asked.

"Aye."

"Are you and Mommy going to get married now?"

"Aye. As soon as possible."

Kate watched Morgan slip the emerald and diamond ring from his little finger and put it on her left hand, where it would always stay.

He kissed her softly, while they treaded water together.

Staying alive in the ocean, getting home again, were only two storms they'd have to weather in life. She knew there would be many more, because as Kate well knew, life was full of tough times. But she and Morgan would challenge those storms together.

Forever.

Off in the distance she heard the whir of an engine. A Coast Guard boat raced toward them. She'd prayed for help, and it was coming.

She'd prayed for Low to disappear, and he had.

She'd prayed with all her heart for Morgan to return, and he was holding her now—and always.

And she'd prayed for one more thing—for Nikki to be okay. Now, as the Coast Guard neared, she saw a pale, rather weak-looking blond slumped at the bow.

Kate smiled, and silently gave thanks for all her answered prayers.

She kissed her daughter, once, twice, half a dozen times.

She turned to Morgan, the pirate who'd become her hero.

"I love you," she whispered.

"With no regrets?"

"None at all."

He kissed her softly, right there in the middle of the calm Atlantic, and she knew that life couldn't be any more perfect.

Epilogue

O'er the glad waters of the dark blue sea,
Our thoughts as boundless, and our souls as free,
Far as the breeze can bear, the billows foam,
Survey our empire, and behold our home!

LORD BYRON
THE CORSAIR, CANTO II

Morgan pivoted, but his attempt to get away from the blade of his attacker was useless. He stepped back again and again as he tried to parry, tried to thrust, until his back slammed against a palm, and the tip of the foil rested victoriously over his heart.

Bloody hell! He'd trained his opponent far too well.

Casey shed her protective mask and grinned. "You're not quite as light on your feet as you used to be."

"Ha!" Morgan tossed down his mask and

ripped off his vest. "I am just as light and just as fast as I've always been." He leaned close to his daughter and whispered, "I was merely giving you the opportunity to impress that new boyfriend of yours."

"He already knows how good I am." Casey winked, and Morgan felt a surge of fatherly protectiveness rise within him.

Bloody hell! He did not like being the parent of a sixteen-year-old girl who'd given up a portion of her love for pirates to the wanton pursuit of athletic young men.

What was a father to do with a girl like that?

Casey dropped her vest in the sand and walked much too provocatively toward the tall, muscular blond who stared at her as if she were a sea witch who'd enchanted him with her charms.

Morgan forced himself to turn away. 'Twould do no good to lecture. Casey, like her mother, had a will of her own.

He strolled across the beach and squatted down in the sand beside his oldest son. This was someone who listened—always.

He was a damn fine storyteller, too. Just like his father.

"Thomas Low was the wickedest, most vile cutthroat ever to sail the seven seas," Joseph said, relating his favorite tale, much to Morgan's chagrin. Many a time he'd asked Joseph to tell something else, but this story seemed his favorite.

Melody, Michael, and Matthew huddled in a

half-circle around their older brother, listening intently to every word he breathed.

"People everywhere were afraid of him," Joseph continued. "Even the pirates who sailed with him thought he was mad. Suddenly Thomas Low disappeared. No one knew what had happened to him. No one really cared. Still, the people were frightened that he might come back and be far worse than he'd been before." Joseph's voice lowered, and Morgan watched his three youngest children lean forward, straining to hear. "One day, the mean, horrid, awful pirate *did* come back."

"What happened then?" Matthew asked, his eyes wide with curiosity.

"The people cheered." Joseph grinned. "They threw parties in the street."

"Why?" Michael asked.

"Because Thomas Low was dead. His foul, stinking body washed up on the beach with a jeweled cutlass running clean through the middle of it."

Melody's lower lip quivered, and Morgan swept his three-year-old up in his arms before her tears could fall.

"Why don't you tell one of the fairy tales I taught you?" Morgan asked Joseph.

"Ah, those aren't any fun, Dad. We like the stories Casey tells us a whole lot better."

He set a hand down on top his son's dark brown hair. "Exaggerations—all of them."

Joseph raised one eyebrow, and damn if he

didn't see his own face staring back at him.

"Obviously you haven't read any of your own books lately," Joseph stated. "Or maybe you exaggerated the truth so you could sell them. Some of those stories about Black Heart did seem a little overdone. No pirate was ever that good."

"He was the greatest, most honorable, gentlemanly pirate ever."

"Impossible."

"Must you argue with me?" Morgan asked.

"Aye."

Joseph's lips angled into a grin, and Morgan laughed so loud he thankfully interrupted Casey's ardent flirtation.

He waved at his incorrigible daughter and her boyfriend, only to suffer her most annoyed leave-me-alone frown.

Turning his attention back to his son, he plopped Melody in Joseph's lap. "Tell your brothers and sisters a fairy tale," Morgan said firmly. "Your mother's not all that crazy about stories of pillage and plunder."

"I've heard you telling Mom some real whoppers when you're alone at night. Casey says sometimes you even dress up like a pirate to entertain Mom. Gosh, Dad, there was even a pirate on top of your wedding cake."

Morgan wasn't about to get involved in a discussion about the stories he told Kate late at night, or the fact that he quite often dressed up as a pirate, complete with eye patch. That was between him and Kate. Talking about something like that could only lead to subjects he wasn't prepared to explain to Joseph or any of his children—not yet, anyway.

Instead, he ruffled his son's hair. "All right. Go ahead and tell a pirate story, but make sure it's about Black Heart, and make sure you don't embellish the truth."

"Cool!" Joseph exclaimed, turning his attention to his brothers and sister.

Morgan rose from the sand, listening to Joseph's opening lines as he walked across the beach in search of his wife.

"Once upon a time there was a mean, swarthy-looking pirate named Black Heart, who had a big, ugly scar down the side of his face. In fact," Joseph's voice lowered, "he looked just like Daddy."

Morgan jerked around. His three youngest children were staring at him with wide-mouthed awe. Joseph winked.

Bloody hell! Had Casey told Joseph the truth?

Morgan looked at his adopted daughter, at her hands wrapped tightly about her boyfriend's neck. It was high time the two of them had a serious talk—and the sooner, the better.

Morgan shook his head in frustration and stalked toward the restored fortress he and Kate had shared as their second home for nearly ten years.

Kate—blessedly beautiful Kate—was sitting in the shade, reading a book. She looked up at him as he neared, and smiled.

"Bloody hell, Kate. You have raised five terribly hopeless children."

"Yes, I'm sure their temperaments are all my fault."

"Damn right."

She'd given in far too easily. She was tired, he guessed, but she'd never admit it, never complain.

That was one of only a million reasons why he loved her so greatly.

He sat behind her, straddling her hips, and pulled her back against his chest, soaking up the warmth and love that had never waned—not for one second—between them. "These two," he said, smoothing his hands over her swollen belly, "shall be mine to raise. They will be sweet, innocent, and totally in my power."

"You said that the last four times. You're a good father, Morgan, but it's your children who have you under their control, not the other way around."

" 'Tis true, I suppose. I often find it hard to believe I ever captained a ship, sailed the world, or . . . or did a lot of things I did. I have turned quite soft, I imagine."

"You're anything but that."

She leaned her head back, and he lowered his cheek to rest against her honey-colored hair.

"Do you ever miss any of it?" she asked softly.

"Nay. I have all and more than I ever desired. 'Tis a blessing that I traveled through time. The Lord smiled down on me that day."

"I think Joe had a hand in it, too."

"Why is that?"

"The night before the storm, he came to me in a dream. It's the last one I ever had about him. He asked me to go to the island. He said I'd find a treasure there."

"But you didn't."

"Oh, but you're wrong. I found the greatest treasure imaginable." She turned in his arms and looked long and deep into his eyes. "I found you."

Dear Reader,

With a new year coming, don't miss a new year of exciting romances from Avon! We've got some of the writers you already know and love, along with some fresh voices you're sure to fall for.

A writer you know and love is January's Treasure author, Tanya Anne Crosby. *On Bended Knee*, Tanya Anne's latest, is an unforgettable love story of passion and promise, and she returns to the Scottish setting that her readers love so well. Don't miss this sinfully sensuous historical love story.

Rachel Gibson's first contemporary, *Simply Irresistible*, made readers sit up and take notice. Now, she returns with another witty and wonderful contemporary called *Truly Madly Yours*. When a young woman returns to her hometown of Truly, Idaho, she never dreams the handsome man she left behind would still be there...laying in wait for her!

If you're looking for a spectacular new writer, don't miss Gayle Callen, author of next month's *The Darkest Knight*. A young woman is on the run from a forced marriage, and is rescued by the one man she can never have in this sensuous, exciting medieval historical romance.

And with a title like *Once a Mistress* how can you resist buying the latest from Debra Mullins? A dark handsome rogue sweeps our heroine off her feet and rescues her from an evil abductor in this wonderfully swashbuckling romp.

Until next month, enjoy!

Lucia Macro
Lucia Macro
Senior Editor

AEL 1298